CHARLIE CHAPLIN'S WISHBONE

AND OTHER STORIES

CHARLIE CHAPLIN'S WISHBONE

AND OTHER STORIES

AIDAN MATHEWS

THE LILLIPUT PRESS
DUBLIN

First published in 2015 by
THE LILLIPUT PRESS
62–63 Sitric Road, Arbour Hill
Dublin 7, Ireland
www.lilliputpress.ie

Copyright © Aidan Mathews, 2015

Acknowledgments are due to the editors of the following publications:
The Brandon Book of Irish Short Stories (Brandon Press), *Arrows in Flight* (Scribner/
Townhouse), *Phoenix Irish Short Stories* (Phoenix), *The Faber Book of Best New Irish
Stories*, RTE Radio 1, BBC World Service, ABC Australia and CBC Canada.

ISBN 978 1 84351 6415

1 3 5 7 9 10 8 6 4 2

A CIP record for this title is available
from The British Library.

Set in 12 pt on 15 pt Perpetua by Marsha Swan
Printed in Spain by Castuera

For my daughters, Lucy and Laura,
who brought me into the world

CONTENTS

CHARLIE
CHAPLIN'S
WISHBONE

AND OTHER STORIES

CHARLIE CHAPLIN'S WISHBONE

If there was any more blasphemy with the skeletons, Charlie Chaplin was over and out.

'I make no bones about it,' my father said. 'Earth calling Timothy. Do you read me?' And he rubbed some aftershave on his tiepin and his cufflinks because his skin was allergic.

'I do,' I said. 'I read you loud and clear.'

'Didn't hear,' he said. 'What was that?' And he dabbed a sting of the stuff on my forehead for fun as if it were a baptism.

'Roger,' I said.

Down in the hotel lobby the gong was sounding for dinner. The same waiter rang it like the Angelus each evening so that, twice already in the first week of our stay, clerics had had to stand at reception pretending to pray for the hour of their death while they waited for room keys.

'They should seal that cemetery good and proper,' my mother said. 'The sand runs off it like an hourglass. Someone will meet

their maker there. When we passed it the first time, I saw something that wasn't human, even if it was a mortal remains.'

I was thinking what I could do with the pelvis in the tallboy of my bedroom. There were pellets of a foot in my leaky snorkel, though you would need to be an archaeologist with an eyebrow pencil to tell them apart from barbecue cinders. But the pelvis had a way of puzzling you until you felt along the bones behind your belt and pulled up your shirt to be sure.

'Ezekiel,' said my father. 'Where's Ezekiel gone?'

'That's a Gideon Bible,' my mother said. 'The Gideon Bible is only the bare essentials. When you stay in hotels, you don't want to be reading about Abimbimoloch and what locusts you can eat with broccoli. So Gideon put in the parts you'd like to read when you feel more spiritual or maybe suicidal.'

Actually the pelvis was like a wishbone: something you would hold in your hands by its light, strong right-angles while you thought of what you wanted most in the world. If I left it where it was stowed, the chambermaid would faint and the smithereens of the lens in her wire glasses would bed in the brown of her eye for ever after. There could be no ophthalmologists in Kerry, unless perhaps one was staying in the Waterville Hotel for the fishing and the golf; but he would not want a public patient to be persecuting him at the dinner table. So her gaze would follow me all my life, without blinking. And who would marry her? Her eggs would go off inside her, with the calendar dates stamped on them. Yet she would know the names of my children and when they were collected from Montessori.

'Ezekiel', said my father, 'had a vision. What he saw was all of the bones of all of the skeletons in the world rising up together at the end of time. All the bits fitting; all the bobs bobbing. The skull knitting with the spine and the collarbone with the ribs. Etcetera and so forth. Obviously, I don't know every bone in the body, but the point is, they're human beings, and they don't want to find that their femurs have gone for a stroll in the meantime.'

'I put the femur back,' I said. 'It was the right grave.'

'You think it was the right grave,' he told me. 'What does the femur think?'

'It was the right graveyard,' my mother said. 'It doesn't have far to walk.'

She had taken off her safari top to put on the ivory blouse. The tan stopped halfway up her shoulder below the vaccination mark. When she stretched her arms to smell the stubble under them, her breastbone stiffened like a starfish. So I took off my shirt and my togs and left on only the waterproof plastic sandals I could walk in and out of the ocean in. She kneeled down in front of me and began to press the ticks out of my skin, one after another, with her pink pincers.

'If I told Charlie Chaplin you'd been fool-acting with people's remains, do you think he'd let you wear his bowler? Do you think he'd let you squirt his buttonhole carnation in the Butler Arms?'

My father's socks had stencilled the white flesh of his foot. It was like the stump of a war wound, all streaked with lemon soot.

'And the Watts,' he said. 'What would the Watts say? He may have bombed the Ruhr in his day, but it still brings tears to his eyes to think of it. Charcoal of orphans. Whole basilicas of cartilage. I saw him in the bar the other night. His eyes filled up. He was only pretending about the smog in the snug. He was thinking about fire storms.'

'Hold still,' my mother said. 'Here be monsters.'

She was pressing a blood-drop from the crease of my navel, the tiny carcass of a creature that the Hollywood Jews might magnify in their movies about the Stone Age and the Stone-Age inhumans running away in their bearskins through the trampled jungles of Liverpool. It stuck to her nail like a bogie and she shook it into the bin among the stones of the peaches and a sodden strip of cotton wool.

'Ezekiel,' said my father.' I wonder would the Watts know Ezekiel.'

What I would do was this: I would wrap the pelvis up in my beach towel after dinner, slip out the back of the hotel where the croquet had been played before they lost both of the mallets, and walk down in a sort of a jaunt as far as the jetty. With a good run and a high swing, I could fling it a hundred yards at least. If they fished it in afterwards, they could call the police; they could call Interpol; they could call the palaeontologists in the National Museum. Salt or fresh, all water washes off fingerprints.

'The Watts? The Watts are Catholics,' my mother said. 'I heard her cursing her corns like I don't know what.'

My father peeled a ribbed white sock over the blades of his toes. It was a moment he hated because it reminded him that he would be tagged after the heart attack, with two L's in his name instead of just one. Even his baptismal certificate was a dog's dinner.

'And there I was treating them like royalty,' he said. 'I'd have sworn on the Bible they were Protestant.'

I wanted to meet Charlie Chaplin more than anything in my life. I would have given two grandparents to touch him in a crowd, and I would have given a complete skeleton from the graveyard on the peninsula to have a photograph of the two of us that would cause everyone I knew to feel unhappy and excluded for a long time after they had handed it back to me in the silver zero of its oval frame.

My mother held my genitals in the palm of her hand and studied them. She blew on them gently from in between her lipstick. Tiny nicks all over me were fading to flesh tones: on my shoulder bone, my breastbone, the pleat of my knee.

'Hold on,' she said. 'This may or may not hurt.'

Round and round the washing line they ran, the fatso with the handlebar moustaches and the ringletted girlfriend. The bowler hat of Charlie Chaplin was bobbing up and down in the empty water barrel, but the bully never noticed. He went on beating his sweetheart like a carpet, raising dust clouds on her back and the small of her back and on her ribboned bustle; and when the broom broke, he took off his belt and thrashed her front and rear while his moleskin trousers puddled at his hobnailed boots.

Actually, it was the funniest thing you ever saw.

'Settle down now,' said the man in the chef's apron who was standing behind the projector where the hotel manager had sprayed eau-de-toilette like a housepainter's blowtorch to soften the smell of keg metal and dehydrated vomit in the games room. But the old gillie beside him had his face lifted to the screen as if he were reading the lips.

'You heard me, ladies and gentlemen,' said the projectionist. 'Loud and clear.'

All the children were shrieking and making rabbit-ears and victory signs and the profiled scowls of thugs on the starched screen with their fists, and two of the boys were standing on the billiard table with the cues in their hands like hunting spears; and a girl at the upright piano was pretending to play the silent-movie score, spiking the keys with her stiff, straight fingers and her flopped, golliwog head in its sawtooth hairband, while Charlie Chaplin rammed a plank from the picket fence into the shaven crown of the walrus would-be killer and then set fire to his feet. The desperado went head first into the dry water barrel with his hooves in flames like rockets.

'Last warning,' the projectionist said, and his shirtcuff shadowed the lens so you could see the tramp's arm brandishing paper chrysanthemums but not the bowler that he pressed to his waistcoat buttons or the way he would genuflect while the woman held his cigarette finger to her lips like a mouth organ.

'What they need is tuberculosis,' the projectionist said to the gillie. 'They need tuberculosis and newspaper in their shoes. Not train tracks and talcum powder. These youngsters all smell like fucking Americans.'

But there were no bones broken. Charlie had linked the lady and they were walking off into the painted mountains while the bully's long johns pedalled at the brim of the barrel. The shadow of those swallowtails stretched out of the picture onto the bump of the boom and shot across the parquet to the empty waders under the empty oilskins on the pegs beneath the empty anglers' hats.

'Not when you hold them over the side so they can shit in a downpour,' said the old gillie. 'They don't smell like Americans then, skipper.'

Over the porthole door the Exit light was hissing, and the smells of the soggy beauty board and the waxed foot rests at the overflow bar counter made the white joined-writing on the screen flicker and fade like the quick-dry copperplate of trick-shop ink as the cricket skips of the reel stopped short in a last hiccup.

'Is there Laurel and Hardy now?' said the boy on the billiard table. 'Is there Laurel and Hardy?' He was the one who had filled a Tupperware to the top with seawater and left it beside his bed to watch it swell and spill over when the moon came out. But he had no stomach for the crab massacre in the dunes at Derrynane. The graves in the sand were beyond him too.

'You're Laurel and Hardy,' said the projectionist. 'And the Three Stooges.'

You could say it to the tramp. Nothing on earth would bowl him over; or, if it did, he would spring up again like a helium dummy, dust his calves, tweak his tach, and waddle into the world. The Pope had watched him in his private cinema, sitting each evening with his prime minister and the Vatican gardeners over the mass graves of their Renaissance ashtrays; and Adolf Hitler had studied the shorts on a crankshaft splice machine, winding the frames backwards and forwards, spooling and re-spooling, letting the poor man drop from the cliff face sheer to the squid and then, just as the breakers jockeyed for his ankles, winching him up again like it was an airlift, like it was Ascension Thursday, raising the dead, reversing disaster, at the very moment that Mr Watt was flushing his cargo from the bomb bay of a Lancaster bomber over a brand-new German city that looked like the ruins of the Colosseum. So you could say it straight out without preliminaries, without pussy-footing: I took a pelvis from a hole in a sandy graveyard where the wind has been nibbling away for ages now at a lot of shallow graves. I found myself a skull and hands too, ribs galore, and other flinty bits I know where to put by feeling myself. But what do I do with them now?

And he would tip his bowler and tap it shut on his head and trot like a convict in leg chains into the brown dustcloud behind the violins that shrieked in the key of seagulls.

'What do you think of the bikinis?' said the projectionist to the gillie.

'Ho, ho,' the gillie said. 'What do I not think is the question.'

'You should mend your nets at the shore,' the projectionist said, 'and you'd get a real Come, Follow Me.'

'I saw a bellybutton yesterday that went out instead of in,' the gillie said. 'I never saw a bellybutton that did that. I thought: would her father have cut the cord, or maybe the mother, and not a proper doctor?'

'Bellybuttons,' the projectionist said. 'I was thinking zips and not buttons. I was thinking how it would look when the sun tanned every part of you the colour of crackling except the covered-up pieces.'

'Step into the shower with me, so,' said the gillie. 'My face and hands are the colour of creosote and the rest of me is as white as soda bread. The nurses had a great laugh in the hospital the time I passed my kidney stones.'

'White meat and brown meat,' the projectionist said. 'Even in the dark, you'd know where to go. The white parts would be shining at you like as if they were road markings.'

'Now, now, skipper,' said the gilly. 'You're only making it harder for yourself.'

The lights came on then and surrounded us on all sides. In the shadowless glare under a tasselled shade on the ceiling rose, I could see for a second the spread bones of my hand in the fat of my fingers.

—

There was silver on the cobblestones in the hotel bar where the day's salmon had been laid out and weighed. My dad was upset in himself over his suede golf shoes with the little flakes of phosphor where the laces trailed; but my mother said she would go on her hands and knees to strip the fish scales off.

'You're not at home now,' he said to her. 'You're in a four-star hotel. I'll leave them outside the door tonight.'

'I leave mine out to be cleaned,' the Frenchman with the crewcut said. 'But I clean them a bit first. I had my feet washed at an Easter ceremony when I was small and my father was away on business, so I am conscious of how unpleasant they are.'

'Be warned. Beware. The girl put polish on a suede shoe last year,' said Mr Watt. 'Or the year before. I couldn't get through to her. You know the kind that breathes through their mouth.'

But Mrs Watt leaned over to me and her breath smelled of fruit cocktail.

'My grandmother was a saint,' she said, 'and she breathed through her mouth. Her name was Saint Ellen Corrigan. She is the patron saint of grandchildren.'

'She may breathe through her mouth,' my father said to Mr Watt, 'but she earns over two pounds a week at the high season.'

'Thirty shillings,' said Mr Watt. 'That's what I took home at the time. There was an extra five bob because, frankly, you were as good as gone in the rear ball turrets. As a navigator, you'd be burning up the brain cells, but you stood a better chance of another night in the haystack. Present company excluded. Gunners were goners. Ergo, the additional two half crowns weekly. Blood money. Plus it passed to your lawful wedded in the sad event. As part of your pension. Not that Penny here was born then. No, she was born long before.'

'I was born yesterday,' she said.

'I jest,' Mr Watt said. 'She was a twinkle in the eyes of the blessed Trinity.'

'And my best friend was a saint,' said Mrs Watt into my ear again. 'Her name was Elizabeth. She was named after another Elizabeth who was named after another one. That is how things go on and on, by going back and back to begin with. My Elizabeth is Saint Elizabeth Robertson. She died of a stain on her skin that I used to wonder about when we played tennis. One of her boyfriends flicked it once with the end of a pencil, and the flap was sore for a week. He kneeled at the funeral service, too, and he was a Quaker.'

'Why was she a saint?' I said.

'I feel it in my bones, funny fellow,' said Mrs Watt. 'Anyone who can dissect a cadaver while she's dying of cancer is a human being; and anyone who is a human being is a holy person.'

'Where was I?' said Mr Watt; yet nobody knew. And his wife touched my cheek with her hand, but it was as cold as a corpse from the ice in her gin and tonic. My father was waiting with his story of how he had helped the Benedictines in the prisoner-of-war camp to make wine in exchange for their tobacco ration and how he had memorized the whole of the Psalms before smoking them, page by flimsy page; but the right opportunity had not arisen yet, and he was getting more upset in himself. The Frenchman had sneaked in out of the blue without so much as a by-your-leave.

'Our fathers died in the First World War,' he said, 'and their sons were defeated and interned in the Second World War. That is the history of France in the twentieth century up to the present moment.'

'From the Belle Epoque to La Bardot,' said my father, raising his glass, and my mother was very pleased that he had had the presence of mind to invent this sentence. I knew from the way she swept her breast for breadcrumbs.

'Now you can see why Indo-China was a fracture, and why Algeria has been a compound fracture,' said the Frenchman. 'It isn't simply that we've lost battles and wars. We have lost face. Unless and until we kill a great many people, we cannot go to bed with our own wives and daughters. Amen.'

'Amen,' said my father because he could not think of the French equivalent. 'But remember Big Ears at ten to twelve,' and he tilted his glass in my direction.

'It's all a question of point of view,' said Mr Watt who was not exactly bear-hugging the Frenchman, 'or, if you want to put it in intellectual terms, it's all to do with relativity. Things are relative.'

'The Benedictines used to say,' my father said, 'that the view from forty is the closest we come to wisdom. Babies growing up, parents growing down. Goo-goo and ga-ga. Yourself in the middle, muddled, putting a bit of flesh on the old bones. The port and starboard of human life. Of course, forty in Hebrew doesn't mean forty at all. It means: a very considerable time.'

Mr Watt thought about this for a moment before he continued with what he had been saying.

'Take a man – no name, rank or serial number necessary – who's dropping propaganda leaflets over Düsseldorf in the ember months of 1939. He's been cutting parcel string with a Swiss pen-knife over the bomb bay, and what happens?'

'He falls out,' I said.

'He starts to read the leaflet,' said Mrs Watt.

'I give up,' said my father.

'He realizes the leaflets are in French and not in German,' said the Frenchman with the crew cut.

'He drops the bale without slicing the string,' said Mr Watt. 'He hopes it will hit a Nazi on the helmet and smash every bone in his body, from his parting to his pelvis and on down to his piggy toes.'

'Did it?' I said. Because I would listen to my father, but this was better than shingles in occupied Singapore.

'God knows,' said Mr Watt, 'but the man who dropped the bale was court-martialled for endangering civilian life.'

'Was he shot?' I said.

'No,' he said. 'He went on to serve for the duration. And the next time he saw Düsseldorf, he dropped three hundred tons of high explosives on the residential centre of the city. He started a firestorm, which had all the colours of a Rembrandt in it. They gave him a medal for that.'

'Saints,' said Mrs Watt. 'Each and every one of them was a saint. Grandparents and schoolchildren. Their bones should be relics. Their city is a reliquary.'

'Do you know Ezekiel?' my father said to her. 'The skeleton section? "Then I saw bones in a desolate this or that"?'

'"My flesh faileth, my bones melteth away",' said Mrs Watt. Her pineapple breath ruffled my sunburn. I blew bubbles like frog-spawn in the bottom of my Coke through the soggy paper straw.

'No, that's not it,' my father said. 'There weren't so many Eths. I'd remember.'

'This boy's anatomy,' said the Frenchman, feeling my vertebrae, 'is the skeleton key to our civilization. It is much more radioactive than ours because he was born after, and not before, the atomic bomb; a bomb that lit up and laid bare the calcium phosphate structures of the scientists in the desert like the apocalypse of the Last Judgment.'

'Actually,' said Mr Watt, 'I daresay that at the Last Judgment, when the graves open and give up their dead, we'll all sit down together, the bombers and the bombed, and have a few drinks, and not go on about things.'

The Frenchman was staring at my mother's lap, at the splinter of ice that was melting in the groove of her skirted legs, until she covered it with her imitation pearl handbag and stared at me. Then her two index fingers shot like a scissors to my kneecap and she gouged a blister precisely. When she held her nail varnish to the bottom of Mr Watt's brandy tumbler, the legs of the sucker magnified whitely to the root system of a weed.

'I missed that,' she said, 'at the tick inspection.'

'Put it away,' said Mrs Watt. 'It makes me think of the house-dust mite. You showed me a picture of a house-dust mite when we married, and it made me bring up my Milk of Magnesia to lie there and realize they were eating me unbeknownst.'

'Speaking of which,' said my father.

'It's time to think about bed,' said my mother, and she blew out the match flame on my knee.

'I wanted to walk to the jetty,' I said. 'It's still bright. It wouldn't take long.'

'It's dark,' she said. 'You'd drown. It would take forever.'

'Earth calling Timmy,' said my father. 'Over and out.'

'Then it's only another day until you meet Charlie Chaplin,' my mother said.

'The little man,' the Frenchman said. 'He is a great man because he is, *par excellence*, the little man.'

'You wouldn't say that if he was French,' Mr Watt said. 'You only say it because he's English.'

'I thought he was American,' my father said.

I knew he was Jewish because I had heard the projectionist say so; but I was not supposed to talk after 'Over and out'. I squeezed past Mrs Watt and my elbow rubbed the bare knob of her shoulder.

The skin was so soft there that you could write your name on its plump vellum as if you were writing with a ballpoint on a rotting banana.

'At Los Alamos,' said the Frenchman with the crew cut, 'the physicists watched Charlie Chaplin in the evening. They cut a hole in the wire around the compound so that the native Indians could slip in under cover of darkness and sit in their blankets on the benches among the tall scientists to watch the little man walk down a lane and turn and look back and disappear.'

Mrs Watt leaned up and put her mouth to my ear.

'Everything they say is a lie,' she said. 'Pass it on.'

—

When it started to rain the old gillie rowed to the island in the middle of the lake where there was the ruin of a church we could shelter at. He handed us ashore, my father and the Frenchman and Mr Watt, and the four of us huddled under a dry-stone overhang at the back of the building. In our hats and hoods and with our hands in the drenched koala pouches of our anoraks we might have been taken for monks. So I hunkered down among the sour smell of men's trousers and sheep droppings and I wrote the date out, between a corduroy leg and a Wellington boot, with one edge of the cube of pink chalk I had taken from the billiard table in the games room: June 20th, 1965. But I wrote it with my other hand, in knuckled jerks, because I had been trailing my left arm in the water and my body was amputated up to the elbow from the numbness.

'There you are now,' Mr Watt said. 'The sky was as blue as be-damned at breakfast. If you peed in the grass this minute, you'd see steam. That's how cool it's got.'

'There's always steam when you pee,' the Frenchman said. 'Even in Algeria. Don't forget that urine is ninety-eight degrees Fahren-heit when it greets the world.'

Water was guttering in over the high gable like the silver fringes of a christening shawl. But the gillie stood bareheaded in the roofless nave of the church with his hat in his hand and could not be per-suaded to come into our pelted heronry. Rain coated him like a caul.

'It's out of respect,' my father said. 'The Mass was said here. The monks are buried around us. Everywhere we walk is a grave.'

'Everywhere we walk on the planet is a grave,' the Frenchman said. 'The whole of Europe is a Jewish plot. The whole of Russia is a Christian cemetery. That's why we have the bumper harvests. It's not pesticides. It's the protein of extermination.'

'Big Ears possibly listening,' said my father, blowing blue smoke towards me.

'Be warned. Beware,' said Mr Watt.

'But it's true,' the Frenchman said. 'In the Revolution we dug up Carmelite skeletons and danced with them in the chancels of cathedrals. That's the Great Rift Valley we come from.'

'Loire Valley, more like,' said Mr Watt.

They stood in the smoke of their cigarettes and watched the gilly pray. His face was running like a watercolour.

'You could put it on a postcard,' my father said. 'It would make a wonderful postcard.'

'That's why I come to Kerry,' said Mr Watt. 'I need to keep in touch with the real world. I need to find time for timelessness.'

'It must be a decade of the Rosary,' my father said, 'though he has no Rosary beads. He's been too long for an Our Father.'

'He's foolish,' the Frenchman said. 'His income for the entire year depends on how well he does in the three months of the high season. He could get a cold. He could get pneumonia. Then where would his family be?'

'He's not married,' my father said. 'He'll sleep with his parents.'

'He's no fool,' the Frenchman said, and he sighed biographically.

'He's as bright as a button,' said Mr Watt. 'I hadn't spoken a word when he called me Skipper.'

'He's a navigator,' my father said. 'He'll survive anything.'

Then the rain lightened and the shiny world lined up for photographs: of the three friends from the three allied nations, of the three friends and the gillie; of me and the gillie at the cavity for the cruets in the east wall where the ancient altar once stood and the priest presided; of my father shaking hands with the gillie at a shallow, labelled font where ancient babies were ladled; and of the three men with their catch at the gravel shore, holding up their fishing rods like rifles over two trout in a tarpaulin. There was no picture of the four of us taken by the gillie, because my father was afraid he would damage the Leica camera.

'Don't look at me like that,' he said to me. 'Ask him when he saw his first motor car. I'd say he was born before the bike.'

But his mood changed when we reached the private jetty and climbed up the beaten fisherman's path among the ferns and the chortling ditches. My mother was standing at the stile beside the sand dune where the golf links petered out, holding the pelvis by the tips of her golf-glove fingers.

'Burke and Hare,' my father said. 'Burke and bloody Hare. That's what you are.'

'I didn't go there,' I said. 'I didn't.'

'A hundred years ago they would have hanged you,' said my mother. 'They strung up grave robbers a hundred years ago.'

'It's not just a sin,' my father said. 'It's a crime.'

I looked down at my drying sandals that would squelch for fifty yards after you left the water and I thought of Charlie Chaplin.

'He's not normal,' my mother said to me. 'Normal boys are squirting water pistols at girls or having a crab massacre. Normal boys don't dig up dead people to play with.'

In the film where he was an undertaker who listened to the coffins with a veterinarian's stethoscope, Charlie had dodged the maniac's shovel by jumping in and out of the fresh graves like they were trenches on a battlefield; and when the priest had arrived in his biretta and bridal dress to read to the fissures in the earth from the book in his hand, Charlie had pretended he was a corpse come back and scurried round the churchyard, kissing the holly and the altar boys, before hightailing it into no man's land and going to ground in the fancy-free credits. He would have twirled his brolly as my parents pulled at their beards like bell ropes and drummed their frosted brassieres. He would have shaken his leg to let the penny drop through the hole in his pocket to the hole in his shoe.

'What is it?' said my mother, peeling off the glove and walking her fingers in the air.

'No idea,' my father said. He was holding it like a steering-wheel. 'Uterus, do you think?'

'I have nothing like that in me, anyhow,' said my mother. 'You can look if you like. I've kept all my X-rays.'

'Whatever it is,' my father said, 'it's a dislocated bone.'

'You'd better relocate it,' she said. 'I'm sure it's alive with things you can't see.'

Then she turned and walked up the hill to the hotel with a half-moon of suntan on her vanilla nape from her bunned hairline to about her second vertebra. But my father and I took the long way round by the sheds and the outhouses until we were at the great garbage containers behind the kitchen where someone had hung diamond-patterned socks beside a dartboard that the rain had swollen until it was warped.

'The point is,' my father said, 'it's part of a human. Part of a human being, what's more. This bone had a mother. It had a father. It may have had cousins. We're in the presence of someone who was christened, etcetera. This is not Papua New Guinea.'

'I know,' I said. My waterproof see-through sandals had walked into beans, and bubbles of brown were treacling into my toes. I was afraid that the beans had been regurgitated by a person or by a cat from the rubbery slipknots of their stomach, but I was not sure if a cat would eat a bean and there was no one in the world that I could ask.

'Earth calling Timmy.'

'Over and out,' I said.

'You don't say "Over and out". I say "Over and out". You say "Roger".'

'I know,' I said.

'I know you know,' he said. 'That's not the point.'

'Roger,' I said.

My father looked at me without blinking. He could do that for almost four minutes by the stopwatch, but my mother was afraid he would go blind. She would clap her hands in front of him like a hypnotist.

'Our Father,' my father said.

'Our Father, who art in Heaven, hallowed be Thy name,' I said. 'Thy kingdom come, Thy will be done in earth as it is in Heaven. Give us this day our daily bread, and forgive us our trespasses as we forgive those who trespass against us, and lead us not into temptation, but deliver us from evil. Amen.'

'Amen,' said my father. 'If you live to be a hundred, you will always be the boy who missed his chance of meeting Charlie Chaplin in the flesh.'

The projectionist stood in the doorframe of the kitchen, looking at us. He wore his tall chef's hat and carried a butcher's cleaver in his wedding hand. His apron was the pattern of my summer pyjamas, stripes of prisoner's cerise. Two little mongrels had lost interest in him, and were moving toward me through a tractor wheel. But my father dropped the pelvis into the garbage drum like a woman would drop a handkerchief from a balcony.

Early in the morning, when the hotel van had left with all the children and two chaperones for Waterville and a picnic lunch on the lawn with Charlie Chaplin, I went down to the jetty and I sat on the shingle with my waterproof shoes in the water. The shallows were copper-coloured and clear to the bottom, as warm as urine. The dead invertebrates decayed there in their grey ghettoes. Little detonations of silt flowered quietly around my feet whenever I shifted them, like the beautiful concussions you would watch from a bomber, the brown soundless magnolias.

'There he is,' said Mr Watt. 'The man himself. I gather the parents had a bone to pick with you.' And he crouched down beside me like a Buddhist squatting, with his tackle and flies in his lap and his maggot box on the sand beside him, which was once a tin of assorted Austrian chocolates you might gift-wrap for a grand hospital visit. But I could not think of anything to say to him.

'I heard,' he said. 'I wouldn't worry. Charlie Chaplin was nothing compared to Buster Keaton. If you saw Buster Keaton or Fatty Arbuckle, you wouldn't stop to look at Charlie Chaplin. My mother adored him, and what good did it do her? She died.'

Then we said nothing for a while, and I wondered if Mr Watt could smell my hair and my eyes and my breath the way I could smell his. So I twitched my toe in the bed of the lake and the silt puffed like a parachute.

'I was always in trouble,' he said. '"All watt and no voltage", the teachers used to say. I went to three schools before the war, and in each and every one of them, there was a teacher who thought of that line. "All watt and no voltage". Of course, electricity was still a novelty then.'

'Did you ever steal bones from a grave?'

'No,' he said. 'The worst thing I ever did was to hide my father's teeth on Christmas Day.'

I lifted my leg from the water and it was dead from the hive down. I could have lit a match under it. But if you were baptized in Scotland or America you had to stay underwater for ages like a swimming test for the Sea Scouts, and there the currents were so cold that fish had been known to throw themselves onto the bank as if they were humans walking in their clothes into the sea.

'Why,' he said, 'is a mayfly called a mayfly?'

I thought about it.

'Because it may or may not fly.'

'No,' he said. 'A mayfly is called a mayfly because it flies in May.' And he opened the lid of the maggot box a fraction and I saw the drowsy heap of wet wings stir minutely in the metal detention.

'But this isn't May,' I said. 'This is June.'

'How are they to know that? It was May when God invented them, and it stayed May until the Pope in Rome reformed the calendar three hundred years ago. I had a friend, a fisherman, and he always called them June flies; but his face turned red one morning, and then it turned redder, until even his wife at the breakfast table was relieved when he stopped breathing. That was in May, too. Now nobody remembers what his middle initial stood for, and the mayflies are still mayflies.'

'What is his middle initial?'

'L.'

I rested my open palm over the crack in the tin and I felt the teasing fuselage of an insect fret at my lifeline.

'They live for one day,' said Mr Watt. 'Twelve hours of darkness; twelve hours of light. They fly in squadrons; they fly solo. When they land, they mate on the water in the creases of the ripples. Their eyes are as complex as the nose cone of a Lancaster, but they have no mouth. Their life is too short, you see, for eating and drinking. And they have never heard of Charlie Chaplin.'

He got up then very slowly, first his shoulders, then his arms, his hips, his legs, letting the dead sensations drain out of him, the sediment of sleep in his limbs. He was not used to crouching for so long.

'The old bones,' he said, and he sealed the scratching container. 'They never let you forget. It only takes a few months to assume flesh; but it's taking me forever to assume bones.'

'Perhaps,' I called to him as he walked away in the high fisherman's boots that breathed like an accordion air pump whenever he took a step. 'Perhaps his name was Lazarus.' But his silhouette only waved to me or shooed flies at his face.

—

My watch was so loud the earwig shrank from it.

Animals could cross the entire country from left to right, from the coral beaches of the Atlantic coastline to the swimming pool in Sandycove in south Dublin, by tunnelling through the Irish hedgerows. Even a field mouse, enormously mourning a paw or a perished sweetheart, could journey from the Venezuelan backwash of the Gulf Stream, say, along a system of trenches as intricate as the Somme, the interlocking rootwork of broadleaf and bramble, barbed wire and abandoned mattresses, and arrive in the fullness of time at my granite doorstep and green weatherboard, a survivor of headlamps and barn owls and the lethal, laid ammonia like a stencil of pollen around the silos.

'Timmy. Are you in there? Say Yes if you are and No if you're not.'

I knew that was true because I had heard it on British television the time my father brought a television into the house on approbation for Hallowe'en and Poppy Day, and I went walking round and round the living room among the chair legs and the *National Geographics* like a radiation expert with his Geiger counter, scanning the mounted mantelpiece photographs with the two tipped rabbit ears, testing the coal scuttle and the picture railings to find the frequency of mercury, until, deep in the woodland of the bookshelves, the picture cleared like a crystal snowstorm, and the Queen of England frowned at the frowning clockwork artillery marching towards her, and my father told me that no feeling person was saying a word at this moment, and that even the perch in the rivers stood still under the shadow of the dragonflies.

'You'll be crawling with things when you come out,' Mrs Watt said. 'You'll be filthy. Filthy dirty. And your mother will be cross with me, you know.'

So I wormed deeper into the ticking wet of the bushes, into the slick pleats that shushed me as I entered them, into the damp tobacco undergrowth of the wild rhubarb and the shivery, chittering ferns, and I counted to sixty. I counted slowly, and between each number I said to myself the words 'Charlie Chaplin' because that was a second in time, the same as 'Mississippi'.

Then I did it again.

'There's hardly any point in my talking to ladybirds,' she said. 'You're obviously not in there. But, since blood is thicker than water, perhaps those dreadful creepy-crawlies that feed on Timmy's flesh whenever he creeps into their crawly headquarters will pass him the message that his mum and his dad will be back for the buffet in about three hours; and while I know them to be holy persons, made in the image and likeness of the Lord, they are not yet saints. They might even, at times, be a mother and a father instead of a dad and a mum.'

'Twenty-seven, Charlie Chaplin,' I said. 'Twenty-eight.'

'Goodbye,' she said.

'Twenty nine, goodbye, goodbye,' I said. 'Thirty, Charlie Chaplin.'

Spiders came and went on the hard bats of the leaves without once stopping to stroke each other. A fly sharpened its legs like a cutler. Two snails climbed the white rungs of a stalk. My eyelashes were growing at exactly the same speed.

When I blinked, I could hear my eyelids part like an apricot.

It was not until the hotel bus drove up the drive and skidded to a stop on the woozy gravel that I stood up and walked out of the jungle. The boy who had borrowed the billiard cue for a spear paddled toward me with a finger in his mouth and his feet at a quarter to three. Then he smiled.

'You missed nothing,' he said. 'He does not look a bit like Charlie Chaplin. He does not even have a moustache. He does not have a bowler, even. He looks like Khrushchev looks, and his voice is all English. He is an old codswallop with a big wig of white hair. All the wine gums in his pocket were stuck together. We should have stayed here. We should have stayed down at the dunes in Derrynane and had a crab massacre.'

Then I walked in my webbed feet through the smoked revolve swing of the hotel entrance and across the wicker cubicles of the tea room down the corridor where the hacked stags snarled from the crucified plaques and their antlers hanked the threads of turf-smoke carbon like a cobweb of grimy wool until I was outside Mrs Watt's room.

'Who is it?' she said. Her voice was tiled from the toilet walls.

'Me,' I told her. The antlers branched their shadows at me like a candelabrum.

'Come in, funny fellow,' she said. 'It's all right.'

There was one big bed and two small mirrors, but they had still paid more for No. 22 than my father had for No. 31 because of the sun all morning until eleven; and my mother understood that perfectly. I sat on the bed in the slump where Mrs Watt had been sitting, and the pouches of the quilt were still warm under the bare backs of my legs. Her private linen lay in the shape of a person beside me, first the brassiere and then the underpants, the dangly pegs and the rolled stockings, with the tasty, clear-headed smell of a banknote that has never been tousled in a trouser pocket.

'I'll be with you in a tic,' she said. 'Wait a moment.'

She was in the bathroom, steeping her feet in the bidet with her slacks pulled up to her knees. I could see her through the fracture of the door and the door frame though she couldn't tell I was watching because she'd bowed her head and her hair had fallen forward and extinguished most of her face.

'My feet swelled in my sandals,' she said. 'Now I can't wear my high heels. The hands are the first thing to go in a marriage. Then the feet. The feet are the second stage.'

'My mother says you have beautiful bone structure,' I said.

'What does your father say?' she said, and she eased her foot out of the bidet so that the water ran from it like wet wax as if it were an exhibit at an autopsy.

'He says that skin and bones is not as nice as flesh and blood,' I said; and she woofed and towelled her foot in one of her husband's vests, and came out then into the bedroom, half hopping, and took a good long look at me.

'I wonder if I ought to sit you into a bath,' she said. 'You're a bit whiffy.'

'Look,' I said, and I took off my shirt to show her the bites on my body.

'Jesus, Mary and Joseph,' said Mrs Watt. 'You're riddled.'

'Look,' I said, and I pulled down my pants and stood out of them, with only my waterproof sandals on me and the tank tread of my belt around my pelvis. 'Look.'

'You're covered,' she said. 'You're covered all over.' And she kneeled down in front of me and touched me here and there, here and there, with her soggy, drowned fingertips. 'You've been through the wars,' she said. 'What possessed you to play in there?'

'They go into me everywhere,' I said, and I gathered my scrotum in my hands. 'Here and inside my legs and between my bottom. I can show you.'

'They don't jump, do they? Like fleas, I mean.'

'No,' I said. 'They go deeper and deeper and then they lay their eggs.'

She stayed squatting in front of me for a moment, considering. Then she got up suddenly and went to the dressing table. I watched the two of them, the woman in the room and the woman in the mirror, two identical twins, inspect the instruments on its smoked-glass surface like a geometry set, projectors and compasses, the clicks and chinks becoming thuds when a steel comb or a tweezers was placed on the solid blotting paper and not on the clouded rink. For a time they were absorbed in a silver cuticle scissors they found there, pricking the white slough of their finger with the edge of one shear. But I was content to sit there with my skin drying on my body like a warm apron of sand after the wave has withdrawn.

'*The Devil Rides Out*,' I said, and I bent over to squint at the other titles in the stack at the barley-screw bedside table. '*Zero at Midday* by Saburo Sakai. *The Bible's Revised Standards*.'

'If you can't close your eyes,' she said, 'a good read is better than fine writing.'

The woman in the mirror said it too, but not out loud: she spoke it to herself, as if she had known the words all along and was waiting, listening for the line of the song on the wireless while she ironed white laundry. Her mouth motioned and smiled.

'My mother fell asleep once in the sun,' I said, 'and the book left a white square at the top of her ribs.'

Slow frog sounds spluttered from the bidet. Wafts from her cottons soothed me. The woman in the mirror had a more beautiful bone structure than the woman at the dressing table. That was the thing.

'So,' she said, turning to me with the bright scissors in her hand. 'Lie on the bed is best. We'd better make you presentable for your mother.'

When I reached the outside wall of the hotel annexe, where the odours of turpentine sharpened the sheep's-wool scent of the eighteenth hole, I could hear a woman's paid screams and the voices of Laurel and Hardy from the games room; so it was teatime for the children, six o'clock or thereabouts, with at least three hours' light left. Across the lake the lamentation of one individual bird intoned the same phrase over and over, the same weakening treble again and again, like a tone-deaf idiot child practising a recorder in the parish hall; and it stayed with me at the shore and under the orange struts of the disused railway bridge and across the anglers' rope bridge to the burnt-down boathouse where the farty bog would snigger as it clutched your gumboots. I trotted on with the hat box under my arm, and the faint blowpipe falsetto darted over the water and the water feathered its flight; and I thought that perhaps the mate or the mother of the bird that was beside itself had been brought in a sheet of the *Manchester Guardian* to a taxidermist in town.

Where the dunes began, I lay low. There were still people about, though the sun was stretching their matchstick shadows the way my mother stretched her imported stockings, and only a few adults were standing up to their waist in the sea, hugging their white abandoned torsos over the liquid jigsaw of their legs. I could hear the clapped calls, the barking of pet names and, closer still, off to the left of me, in the crumbled gully where I roller-coasted on tea trays, girls' voices going mad.

'You must have done a gallon.'

'I've more to go.'

Through the quills of stiff seagrass I could see the two of them in a giggly conga churning the sand with their bare feet while the pee spread faster downhill, and laughing like gods as they yanked at their swimsuits under their skirts.

'Don't make me laugh,' one of them said. 'I've a weak floor.' And they rolled down the slope and lay at the bottom, screaming and crying.

I gathered up my hatbox and went on behind the gully and beyond the canvas windbreaks where the seminarians sheltered, bus tickets for bookmarks in their Penguin paperbacks and jam sandwiches with the crusts cut off them in a housekeeper's tin-foil folds; and farther again, where a woman was burying her husband in the grey, damp sand and patting his chest with the flat of the spade as she called her toddler.

'Look, Gregory, look. Isn't Daddy silly?'

'This is ridiculous,' the father said. 'He's a year behind his age.'

'How is he ever going to learn anything if he hears you saying things like that?' she said. 'You've been saying things like that since he was born. Look, Gregory. Stupid, stupid Daddy.'

But the father sat up straight and the sand fell off him in breast-plates, and he had no hair on his chest and the same religious medal-lion that my own father wore except to the swimming pool in case it got rusty. Then the mother kicked sand in his face and Gregory swung at her with the seaweed in his bucket as I jumped into a trench and ran along its length to find a windsock in the overgrown wire fence that would bring me into the fortified churchyard.

Down where the land and the sea leaked into each other in a little denuded triangle of ground, an eroding ochre domain of wildflowers and metatarsi, of bumblebees and human remnants, were the rock pools of the mauled Uranian crabs; and the break-water concrete slabs were still crunchy with the numbered armour of the smashed hostages from the last crustacean massacre in the Derrynane dunes on the evening before my parents had read me Ezekiel's lecture from their memory cells. Even now, I could see some blackening claws that the gulls had not yet come for. They lay where they had been pulled off during the race to handicap the fastest crabs in the derby.

There, when I parted the prickly, saline grass with my two thumbs, was a hole I could squeeze through.

Suddenly there was a noise, a rattling, and the bones came together, bone to its bone. I looked, and there were sinews on them, and flesh had come upon them, and skin had covered them; but there was no breath in them.

That was what it said in Mr Watt's Service Bible on the page that I had worked loose from its binding with the edge of the cuticle scissors. I read it at the speed of the ambo where the elderly canon counted to four in an undertone at every colon, although it was difficult because the print on the opposite side of the cigarette paper piggybacked each gothic letter as if the real message were being deciphered at dead of night painstakingly over a floating wick.

Thus says the Lord God: I am going to open your graves, and bring you up from your graves, O my people; and I will bring you back to the land of Israel. And you shall know that I am the Lord, when I open your graves, and bring you up from your graves, O my people.

The pelvis smelled of potato skin and spaghetti from the bin at the back of the hotel, but it was glad to be home. It twitched a bit in my hands like a water-diviner's fork, sensing its underground source. I was not sure if it was a man's centre of gravity, or a woman's, or if it spoke English at all. It may have been washed ashore from a Hungarian shipwreck, or belonged to one of the Africans who had been adopted for a pound, ten shillings a week, by the farmers with cattle grids. But I blessed it and kissed it and stooped into the hole.

I will put my spirit within you, and you shall live, and I will place you on your own soil.

'How long more?' said a voice from the other side, from inside the churchyard, from deep within its prohibited, lumpy precinct; and I thought at once of the muslin sleeves of the rain trailing across the gable of the oratory to where the old gillie stood in the science-fiction thistles, rotating his hat brim like a rosary. It was the same muffled mouth, as if the flour of too many scones had coated his gums. But the truth was he had no teeth: they had been strewn across the universe, and his diet was down to boiled pears.

'Eternity takes time,' said a second voice; and this voice, frank and Yankee, the voice of Paramount and Universal, was American.

'You're as long as the priest,' said the gillie. 'Do you know that?'

'No, I don't know that. As long as the priest at what?' the American said.

'At funerals, anyway.'

'This is not a funeral. This is the opposite of a funeral.'

'It'd be my funeral if some artist turned up with his paintbox. They're always coming here to paint. Then they do a dance when it rains.'

We're not grave robbers. Do you see yourself as a grave-robber, Kenneth?'

'No,' said a third voice, lighter, more lenient. 'I don't see myself as a grave robber. I see myself as someone who's filling cradles for the dormitories of the Lord.'

'Amen,' said the other American.

'Amen,' said the gillie. 'Mind your step at the MacCarthy vault. There's a rabbit burrow that could sprain your ankle.'

I wedged the hatbox into a cage of roots and I worked my way forward on my belly until I could peep up over the hedgerow where it sank steeply, suddenly, surprisingly, in a pink dyke. Across the semi-desert of the cemetery, among many wall-fallen head-stones, sat the bareheaded gillie. He was leaning his side and shoulder against the pillar of what had been a stone cross or a megalith, maybe, and you would have imagined he was about to milk a cow or to hear a confession. He had made himself that comfortable.

But the two Americans were moving among the graves.

'How about this individual?' said one of them. In their creamed and gleaming skulls, their accurate, black, scholastic jackets, and the burly books they portered like brickbats in their pale right hands, it was hard to tell them apart.

'Who is it?' said the gillie.

'McHenry, Charles. Charles T.P.'

'Charlie was a great friend of my father's,' said the gillie. 'He ran away to sea at fifty, and he came back five years later. There was no other woman. It was ships and the sea.'

'Was he a relation?'

'I always called him Uncle Charlie,' said the gillie. 'After he came home, I called him Mr McHenry. My mother felt we owed it to his wife.'

'Was he bloodline?' said the American. 'We can only baptize the bloodline.'

'We've been over that ground a good few times,' said the other. 'It's not negotiable. We want to be sure that every cot in the dormitory is properly tagged.'

The gillie stared into the inside of his hat on his lap. My father had said it would go up like a Molotov cocktail if you threw a lighted match into it. It was as volatile as gelignite with ancestral grease.

'He was,' the gilly said. 'He was a relation. He was immediate family.'

'Then we'll baptize him too,' the American said. 'There is room at the Lord's table for Charles McHenry.'

'Not just room,' said the other, and he seemed to be loosening the screw top of a flask as the other balanced his book in the palm of one hand and let it spread its heavy halves like a conjuror's paper bouquet.

'Not just room,' said the American. 'A place of honour. Even for those who go down to the sea in ships the Lord offers a lasting anchorage.'

'Amen,' said the gilly.

'OK,' the American said. 'Then we're done.'

'It's just that they do come,' the gilly said. 'I tell them they should paint the sunrise, but they say, no, no way, not at all, you can tell a sunrise from a sunset even in a photograph. These are people who wouldn't stir until the middle of the day, do you know? It'd be easier to wake the dead.'

I reached back to the hatbox and lifted out the pelvis. It was already within ten yards of consecrated earth. If you could hear a valid Mass on the steps of a church without once going in, you could trust that the vicinity of a graveyard shared in the sacredness of the burial ground. I could do no better; I could do no worse. Besides, any passer-by or picnicker who discovered the fragment would be nearly naked for another day at the beach, all flip-flops and synthetic trunks and cooking fat for a swift tan, and they would be unlikely in that state to touch what might have been the jawbone of a mule or the back passage of a pet camel. I lobbed it into the soft smother of nettles and stole away in the evil squelch of my sandals.

'Charles T.P. McHenry,' the American was saying. 'As you lie here today in this beautiful churchyard awaiting the resurrection of the flesh at the Last Judgment, when the Christ of God will summon you before him to disclose the totality of your works and days, do you of your own volition, without coercion or constraint, proclaim the risen Jesus, Emmanuel Sabaoth, as your personal Saviour, and so seek baptism by water and the power of the Holy Spirit through the presence of a proxy of your bloodline?'

'He does,' said the gillie.

'Charles T.P. McHenry, your gravestone reminds us that your eternal life began about nine months before January 17th, 1878. Do you acknowledge that everything since then and so far has been corruption and darkness?'

'He would,' said the gillie. 'He was always straight.'

I went in a wide arc that took me down and around the foreshore and along the headland, over slithery kelp and a dumped Volkswagen to a village of soundless rhododendrons where a feeding bird could not have been bothered to glance at me as I passed him. Only the grass that I walked on made a sound, as slight as a smoker exhaling:

only the grass, and the coal-fire fretting of scratchy heather, and the bubbly chuckles of my shoes if I forded wetness. So I slowed to a tramp until I could breathe through my nose.

'One, Charlie Chaplin. Two, Charlie Chaplin. Three.'

The gillie was standing in front of me with his hands in his pockets.

'Hello, skipper,' he said.

'Good evening,' I said.

'It is,' he said. 'Thank God.'

And we stood there for a while, looking at each other. A planet of midges condensed in the shimmer between us. They flicked my skin like a party sparkler, but I did not blink or groom my face.

'When was the first car you saw in your life?' I said.

The bird who was mentally ill was still at it, the whiney piping. I had come that far.

'It was before the war,' he said. 'It was before the Great War. I was walking in a Corpus Christi procession and a car stopped to watch us. Then we stopped to watch the car. Even the priest who was carrying the Real Presence turned around to look. It was a high, open car, with lamps like a lighthouse. The women were dressed like bee-keepers, with long veils that hung down to their laps. My father said to me: "You've seen everything. Go on now"; and I did.'

'All right,' I said.

He took his hand from his coat pocket and stared at it as if it were the embryo of a pigeon that had fallen out of a pylon and lay in its fossil goo in his palm.

'When I was your age,' he said, 'a man came to my town with a tripod and a projector, and the parish priest gave him the loan of a sheet from his own double bed in the presbytery to use as a screen. But I'd gone and done something wrong, and I don't know what it was. My mother fetched me home. She was in there darning socks with a wooden mushroom while the whole peninsula carted church-benches out into the open air to watch Charlie Chaplin trick on a tramcar; and they brought the upright out of the presbytery too and the organist, Mr Barlow, played a ragtime tune. He had more than hymns, you see, in his sheet music. The way they were laughing would have woken the dead. I never in my life heard laughter like that. I was not myself, Skipper. I was beside myself. I hit the wall with my fist, and my mother said: "Serve you right, you scut." It was the hardest blow I struck, then or later.'

The flies were in my hair, my eyelashes, my lips. I was being eaten alive.

'The little bones were never the same,' he said. 'My hand still hurts when the mercury sinks. Winter, it's a numb class of a throbbing; summer, a sort of a scalded ache. There are injections, of course.'

My shoulder was not itself. That was from throwing the pelvis the way I had. My armpit would pain me for three days now. It had happened before.

'I am not saying a bad word about my mother,' the old gillie said. 'She was a saint in her own right.'

He reached out in the smell of shag and vase-lined spinners and brushed the flies from my face with the front of his hand.

'Go on now,' he said. 'You've seen everything'

From there to the dirty foxhole where the buried father wrestled with the elastic of his underpants beneath his towel and stalked away in a pet from his child in tears, I did not turn back; as far as the gully where the girls cavorted, I did not look behind; well within spitting distance of the rope bridge and the boat-house, I waded in my waterproofs without swerving or stopping. But then my sandals smarted and hurt me, and I sat down and unstrapped them from the criss-cross patterns of sunlight and moonlight that the weave of the plastic had imprinted there. I inspected them like that for ages, the two shuddering animals that had landed me here; their alien, holy swellings. They had walked me into it, the sensible world.

I coaxed them into my lap and cradled them there.

ACCESS

And back he comes from the queue at the counter to the table where I'm sitting waiting, because he hasn't any cash, the same as last Saturday and in the same McDonalds too; but I say instead:

'Dad.'

I haven't called him Daddy for a long time. It was Dad by the time he left; it was Dad for ages before that, even. It just happens at a certain stage, ten, eleven, sooner for boys, I suppose, and you don't notice. First you stop saying Dadda, then you stop saying Daddy. Perhaps there's a point when you don't call him anything at all.

'I'm sorry, Wagsie,' he says. 'I'll go to the pass machine.'

And off he rushes, slipping in between all the other separated dads carrying trays ahead of their children, with his rolled-up newspaper jutting out of his pocket in the long navy coat that he wears when we meet at the weekend because I hate his anoraks that make him look poor.

I still haven't decided to tell him my news.

'Can I sit here?' says a mother, bossy with sundaes and tea bags, and I explain:

'My dad is sitting here. And my mum. My dad's gone to get money.'

'You can't reserve seats,' she says. 'It's not fair.'

She has hairs on her cheeks like sideburns. She smells of apple-flavour toilet freshener. But I say to her:

'My dad will be back in a minute.'

In fact, the pass machine isn't working and my dad has to traipse across the road with a bus beeping him, into the newsagent where he buys - this is true - a fart cushion for me and a copy of *Sugar* to get cashback for our Happy Meal.

'I don't want a Happy Meal,' I say to him. What I want is a cheeseburger, a caramel sundae and a medium diet Sprite.

'I'll have the happy meal,' he says. There's a character from *Lord of the Rings* in it. I thought you loved *Lord of the Rings*. We saw it twice.

'I'm too old for a happy meal,' I say. 'All the people getting happy meals are about two. I'm in sixth class. I have to read an article out of the *Irish Times* every week. Then I have to do bullets about it on the board.'

'Well,' he says, 'if you're so enormous, you can get the grub.'

He has shaved everywhere except around the psoriasis beside his ear, and he looks nice really without the scruffy beard. Also he has cut the bits of skin that stuck up around the moons of his fingernails. I watch him from the queue as he punches his newspaper out in the middle. And I wonder what he'd say if I did tell him. He would be over the moon, actually. He is not like other dads. My mother wishes he were. At least she wishes he had been.

'*Shay shay,*' I say to the Chinese man who hands me our lunch, because *shay shay* is the Chinese for thank you, and it must be nice for them to hear their own language.

'I am not Chinese,' he says. 'I am Korean American. But fair play to you.'

And I take my change from him, all the euro bits and pieces that come from other countries, Germany and Greece, places I am going to go to university in some day, and then I shove and push my way back to the table through the other waiting dads. Some of the other dads look younger than my dad does, because my dad hasn't shaved his head or bought slitty glasses like an eejit. He is not ashamed to say that he watched the first landing on the moon.

'Earth calling Dad,' I say, and I settle the tray.

'Listen,' he says, studying his paper like it was a treasure map. 'Do you remember that terrible train crash?'

'No,' I say. 'What terrible train crash?'

There is a Gandalf figure in the Happy Meal. A child would love it. I take it out and examine it a bit. Somewhere at home I have a model of Obelix, the funny fatso who carries huge boulders on his back, and it almost choked the dog and my mother had to boil it for ages afterwards in the kettle. But that was long ago. It has faded like Polaroids do.

'In this terrible train crash,' my dad goes on, 'there were dreadful casualties. People were burned to a cinder. There was one man they thought had been burned to a cinder, but he hadn't been. Instead, he survived the crash and slipped away before anybody noticed.'

'Why?' I say with my mouth full. The chips from the Happy Meal are pretty good, actually. I am hungrier than I thought I would have been.

'To start a new life,' says my dad. 'To begin again. To begin all over. To rise up from the ashes.'

'That is not so brilliant,' I say. 'What about his family?'

He thinks about that for a while, hunched over the paper and staring down at the leaky, wrecked ketchup sachet.

'He probably felt', my father says, 'that it was the best thing he could do for them.'

My dad always sounds like a priest when he says something unintelligible, so I knock back the Sprite too quickly and it soaks the collar of my sweater. But the lovely icy slush seeps through my train tracks onto my tongue.

'Would there be a coffin at a funeral if there was nothing left to go in it?' I say. 'Or would there be a jewellery box?'

'I don't know,' he says. 'You could bury a photograph. Or a change of clothes.'

'That's why Mum went mad,' I say. 'You say weird things in a priest's voice.'

My father stares through the window at the other dads in their shirtsleeves smoking outside in the carpark.

'How is she?' he says. 'How is Mum?'

'There was a diet on the radio and she lost weight. She lost five kilos.'

'I can't do kilos,' he says. 'I can do stones and things. I can do tons.'

'There is less calories in chocolate gold-grain digestives than there is in Weight Watchers,' I tell him. 'She was pretty pleased about that. She has gone back to dunking them.'

'Don't you worry about Weight Watchers,' he says. 'I work with women who wear their overcoats when the central heating's on, because they won't eat anything. Skin and bones, the lot of them. Skeletons in kindergarten smocks. Their breath is bad from the lack of food. Rocket and broccoli, and a half a stick of KitKat at the water cooler on payday.'

Sometimes it is pashminas and lemongrass, but today it is smocks and broccoli. The KitKat is completely new.

'I don't want you ending up anorectic,' he says.

'It's anorexic, I tell him. There's an X in it. I looked it up on Wikipedia.'

'What's Wikipedia?' he says. 'I looked it up in the *Oxford English Dictionary*.'

There is a streak of ketchup on the face of the girl on the cover of *Sugar*. He makes it worse for a while by scraping it with a fork. The daub becomes a doodle. He is not just thinking, you see. He is thinking to himself.

'And how's the boyfriend?' he says at last. 'How's Raymond?'

'Redmond is Redmond,' I say.

'Is he around?' says my dad.

'You know he is,' I say. 'When he is, I sleep with Mum. I sleep on your side. He sleeps in my room. Mum won't change my sheets afterwards, when I ask her. She says if I don't change them for a dachshund, she's not going to change them for a human being.'

'He's all right,' my dad says. 'He wears corduroy on his elbows of his jacket. Corduroy on the elbows of your jacket is cool.'

'Corduroy is all right,' I say. 'He wants you to think that he's a lecturer somewhere and not just a geography teacher in a school.'

But my dad hides behind the weekend supplement because someone he shared a room with in the alcoholics' unit in the hospital on the other side of the junction from the shopping centre has taken off a crash helmet at the counter.

Suddenly I decide to say it. There and then. Out of the blue. It wells up.

'He won't remember you,' I say. 'That was when you had the scruffy beard. Listen. Do you know what? I had a period.'

He comes out from behind the weekend supplement.

'No,' he says.

'I did.'

His face smiles and all the lines go out of it, except for the line from the stitches when he passed out in the taxi. Then he walks his fingers slowly across the table until they touch the charm bracelet on my wrist. His nail is still stained from cigarettes; but it will grow out.

'My little woman has become a big girl,' he says.

'It's really the other way round,' I say. His fingers climb up on my hand and hold it.

'If this was India, we'd have a feast,' he says. 'But it's only bloody Ireland.'

'We could go to *Lord of the Rings* again,' I say, 'and have popcorn.'

'We'll do better than that', he says. 'Much better. We won't have a feast, but we'll have a field trip. We'll go to the dolmen.'

And we get up and go, just like that, like we always do, while the man with the crash helmet is hiding his face from us with his gauntlet and the separated dads are taking the burger bread and breaking it and giving the pieces to their children.

Access to the dolmen is through a long passageway, a lane between wooden Americany houses with flat roofs and eucalyptus trees on a ridge that looks down over Dublin. You could stop and pick out the shopping centre, and listen to the low, throaty sounds of the motorway, but guard dogs growl at you as you go by and wedge their noses between the planks of the partition fences, so that you run past them. I am a bit too old to hold my dad's hand, but I hang on to the button of his coat sleeve.

'Imagine,' he keeps saying. 'My little woman has become a big girl.'

It has been a year at least since the last time we visited the dolmen, but it is still there, as quiet as ever, the shiny capstone long enough to play hopscotch on, and the two big, dogged uprights where a family sheltered during the Famine and where we ate a box of After Eights in the rain on my first Holy Communion. At the far end of the field where a metal plaque on a post reads Office of Public Works, a horse is rubbing its tail end against it. Drool is running from its mouth like a sort of yoghurt.

'I was always saying to the priest we should come here early on Easter morning and read the Resurrection stories,' says my dad. 'But he thought it'd be too cold.'

'Dad, 'I say, 'I don't like the horse. Why is he rolling around in the nettles?'

My dad looks at him. You would think he was a vet, examining a specimen.

'He's a mare,' he says finally. 'He's having a foal. Look at how big he is.'

'Let's go back,' I say. 'Look at her dribbling.'

'We'll go round the other side,' Dad says. 'We'll circle her.'

But when we reach the dolmen at last and Dad goes into his druid mode, resting his palms on the side of the capstone, and then his forehead too, the horse straightens and stands up and looks at us. I do not think she is in search of a sugar lump.

'Dad,' I say. 'She's walking towards us.'

'There's room in the world for the three of us,' he says. 'Not forgetting the foal.' He's back in the days of picnics here and me squatting behind the trees when I had to.

'The people who raised these stones are still in our bloodstream,' he says. 'You can hear them with a stethoscope.'

Then the horse quickens towards us and lowers its head like a bull would. Like a bull it charges at us, and I let my father's coat-sleeve drop and I run away. I am running so fast I cannot hear my feet or my legs or my body, only the wind and the sky. When I stop, I hear the world again. I look back.

'Get out of the field, Wagsie!' my father shouts. 'Get out!' He's walking backwards between me and the horse, holding his hands up like a soldier surrendering. Then he trips and falls, and the horse rears up over him, whinnying, rolling its eyeballs, goo peeling like white of egg from its gums, and its mad hooves pedalling the air.

'Daddy,' I say. 'Daddy.'

The horse soars, stops, swerves to the side, and canters off. Midges are settling on my skin. My dad comes scrambling to me. His face is as red as if he had been drunk. And we do a sort of three-legged race to the car, the two of us, to the fart cushion and the magazine and all the empty takeaway cartons that are the middle of God.

'My little woman has become a big girl,' he says, but his breathing is still in ruins and his hands twitch on the steering wheel. I know that I am much older than he is and that he is already aged.

I bleed for him. My big daddy has become a little boy. I walk my fingers slowly over his arm until they touch his watch-strap.

'We'd better not let your mum find out about this,' he says. 'The next thing you know I'd have to see you with a social worker.'

The moon has come up on the left hand side of the car although the sun is still shining down on Saturday afternoon.

'I'll tell her we went to *Lord of the Rings*,' I say. 'For the third time.'

'For the third time,' he says. 'But she'll try to catch us out. She'll ask: "Which episode did you go to? Was it Episode 1 or Episode 2 or Episode 3?" She'd go and check the bloody CCTV.'

I rub the hairs on his hand backwards like a parent should. There is a bit of a hangnail on the moon of his left thumb, and a dent on the thumb where the French door slammed at the Holy Communion party. Once upon a time I used to suck his cigarette finger for the taste of it, the garden shed and summer evening of it. If I did that now, of course, they would come and take him away. So I rub the hairs on his hand forwards again.

'Dadda,' I say. 'Dadda.'

BARBER-SURGEONS

To begin with, they had nothing in common, the surgeon and the barber, although Mr Bevan was a great devourer of newspapers and could always find something in them, so long as it wasn't the sports page, to entertain a customer.

'I see,' he said, 'that Pope John has gone and excommunicated Castro.'

'Has he?' said the surgeon. He was staring at his hands in the mirror, and wondering if he should insure them. Look what had happened to the child's finger in the car window. Even across in London they could have done nothing.

'He has,' Mr Bevan said. 'It's not like Pope John to do that. Even Protestants think he's a pet. But I suppose the whole Cuba business is beyond the beyond.'

'Has he excommunicated Chairman Khrushchev?'

Mr Bevan thought about this for a while as he clipped briskly at the base of the skull where the surgeon's hair oil had pollinated his shirt collar.

'Khrushchev,' he said, pronouncing the word as his client had, with the stress on the second syllable and not on the first, which was strange, 'may not be subject to Pope John's jurisdiction. Would he be a Russian Orthodox?'

'Quite.'

Then there was a silence for a space, and the surgeon stared in the mirror at the barber's girlish wrists, at the one recessed knuckle bone from an old collision, and at the hands themselves then, which were quite middle class, really, for a cutter of hair; and the barber listened in turn to the vertical rain in the little street upstairs, the great crashing glasshouses of it that gave him always a queer pleasure. Something wonderful must have happened to him once in a downpour. That was it.

'And Eichmann is for the high jump,' he said. The man in the chair was wearing a cheap chain of some sort round his neck. Perhaps he was a Catholic after all, though you would not think it from the genteel things he did, such as taking off his chamois glove to shake hands or saying Quite where he might as easily have said Indeed. Good manners was always a giveaway.

'Eichmann,' the surgeon said. 'I imagine he's happy to be hanged. I imagine he's been waiting for this for almost twenty years now. He must be the most miserable person on the planet.'

'There's that. It would certainly make you think.'

Mr Bevan's breath whooshed loose small hairs from the doctor's neck. There was grey among the auburn and it served him right, too. In or out of a barber's chair it was discourteous to say something that was so paradoxical as to be unintelligible. But the barber let it pass. Better to lose the conflict than the custom.

'Mr Horngrad,' he said, 'who comes into me each and every month for a trim and a talk has a tattoo from the camps. Don't ask me which one. It's not Belsen. It's not Buchenwald. Anyhow. There's more hair on his arm than on his head, but you can see it. Now, sir!'

And he whisked the green gown away like a toreador's veronica, pedalled the chair down to the dismount level, and steadied the surgeon as he stepped out on to the magpie rug of hair on the new linoleum. It was a good day when he had to sweep that floor before lunchtime.

'I'm tired of the Second Vatican Council before it begins and I'm tired of the Second World War since it ended,' said his customer. 'But I never get tired of the cinema. I went to see a film the night Kennedy talked on TV about the missile sites. Had the whole place to myself too. Have you seen *Dr No* at the Capitol?'

'Have I seen *Dr No*?' Mr Bevan said. 'I've seen it twice. The queues!'

'The dialogue. Or at least the *double entendres*.'

'And the stunts,' said Mr Bevan. 'Lord above!'

'And the girls.'

'And the girls, God bless them,' Mr Bevan said.

'Bless them and breed them,' the surgeon said. 'We could do with a few.'

But that was the slightest bit off colour, and Mr Bevan metabolized it slowly, putting the clippers away awkwardly among the sterilizers.

'And Connery, of course,' he said then. 'Cometh the hour, cometh the man.'

'Beautiful body,' said the other. 'If I had that body on my operating table, I think I'd call the College of Art instead of the College of Surgeons.'

It had stopped raining. Mr Bevan looked up the narrow stairs to the street. It was as if his ears had been syringed. The pond of his hearing quivered and cleared and became sky. Sun broke through.

'You're a doctor?'

'I'm a general surgeon,' he said. 'I work around the corner. I do mostly the throat to the privates. The odd one survives me. My name is Roper.'

'My name is Bevan, Dr Roper,' said the barber. He still had the gown in his hands too, with a long yellow nail on his index finger.

Anyone would think he was a smoker or dirty. But it was only the strong rinses gave you the soggy, stained palps.

'Surgeons are never called doctors,' Mr Roper said. 'Don't know why. It's just a thing. Anyhow, I'll be your outpatient in future, Mr Bevan. I'll ask for you specially.'

'I'm the only one here,' the barber said. 'I inherited the second chair and the name of the shop. I wouldn't have chosen The Barber of Seville myself. It's a bit loud. I would have chosen something more subdued.'

'Why not the girl's name from *Dr No*? Was it Honey Ryder?' And the surgeon hummed a few phrases from the film's theme as he sank into his saturated coat. Wet or not, it was as good-looking a garment as any undertaker's.

'Goodbye now.'

'Goodbye, sir.'

Mr Bevan watched the consultant taking the rubbered steps two at a time. There was no price inked indelibly on those shoes. The handmade leather shoes from God knows where waited an instant on the mat at the metal door saddle, and were gone.

—

After that it was mostly plain sailing.

'I'm wrong,' said a waiting customer from a bentwood chair in the tiled corner, and he coughed productively. His nose had been set by an intern at some stage and not by a registrar. It was still deflected, as if pressed against a tumbler. 'It's not two thousand. It's twenty thousand. Sure I'm wearing my brother's glasses. No wonder. Twenty thousand dead in a landslide. See for yourself. Page three, top of, right-hand side. What kind of a fucked-up faraway place is South America?'

But Mr Bevan and Mr Roper were gone off to other latitudes.

'How they get away with it is the question,' the barber said, slicing through a silver strand at the scalp. 'Pussy Galore, how are you? The censor must have been born in the bogs. Even I knew that much growing up in Stoneybatter.'

'Did you ever hear "gobblejob"?' said the surgeon.

'That's typical Liberties English for you,' Mr Bevan said. 'Stoneybatter set a higher tone to things.'

'I heard gobblejob on my ward rounds yesterday,' Mr Roper said. 'First sighting in twenty years. Thought it went out with Chaucer. None of my students cracked it. They're all from the suburbs, you see. Of course, they all knew Oddjob.'

Mr Bevan snipped considerately along the curve of the ear where the morning's razor had forgotten to. There was a pink linear indentation there. That, of course, was from the elastic of the mask he wore in surgery.

'Oddjob the Jap,' he said to the doctor. 'Oddjob and his bowler hat I met a fellow who was a POW in I don't know where. Maybe Burma. He used to memorize a page of the Bible and then use it for cigarette paper. By the time he was freed he could have gone for the priesthood. But he wasn't able to sit through *Goldfinger*. He's put up with beriberi and beatings, but the mere sight of a Nip was enough to make his hands sweat.'

Mr Roper looked at the large wall mirror in front of him and saw in its reflection the further reflection of a small hand-mirror held behind his head for a customer's close inspection of results. The capillaries were definitely whitening like cradle cap. His testicles would be snowy in ten years' time.

'Kennedy would have loved Pussy Galore,' he said to the barber. 'He was a genius and a great man, of course, but he was also what they call in the States a fraternity jock. He would have gone for Honor Blackman. He would have gone through Honor Blackman. In fact, I think he may have seen the movie at a private viewing before he went to Dallas.'

'Would you believe that it wasn't even made then?' said Mr Bevan. 'No, it was the earlier one with Robert Shaw as the gentleman caller from Spectre. That was *From Russia with Love* and JFK previewed it in the White House, only a week or ten days after I waved to him in Winetavern Street. I was so close, Mr Roper, I could almost smell his aftershave. Sure the bodyguards were hugging the kiddies. It was like a Corpus Christi procession gone mad.'

'He was my age exactly,' said the surgeon, standing on the footrest. 'Give or take a few weeks.'

'Me too,' Mr Bevan said, 'give or take a few months,' and he stood on his toes to brush scintillating debris from the surgeon's shoulders. Was it destiny or the few quid that made the specialist's skin supple and his scaly? 'He was the only man you could stand up in public and say *I love him*, and get away with it.'

'Sometimes I loved him, sometimes I hated him,' Mr Roper said eventually. 'Role models have an awful way of turning into rivals. Today's outstanding examples become tomorrow's enemies. I prefer a world without Gods. A world without Gods is entirely human.'

'There's that,' said Mr Bevan. 'It would certainly make you think. I'll get your jacket.'

'Listen to this,' said the waiting customer with the deviated septum, and he looked up at them. 'Page four, middle of, left-hand side. The Supreme Court in America has banished prayer in the classroom. There you are in black and white. No more Our Fathers, no more Faith of our Fathers. What sort of a fucked-up faraway place is Yankee Doodle Dandyland?'

But Mr Bevan was noticing sweat stains on the lined armpit of Mr Roper's jacket; and Mr Roper in turn had seen the tremor in his hand as he reached up to the antlers of the coat-stand.

'Middle age,' said the general surgeon to the general barber, 'is neither one thing nor the other. You can't see the starting line; you can't see the finishing tape.'

They looked at each other briefly, the brown and the blue eyes.

'Old age thinks well of the halfway stage,' said the barber. 'A man in the Incurables said to me once he'd rather be sick and thirty-five than well and seventy.'

'You meet a wise class of patient in that place.'

'There was a lovely thing I saw in the *Reader's Digest*,' Mr Bevan said, although he had really been saving this for the next visit. 'It said that the sun itself is a middle-aged star, so perhaps we're in good company.'

And even when the doctor had gone, laughing his way up the stairs and out of earshot, into the lanes of prams and the glaring winter, and Mr Bevan was slapping stinging water on the sandpaper skin of the man with the concave face, he still loaded and reloaded that parting shot. It had been perfectly timed and thought through. It was almost worthy of 007.

———

Then the screen faded and the houselights came up and the barber in the back row under the projectionist's lens condensed again into Terylene trousers and a single sibilant denture. Why did they ruin it for everyone with an intermission? It was a terrible thing to step from the clarity of Caribbean waters, in the company of Dominique, and into the chlorine of a sterile public baths, from coral to parterre in the sunspot of an instant. It was a kind of death beside which dying itself could seem lively.

Thunderball, he thought. Even the title was stylish. Masculine and concise with a slipstream of slyness from its submarine innuendo. But how had Bond twigged that the wraith in widow's weeds was a lethal transvestite? Yet you couldn't really cavil: wit, killings, bikinis — they accomplished an infinite trinity. And there was a fifth film promised already, its première to be held in the Queen's presence. So much for the scoffers and sneerers. So much for the bald-headed bishop of the Church of Ireland who had cut him as he started small-talking Bond business the week before during a ten-minute tonsure. They could laugh their varsity hearts out at the daft plotlines and bedlinen, but that had not prevented *Goldfinger* and *Dr No* from being tremendous and true, at least as much as the sagas of round towers and round tables.

It was that very truth which challenged Mr Bevan now. Why had he never considered the secret service? He was old enough to be entitled to a British passport. To be sure, he would slaughter more sparingly than James, and afford each foreign agent opportunities for prayer before the necessary ballistic climax. But it was all too late. There was too much water under the bridge. Indeed, there were too many bridges under water.

Would he chance a packet of Rolos? They had stuck in his plate last time.

When he angled his distance glasses on the bridge of his nose, he saw the doctor at once, a beige, slightly italicized figure, buying an ice-cream tub from a teenage girl with a tiered refreshments tray at the fire exit; and his first instinct was to stand, because his body had known no other relationship to the man. Then, because he was standing, he waved; felt foolish, hunched, and hid.

The chandeliers were going out again. It was just as well. Mr Roper might be with children or with their mother, if he had a wife, or with a housekeeper, even. The lack of a ring on his wedding finger meant little. Clearly, no man who dressed as smartly could live alone. There was a slavey somewhere. At any rate, he couldn't greet a camel-haired consultant in a duffle coat. After all, courtesy wasn't a code. It was awareness of the needs of the other. You did not cause embarrassment.

Mr Bevan softened the salt-and-vinegar crisp in his mouth for a long time before scrunching it. That was out of consideration for the fellow in the next seat, because the munching would be too audible otherwise. Actually, you could be a saint in all sorts of situations. Indeed, if you were striving for sanctity, you shouldn't be deterred by social form. Therefore he would in fact salute the surgeon, but on the way out. He would do it visibly. He would do it vocally. It was his human right.

Later, though, as the radiant congregation descended the blinding, balustraded staircase that had been built for the *Titanic* and never installed, he saw no sign of the head that he had shaped so often but could not see inside.

Cut to the Barber of Seville and enter Mr Horngrad.

'Watch now,' Mr Bevan said in a breathy whisper to the surgeon's ear. 'You'll see for yourself. On a warm day like this one, he'll wear a short-sleeved shirt. The tattoo is on his left arm. Or is it his right? The mirror reverses everything.'

'Quite so,' said Mr Roper.

'You'll be sad to learn,' said Mr Horngrad, his voice a cadenced counter-tenor's as he sat with a three-coloured ice pop in his fist, 'that Stan Laurel has passed on. But I can't remember if he was the fat one or the thin one, so I don't know who to grieve for.'

'The skinny sidekick. Let me take your jacket,' said Mr Bevan. 'Did you happen to hear on the radio about the Crucifixion?'

'I heard about it before radio was invented,' Mr Horngrad said. 'I have been hearing about it all my life. I gather I am somehow to blame.'

'That's the point,' said Mr Bevan. 'You're not. Pope Paul has just apologized on all our behalves. Roman Catholic and Reformed Catholic. So there.'

Right enough, the man was tattooed. It was the sallow hallmark of his mettle, the badge of tragedy. But why didn't they go for a skin graft? Skin grafts were two a penny these days. Hadn't that manic stevedore burned his sweetheart's image off his elbow with an oxyacetylene torch, and lived to strangle her later with the same arm? As a matter of fact, many a guinea pig from the war years wore his own behind on his beaming face. But even in a godless world, the surgeon reflected, we idolize our afflictions.

'And who is to be the new scapegoat?' asked Mr Horngrad. 'Did the Pope indicate that?'

'The Italians, I think,' said Mr Bevan.

'The Italians,' said the waiting customer, 'are a most fucked-up set of foreigners. Not like your folk in the Sinai, Mr Horngrad, blowing the bejasus out of the Arabs. Six days, no bother; and on the seventh, I suppose, they hit downtown Tel Aviv.'

'No politics or religion in this club,' said the barber.

'The Arabs,' said Mr Horngrad, 'are all faggots. They can't face a fight.'

'Faggots?' Mr Bevan said. 'You mean they're for burning?'

'I mean faggots,' Mr Horngrad said. 'Bum boys. Men for pleasure, women for breeding. That's an Arab proverb.'

'I know a man who was that way,' said Mr Bevan. 'I know a man who was a faggot; and he had a DSO. He had a Distinguished Service Medal.'

'He was a fiery faggot, so,' said the man with the camp tattoo.

With a flick of his foot, Mr Roper spun round in his seat and addressed them. His accent mentored and tormented them.

'Faggots saved the West at the battle of Thermopylae,' he said. 'Three hundred Spartan faggots stood between us and ten thousand well-adjusted Asiatics.'

'*Touché*,' said the barber.

'There you go again,' said Mr Horngrad. 'First you charge me with murder; then you charge me with bigotry. I can't win. I'm always being accused of something.'

'Be honest now,' said the waiting customer. 'Do you think that Cassius Clay has a soul?'

'I don't think anyone has a soul,' Mr Horngrad said. 'We've been down this road before. But I respect Cassius Clay and I would break bread with him. He's a magnificent creature. He's Michelangelo's *David*, for God's sake. He inspires me.'

'Do you know who inspires me?' said Mr Bevan. 'Sir Francis Chichester inspires me.'

'*D'accord*,' said the surgeon.

'You don't have to go to Cape Horn to feel crestfallen,' Mr Bevan said. 'There are times down here when I don't feel I have the strength to go on any longer. After all, the Barber of Seville is not the be-all and the end-all of the world that God created. It's not on any Cook's tour. But then I think of this old man out there in the middle of the ocean, washing his Y-fronts over the side and steering by starlight. And what does he eat? The hold of the *Gypsy Moth* is full of Irish potatoes. So you see.'

'See what?' said Mr Horngrad.

'His dignity,' the barber said. 'His daring. His derring-do, if you want.' And his facial colour rose a tad, and sank again. 'Being broken down, I suppose, and still standing up. That's what I mean.'

He swivelled the surgeon round and resumed his clipping. Actually, Mr Roper hardly needed a cut at all. Why had he bothered to come? You took an awful chance on those steep stairs.

'Who inspires you, Mr Roper?' he said then. But he said it in a jocular fashion that took the familiarity out of it, so that the doctor thought about it in a genial way with his eyes closed. The cold sore at the corner of his mouth had dried and disappeared since the last time. Then he laughed out loud.

'You do, Mr Bevan,' he said. 'You keep the show on the road.'

'Did you see it yet?' said the barber, and his elated scissors circled a little mud stain of psoriasis that was probably all due to anxiety. '*You Only Live Twice*.'

'Spare me the details.'

'You'd love it. I swear to God.'

'I'm an aficionado,' said Mr Roper. 'I'm not an addict. Desist.'

And Mr Bevan let it go at that. He tucked the label of the surgeon's shirt down inside the collar carefully. It was one of those drip-dry affairs that people with Pyrex dishes bought. More to the point, it was the first time he had ever seen his personal hospital consultant wearing anything off the peg.

———

On the other hand, it wasn't always a charmed relationship. There were times when you could sense something between a rift and a rupture in the sedimentary deposits of their banter. It might even be defined, given the venue of their meetings, as a hairline fracture.

'What do you make of this man Christian Barnard?' said Mr Bevan one Tuesday afternoon at about ten past five. He had actually closed for the day when Mr Roper clattered down the stairs in a De Valera cape.

'A chancer,' the surgeon said. 'A charlatan. He jumped the gun to be centre stage at a photo opportunity. The English team were just about to make the first incision. I suppose you think he's Dr Schweitzer. Well, he isn't; and neither was Dr Schweitzer, either. He was a complete cunt.'

And that was upsetting from a professional person who had won a gold medal in some ology or other in the Royal College of Surgeons, and who was never supposed to take a sabbatical from suavity and seriousness. In fact, if you were to post a letter to Mr Roper, FRCSI, Bedside Manor, Dublin, it would be sure to reach him. It was very wrong of him to utter cornerboy English.

'Enid Blyton has gone to her rest,' said the barber one Thursday morning when the chair was still warm from the buttocks of Mr Horngrad. 'I heard on the BBC that she authored – that was the word – nine hundred books. Can you imagine that?'

'Everything about that woman is unimaginable,' Mr Roper retorted. There was no other word for it. 'She was a silly little snob who was married, I gather, to a surgeon. That, at least, argues a degree of discernment wholly alien to her written inanities.'

Mr Bevan had only asked in order to prise domestic detail from the most recalcitrant customer he had ever invested affection in. But it was no use. After how many years, four, five, six, the man was still an enigma. Yet he had begun to write down snatches of Mr Roper's small talk because there were words in it which he had never witnessed outside crossword puzzles.

'Discernment, indeed,' he said, batting it beautifully. 'How discerning was Jackie Kennedy the other day? I could have wept. I could have. But I was at work.'

'You should have,' the surgeon said. 'People are supposed to cry at a wedding.'

'Oil money is all he has going for him. You may call him Aristotle or Plato or whatever you like, but it's all about petro-dollars.'

'Onassis? He won't have long to look at her,' said Mr Roper. '*Myasthenia gravis.*'

'It would make you think all right,' said the barber, who was very pleased that he had got into petro-dollars. It was still in quotes in both broadsheets.

'He has his eyelids bandaged back already,' the surgeon said. 'Otherwise he has to hold them up with his thumbs. He's feasting his eyes while he can, greasy little adhesion that he is. All the oil in the world won't help him now.'

This was not right. It was not righteous. There was a point at which you passed from mischief into malice, and they had passed it. So Mr Bevan searched among his witticisms for some passage into leniency.

'He sounds like the baddie in the new Bond film.'

'Have you seen it?'

'I'm saving it for the weekend.'

'Hamlet without the Prince. The new Bond ponces around in a kilt, but he's no lookalike. You don't believe he's a killer: you don't believe he's a ladykiller. Ergo: no go. It's all set in a rotating restaurant that's cemented to a summit miles above Wengen in the Swiss Alps. I've been there. Five pounds for a cup of coffee and a Cinemascope view of Toblerone mountains. Then you can ski all the way down the cordoned learners' piste at fifteen miles an hour to the nursery slopes where the cable cars start from, and pretend you're on Her Majesty's Secret Service while you're at it. But there is this vicious old dyke in the film who looks the image and likeness of my anaesthetist. It was worth it for that.'

Then he smiled, relaxed, relented. His fist became a hand again. A shaft of sunlight minted its way through the glass door of the premises, down the peculiar staircase, and lay at their feet on the lino like an oblong ingot. And Mr Bevan's being rose up like a *Magnificat*, for this was what he loved: when he could groom the cherished head until it gleamed like the bobbing skull of a seal, all tweaked and squeaking, from the domical forehead through the perfect parting, as straight as any Roman road, to the anticlockwise origins of hair near the old, abandoned fontanelle.

'You could leave it a little longer at the sides,' Mr Roper said. 'Maybe the back too.'

'You're not going to grow sideburns, are you?' said the barber. 'I think they're very common.'

'I won't wear sideburns,' said Mr Roper. 'But my students have ponytails. You have to move with the times.'

He bowed his head to the barber's clippers.

'Do what you will,' he said.

Mr Bevan thought of what a canon had said to him years before. Not an Irish canon, of course, but a Canadian, and possibly even a French-Canadian one at that, so you had to take his words with a pinch of salt, as coming from the hillbilly hinterlands and not from the bench of bishops. Yet he had told the barber that the beloved disciple of Jesus in the Gospel of Saint John would have been the Lord's closest friend, his confidant and sleeping companion in the perishing small hours of the Galilean winter, and that they would have deloused each other, God and the man, under the shrieking olive trees in the atrocity of the midday heat outside Jerusalem. The fingers of the beloved disciple would be roaming the Master's hair, splitting the head lice deftly between his nails, listening for the brittle report of the puncture before casting the broken fuselage to the ground, and inhaling all the while the sour sephardic pungency of the body of Christ.

The surgeon hadn't been to the Boat Show at the Royal Dublin Society since the time, three years before, when he had finally sold his folk boat, remaining on at the yacht club only as a dining member who dropped by for an occasional game of billiards and a browse through current issues of *Punch* and the *Spectator*. Whatever drew him now, it was certainly not the motor launch from *Dr No* or the Spectre-manned torpedoes that a few redundant London models were piloting in a prefabricated glass aquarium until half past four each evening as hooligans ogled their adipose tissue.

'A pound? It was twelve and six the last time.'

'It was twelve and six when my granny was a girl, sir.'

Kayaks to catamarans. He walked among them, their landlocked, stationary yearnings. Worse, there was a saline smell from the breakers less than a mile away at Sandymount to torment them. Tides slipped at the sea wall twice a day as its pennants stiffened under the halogen lights.

'That one's got hairs under her arms. Lookit!'

When he found himself there by accident, at the shallow end of the sci-fi waterhole where swimsuited centrefolds were entertaining a heterosexual press of boys at puberty, Mr Roper saw his man immediately. It was the barber in civilian life, Bevan at large in the lit, incongruous domain of everywhere that was not his basement practice. A hooded coat with wooden pegs for buttons made him monkish and stunted. His moccasins too were spattered a darker shade in places as if he had sprinkled himself at a urinal. Under the canopy of his discoloured ceiling he seemed always endearing in his eccentricity. But this was not it.

'Not that one, you spastic. The bird with the gun.'

The consultant veered discreetly to the right and slipped among the hulls of ocean-going cruisers with their slanted names at bow and stern. *Birthright. Salamander. Gemini.* Their impervious emulsions fashioned his flitting outline as he waded through buggies and paper windmills to the door marked Exit.

—

'And where did you disappear to in the last fortnight?' said Mr Roper, settling into the chair without a say-so, and arranging the spaghetti strings of the apron around his own neck as Mr Bevan swept the detritus of a dozen clients into a balsa-wood fruit box stamped 'Fyffes'. He was always afraid that the sight of so much human hair strewn about might disconcert Mr Horngrad.

'I had to go for a check up,' Mr Bevan said, but he had taken a long time to commit such a small sentence.

'Three times I came by,' said the other, 'and the sign still said Open. In the end, I went off to the salon in the Shelbourne. There was a man there with a white streak in his beard like dried Milk of Magnesia, and all he could talk about was parking meters.'

'That's the way,' said the barber.

'Page two, top of, left to right,' said the waiting customer, coughing. 'Israeli archaeologists have dug up the skeleton of a crucified man.'

'Don't blame it on me,' Mr Horngrad said in a striped and long-sleeved shirt with matching tiger's-eye cufflinks. 'Everything ends up on my desk.'

'Are you all right?' the surgeon said.

'I'm all right,' said Mr Bevan. 'I just got a bit of a fright.'

'That's a Jewish plot if ever I heard one,' said the waiting customer. 'That stinks.'

'The whole of Europe is a Jewish plot,' said Mr Horngrad. 'A Jewish cemetery from Brittany to Belorussia.'

'Come into me and I'll have a good look at you,' said the surgeon. 'Come in Tuesday. Will you do that?'

'I feel fine. I look fine. I am fine,' Mr Bevan said.

'That's what worries me,' said Mr Roper. 'Everyone blooms in the mortuary chapel.'

'Skeleton of a crucified man. Very fucking convenient,' said the waiting customer. 'That really takes the biscuit.'

'Did I dig him up?' Mr Horngrad said. 'Am I suddenly an Israeli grave robber? When I came in five minutes ago, I could have sworn I was a white-collar worker from the South Circular Road.'

Mr Bevan snipped a long hair from the consultant's eyebrow with a cuticle scissors. He must get silver tweezers at some stage. Eyebrows could be more ageing, actually, than nasal hair, though the worst of all was what grew out of your ears. That was the body calling Time now please, gentlemen.

'What did you think of the new one?' he said. 'Now that Connery is on the job again.'

'*Diamonds are Forever*? I liked the song. I loved the silhouettes at the start.'

'And Plenty O'Toole. Was that her name?'

'It was. Not nearly as good as Pussy Galore, mind.'

'Not at all. Pussy Galore was in a different league all together.'

Mr Bevan set aside whatever he was doing and looked at the surgeon in the mirror.

He could hear the distant bronchitis of the two customers arguing.

'The two fellows,' he said. 'Mr Kid and Mr Whoever-it-was. I can't remember now.'

'The fairies?'

'Whatever. Fairies. Queers,' said Mr Bevan. 'Ponces. Nancyboys. Homos. Homosexual is a bit long. Gay is a bit short. Maybe something in the middle like: people. Do you know what I mean?'

'I do.' You could tell by his voice that the surgeon was astonished.

'Because I was loving the film until they turned up in it. Then there were catcalls whenever the camp one opened his mouth. Cornerboys in the balcony. I just thought.'

'You thought justly.'

'I don't know what I'm trying to say,' said Mr Bevan.

'Never let that stop you saying it,' Mr Roper said. 'It never stopped me.'

Mr Bevan picked up the clippers. But what he wanted was the stainless-steel comb.

'Do you know,' he said, 'I'll be charging you in decimals after Christmas.'

'You will,' said the surgeon. 'If the Lord preserves us.'

'Take it from me,' said Mr Horngrad, butting in, the bloody fellow. 'If there is a Lord, the only thing He preserves is silence.'

—

'... will warrant further comma more vigorous comma attention.'

Friday at six o'clock as the pre-recorded *Angelus* played from the campanile of the nearby parish church, Mr Roper set aside the Dictaphone and rubbed his eyes because he had seen Burt Lancaster do it so often in American films. Like it or not, he would have to reconcile himself to the new technology of pocket-sized recorders. He would miss the deference and reverence of the convent schoolgirls he had kept supplied in Coke and Cadbury's while they touch-typed complex case histories, but since the nuns had stopped teaching Latin, no one could be trusted to spell correctly the metaphysical intimacies of the body. Besides, the cassettes were cheaper, though he would have listened more alertly to his English master in his early years if he had known that the mysteries of punctuation would so terrorize him in his later ones. Only the colon made complete sense to him. The semicolon belonged to particle physics; and the simple dash had already garbled many a medical court report.

He twirled in his swivel chair among his certificates. Outside the window there was a moon. On the moon there was a man. Two men. He had forgotten their names and their likenesses before the bulletin announcing their arrival there had ended. They would splash-land in the ocean just like ooʃ, close to the Stone Age tribesmen of New Guinea, in a day or in two days. They had left clean shaven and would return bearded. That was as much as could be said about any male experience in or out of this world. Growth on the cheeks was truly astronomical.

Bevan, he thought. He's a loveable fellow.

Mr Roper, the barber thought. Where would I be without him?

Those bells from the church were only beautiful. Better recorded music than live noise had always been his position. Best of all he had loved being swept off his feet at the consecration when the adolescent bell-ringers in the Jacobean belfry proclaimed the Risen Lord in their early morning Sunday service of Holy Communion. And to think that their Roman Catholic neighbours still regarded them as Protestants.

It was time to go home. He would do a fry, white pudding as well, and listen to the astronauts. They were at prayer in the firmament, and doing some measurements too. It was nice to hear them read from the Authorized Version, though it was a pity about the American accents. Genesis did not seem the same when it was read in Texan by a youngster. They should have brought Alec Guinness with them in the lunar module.

I must look at my underpants, he thought. I must see if I leaked through the first pair into the second. Thank goodness it is blood and not the other. Thank goodness it is not excrement.

He twirled in the barber's chair, and the surrendered hair on the lino rotated with him, Horngrad's and Mr Roper's the dun, the chestnut and the auburn, carrot and caramel, russet and sand; copper, jet, dove grey, slate grey, and the thousand shades of ash. All the walking wounded between the canal and the river had found their way to him. And for what?

He faced his reflection.

—

In spite of the fact that his life had been saved at the public expense three years before by a quick-witted surgical intervention, the pump attendant did not favour his benefactor above other motorists, and Mr Roper was therefore obliged to queue for his petrol along with at least a hundred other cars. Yesterday's customers had become today's clients, and the proletarian was blithe.

'Don't give out to me,' he said to the surgeon. 'Give out to the Jews. If they let the Arabs win once in a while, there wouldn't be an embargo. Besides, if I move you up to the front, there'll be a pogrom.'

So it was almost three o'clock when Mr Roper parked in a consultant's spot outside the Catholic hospital with its sanguinary carving of a saint or an archangel, perhaps, decapitating a Chinese dragon with a drowsy sense of reciprocal pleasure. If it were the third hour on Good Friday, the chaplain would be in procession at this point with a lifesize cross that spent the remainder of the church calendar outside the brick incinerator at the mortuary chapel; and sick men would be struggling from their beds, with their goitres and their gall bladders and their golf-ball growths in their scrotums, to honour the Passion of Christ by kneeling on the bare planks of the ward. Thirty years before, when he was a senior house officer with his churchwarden pipe and cravat, he had found it moving, Mediterranean without the ultra-violet. Now it saddened him that even the most important human pain – loss, leave-taking, all the lethal forms of finitude – cried out for the anaesthesia of pantomime.

The stairs as they were, one-hundred-and-two marbled steps from the lobby to the nurses' station on the second floor, a Via Dolorosa for the pensioned charladies with their black, bandaged legs; and the elevator too unaltered, the crash of its old accordion doors meshing and buckling as the trolleys crackled. And then the age-old, old age odours of the male surgical ward: Lucozade, secretions of the armpit, Woodbine, warm, carpetless wood, disinfectant fluid, the perfume and periods of the trainee nurses. It is harder to quit a place than a person. He realized that too.

'*Voilà*,' he said, and drew the curtain with unconscious clinical expertise behind him.

The swollen, simplified face of the barber turned to him. It beamed with embarrassment.

'Mr Roper,' it said, 'There is no doubt.'

'Dr Bevan, I presume,' the surgeon said

'The same, in spite of appearances. Shaken but not stirred. I am sorry for not standing. And I apologize for my five o'clock shadow. I hadn't got around to shaving.'

'Absolutely,' said the surgeon. 'Absolutely.'

There was nowhere to sit, of course, and he did not want to camp on the bed. At least if you went private, you could keep your dignity. There would be an economy armchair under the fake Constable on the social side of the bed, with your own private business in the pinewood closet on the other. Civility of that sort mattered more in this world than all the awful feel-me-heal-me histrionics of the distaff side. But what could you expect? Unmarried women were running all the committees.

'I'm afraid I can't ask you to sit on a chair,' said the barber. 'And the little table's a bit nervous. But please ... the bed.'

Mr Roper took his overcoat off slowly in order to think through the whole decision-making process. He had never anticipated this circumstance.

'Actually, Mr Bevan,' he said, 'I've never seen you not standing. In all our conversations over the years, I've been in the chair. You might say that I have been the chairman. This is a complete reversal.'

'It is that,' said the sick man.

Mr Roper lay out his folded overcoat on the bed as a compromise.

'I saw Mr Horngrad the other day,' he said. 'He looked badly in need of a cut and a shave.'

'I think there's a time in the year when Jews don't shave,' said Mr Bevan. 'Or is that the Sikhs? You've had a bit of a trim yourself, I suspect.'

'Never.'

'I'm a wise old bird. Somebody else has been at your hair.'

'The Shelbourne,' said Mr Roper. 'I pretended to be Finnish because I got that bloody bore again. Parking meters, remember? And he kept saying: "I could swear I've met you somewhere before." So I said: "*Nodicke, nodicke, dicke.*" And do you know what he said then? He said: "You poor fuckin' poof, wait until you get back to your car and see the summons."'

'That's the Shelbourne for you,' said Mr Bevan.

Mr Roper was examining the chart at the bottom of the bed. He hadn't for a moment intended to, but his hand could not withstand its own instinctive mapping.

'I know the man you're under,' he said. 'Good pair of mittens, too. Mind you, he borrowed a signed copy of a book by Oliver St John Gogarty from me the time of the Suez affair, and he never brought it back. There's no statue of limitations on my resentment, you see. He borrowed a girlfriend as well during the war, but I don't mind that. She hated shaking hands with a man in case he'd been to the toilet and the last thing he'd touched was his penis. "They don't wash afterwards," she'd say. "That's the long and the short of it."'

'I'll tell him,' Mr Bevan said. 'About the book.'

Mr Roper sat down on his own coat on the bed. Why was he rabbiting on? There was no way around it.

'How are you, old man?' he said. He remembered the theatre faintly.

'Ah. You know yourself.'

'I do?' Of course that was then. It had probably been modern ized since.

'You read the chart.'

'That's only there to impress patients. Did you not feel the fear of God when I was looking at it?'

'Well, I didn't feel I was going to take up my bed and walk.'

'Proves my point. The surgeon has to mind his mystique.'

There was a child squealing with excitement outside the linen drapes around the bed, out there in the spacious world of the male surgical ward with its blue sash windows open to the cumulus nimbus. Mr Roper hoped it didn't belong to the man in his mid thirties with the tracheotomy tube. Even if it did, the mother might be young enough to marry again. So much depended, though, on her features and her figure. Truly life was a bitch.

'I thought it was haemorrhoids for a long time,' said the barber.

'I had haemorrhoids for years. They'd come and they'd go, like.'

'I understand,' said the surgeon. 'They're a pain in the arse.'

'It was only spotting for ages,' Mr Bevan said. 'I thought, if it was anything serious, then I'd be in pain. But I wasn't in pain. I was as happy as Larry.'

'I know,' the surgeon said. They would have done the operation in fifty minutes; the biopsy within twenty-four hours.

'I was happy in my work,' said the barber. 'I was happy in The Barber of Seville.'

'We were all the same.' The statistics were as bad as the lung but not as bad as the liver.

'Then the spots were more like stains; and the stains were wetter.'

Mr Roper looked over his reading glasses in Mr Bevan's eyes. He had been doing this for almost three decades. In fact, he did it very well. There were times when he had been as moved by himself as by his patient patients. But not now.

'You'll be fine,' he said. 'When you're better, we'll go and see *Live and Let Die* together at the Capitol.'

'I'd like that.'

'I'd like that too.'

'It's a date so,' said Mr Bevan.

'Absolutely it is,' said Mr Roper. 'Now I have to admit that I've seen it already, but I'd love to go again. There's a terrific crocodile sequence and a state-of-the-art chase, with this sadistic black ball-breaker, a right-hand man who doesn't in fact have a right hand at all, only a prosthetic pincers. Roger Moore, the new face, isn't too bad. Admittedly, he wouldn't be my type; never was, even on TV. He just can't play patrician; he can't play privilege. Of course you wouldn't want him to try to be Connery. Connery is *sui generis*. Connery is God. If not God, the Son of God. The most you can ask, I suppose, is that he won't be as lamentable as Lazenby, though even Lazenby has been pilloried disproportionately. Generally, the whole style of the series has gone completely camp and caricatural. It's *The Saint* to the power of *n*.'

'It would make you think all right,' said Mr Bevan from far away. His eyes were playing slow table soccer with their motes on the arctic whiteness of the ward ceiling.

The man in the next bed down, or perhaps in the second-next one because they were all so close together, like in the dormitory of an orphanage, was imitating Peter Sellers imitating Clouseau and Dr Strangelove and the Indian fellow who chanted the 'Doctor, I'm in Trouble' duet with Sophia Loren sometime back in the early sixties when her breasts were one of the glories of Western civilization alongside Brunelleschi's dome and Einstein's Theory of Curved Space. But he was singing to amuse his callers or was he whistling in the dark, shaking a leather tambourine in the breathing labyrinth?

'Do you know this part of the city at all?' said Mr Bevan.

'I know it well,' the surgeon said. 'I was educated down the road.'

'By the Brothers?'

'By the Fathers. The Jesuits. In Belvedere.'

Mr Bevan's face lit up. 'Sure we got food parcels from Belvedere every Christmas in Summerhill,' he said. 'That's why my grandfather called it Wintervalley. Plum pudding, Madeira cake. We got presents as well up to Confirmation and then nothing You were on your own after that.'

His left eye scored a penalty. Several of the key players had drifted into the stands.

'My father used to cycle through the Monto every day for years,' said the surgeon, talking to the curtain material in front of him. 'He was supposed to go two sides of a triangle from Sandymount to school, but he cut straight through. One time he peeped into a girl's ground-floor room, and it was wallpapered with holy pictures. It was more of an oratory than a bordello. I don't know how anybody managed an erection in a place like that.'

'My da used to fetch messages for the girls,' said the barber. 'That was after his Confirmation. They bought him a pair of shoes one time that shone like the Poolbeg lighthouse. Then this particular prostitute got sick and she was dying, and he had to carry her downstairs on his back, at thirteen years of age, out into the street where the Catholic priest from the pro-cathedral was waiting to give her Extreme Unction. But it was the sleet and rain of the outdoors and the night air that killed her with double pneumonia on top of the tuberculosis. He had his top hat and his cloak on. My side was as bad, of course.'

'Your side?'

'Protestant,' said Mr Bevan.

'Church of Ireland?'

'Church of Ireland. The Church in Ireland is the Church of Ireland. That was my da.'

'Me too,' said Mr Roper.

'Go way,' said Mr Bevan. 'I often wondered.'

'Long story. Mixed marriage. Four services on a Sunday.'

'Eucharist, Morning Prayer, Mass, and Evening Prayer.'

'Something like that,' Mr Roper said.

'Roper could be either,' the barber said. 'That's what had me wondering. I knew a Roper in the Third Order of Saint Francis; and I knew a Roper afterwards who was a Freemason. It's handy, like. You'd need to know the Christian name to be sure.'

'Gregory,' said Mr Roper. 'My mother called me Gregory the Great when she was pleased with my homework. She named me after a Pope, you know. She had certain expectations. More to do with prestige, I imagine, than with prayerfulness. Women know what's what.'

'Gregory could be High Church too,' Mr Bevan said. 'Gregory could easily be bells and smells.'

'Bevan is both,' Mr Roper said. 'Catholic and Protestant. And Jewish, for that matter. Am I right?'

'Not with Christopher de Valera in front of it,' Mr Bevan said.

'I suppose not,' said the surgeon.

Then they said nothing for a while as they thought about things. Things in general and things in particular. Visiting time must have been coming to an end because the shadows of people were passing the screen, and two of them were carrying children, and one of the children called out: 'Byebyebyebyebyebye'; but an adult voice from the far corner of the male surgical answered: 'Shhhhhhhhh. Don't wake the dead.' And Mr Bevan was deciding that loyalty was a quiet form of love, an undemonstrative cornerstone, and that not enough had been said about it, really, by those who studied the behaviour of the heart in its covert operations; and Mr Roper was remembering how the affection of equals had been taught to his class by brief allusion in a course on forensic medicine, which was optional for females.

'You'll have to go,' said a student nurse, inserting her head between the folds of the curtain and making an impromptu guillotine around her spotty swan neck. 'It's half past.'

'This is Mr Roper,' said the barber. 'He's a surgeon.'

'Is this a consultation?' she said. Now that he looked, she had a sebaceous cyst among all those hairclips. He used to love squeezing them.

'It's only a visit,' said the surgeon. 'It's not a visitation. I haven't worked here since the Second World War.'

'You must have been a very young student,' she said.

'This ward would have been jam-packed in February,' he said. 'Pulmonary cases, mainly.'

'It still is,' she said. 'And the private hospital is full of skiing injuries until Easter.'

Then she was gone, leaving the faintest watermark of something astringent in the atmosphere.

'Hydrogen peroxide,' Mr Roper said. 'She's bleached the hairs on her lip.' He could get up and leave now. There would be no shame in that. He had done enough.

'Could I ask you something?' said Mr Bevan. 'But stop me now if I'm intruding.'

'Ask away.'

Silence had resumed in the ward outside. Real illness was always speechless. When they were garrulous, they could go home.

'Were you married at all?'

'I was married. I am married. I have a wife and four sons. Hamburg, London, Stepaside. The youngest has terrible cerebral palsy and shouldn't have survived. He looks like the wreckage of a head-on collision. But that's the tragedy of modern medicine. It saves too many lives. I save too many lives. It's wrong.'

'And your wife? What does she think?'

'For the last seventeen years, my wife has decanted all her pity and all her anger into remains in a wheelchair. It leaves very little for anyone else.'

Mr Bevan ran his recessed hand through the frail strings of his hair and across his stubble.

'Still and all,' he said, 'there's something nice about a home with, maybe, pipe cleaners on the mantelpiece and slips or a pair of stockings on the clotheshorse. It seems to outlast everything. The Roman Empire, the British Empire, even the Holy Roman Empire although I know that it was neither holy nor Roman nor an empire.'

Whitest of feet in flip-flops with a plastic daisy padded past the hem of the curtain.

'Have you a scissors handy?' Mr Roper said.

'A scissors?'

'And a razor.'

'I have a scissors,' said the barber, 'and I have a battery shaver. But you look very spruce to me.'

'It's not me I'm talking about,' the surgeon said. 'I'm talking about the barber from "The Barber of Seville".'

'You must be joking. Is it me?'

Mr Roper yanked at the door of the metal bedside table and

found inside it two paperback novels by Ian Fleming, a bacon scissors of sorts, assorted batteries, one shaver wound in its own helical flex, jelly babies, the Book of Common Prayer, and a dull service medal from the desert campaign.

'Did you know,' he said as he sat on the tuck of the regulation bed sheet near to his patient, 'that once upon a time, and a very good time it was too, barbers and surgeons belonged to the same brotherhood.'

'Did they?'

'They did. The barber's pole, you know, was the surgeon's sign. White for bandages and red for blood.' And he ran the shaver lightly over the chin and the jaw; then, with more weight and agility, into the groove of the throat and over the Adam's apple across to the long lobe of the listening ear.

'They were neither surgeons nor barbers but surgeon-barbers. Surgeon-barber Bevan and surgeon-barber Roper.'

'Imagine.' Yet he yawned as he said it.

'Nothing imaginary about it,' said Mr Roper, and the blades of the shaver sipped at the hairs on the upper lip until Mr Bevan drew it down over his top teeth to bare them. 'They were feared the length and breadth of Europe. It was the surgeon-barbers who carried out autopsies on the cadavers of criminals. It was the surgeon-barbers who performed the anatomical demonstrations at the universities where mere medical doctors commentated behind their pomanders. And it was the surgeon-barbers who amputated the arms and legs of wounded soldiers in the aftermath of carnage.'

'Dear me,' said Mr Bevan. 'You make us sound like Burke and Hare.'

But there was a tear, as slow and solid as mercury, snailing along the chafed overhang of his cheek.

'Never,' the surgeon said. There had been friendship between them, and that was something. Muted and minor, perhaps, but what about it? Closeness was too costly. One's near and dear were pathological partners full of resentment and sentimentality. This, in the dignity of its distance, had been pure; or, at any rate, purish.

When the barber drowsed and dozed and fell asleep, his denture whistling modestly in the half-open orifice of his voice, the surgeon sheared soundlessly at the damp, disordered twists of hair, picking the coils from the pillow as he worked, tidying the sides and the little, delinquent spikes, thinning the springy fringe. It was strange to be so intent without boots and gloves and a fragrant scrub nurse and the solar ferocity of the overhead lights like the panels of a satellite in space. Yet he hummed as usual.

As he left, the nurse smiled at him from a trolley of bottles. Many men would mount her.

'Thanks,' he said. 'You're great.'

'No bother. Do you want to talk to the consultant's houseman?'

'No,' he said. 'I'll get back to him. You could say I was in. Roper.'

'Maybe I oughtn't to tell you,' said the nurse. 'I got into trouble once over telling. But they didn't operate. There was nothing they could do. It was too late.'

'They opened him up?' said the surgeon.

'They opened him up, took one look, and closed him again. That was it. He was back in the bed before the Gay Byrne show was over. Gas character. Are you good friends?'

Mr Roper thought about that. Because it would be reported back. It would be relayed forward. It would have its own precarious itinerary among the strict witnesses.

'We were very close,' he said to her. 'We came within a hair's breadth of each other.'

CUBA

When the Mass ended, the Holy Ghost from the Ukraine took off his chasuble at the altar, folded it over my arm without saying a word, and walked out of the sanctuary in his surplice up into the pulpit. Nobody in the church looked at him because Jesus was still inside them for fifteen minutes more. I lay down again on the marble steps.

'Friends,' he said. 'Some of you may have heard the President of the United States on the radio late last night. Some of you may have seen and heard him on BBC television, even, because the wind came from the direction of England. Now I know nothing of the rights and wrongs of Cuba. But there is always the possibility of horror. In my own country we lost half the male population in less than twenty years, twenty years ago; and Nikita Khrushchev, the General Secretary of the Communist Party of the Soviet Union, choreographed part of that atrocity. But there is always hope as well. John Fitzgerald Kennedy is an Irishman and a Roman Catholic, and his nationality and his religion are potent sources of moral authority. God is always looking for ten just men in Sodom to spare the city-state. Let us pray that He will find them in this year of Our Lord. Amen.'

'Amen,' I said. My body was a bit dazed by the fast from midnight. Its stomach lurched and hurt under the breastbone, and its left foot hummed with pins and needles inside the shoe leather. When I blew on the palm of my hand, my breath was bad too.

'Because of the imminent threat of thermonuclear doom,' said the Holy Ghost from the Ukraine, 'there will be exposition of the Blessed Sacrament from three o'clock, continuing indefinitely, with confessions from five onwards. Rosters for the vigil are in the church porch. The parish old folks' club will be touring Guinness's brewery this day week, and the coaches will arrive in the schoolyard at a quarter to two exactly. Mind the step wells, please. Mrs Henderson is still not over her fall. Amen.'

Down in the posh transept where the doctors' wives met, and the families of those who had voted for the Treaty sat together, my mother wasn't kneeling although she had gone to Holy Communion a minute before without even smiling back at me as she tucked the altar cloth into her camel-haired coat and stuck out her tongue over the paten I was holding. She was mad, of course, that her Hallowe'en party would be wrecked by the atomic bomb. But a Labrador dog came up through the golden gates of the rails around the chancel, and lay beside me for a scratch. When he turned over I could see his nipples, as hard as the beads on a rosary, all glittery with slobber from a wet litter.

———

I cycled home with Shylock. He was a Jew who read the *National Geographic* during Religious Knowledge class. Father Bruno would ask him about the Hebrew Bible, and Shylock would shrug and say, 'Do you mean the Old Testament, Father?', and Father Bruno would say, 'There's nothing old about it, Yitzhak,' and Shylock would say, 'Isaac is bad enough, Father. I prefer Shylock,' and the whole class would chant the name – *Shylock! Shylock!* – like in a rugby final when the prefects conducted the stands, and Shylock would bow and blow kisses to us. Then Father Bruno would run his fingers through his loose grey hair, and the chalk dust on his hands would colour his head yellow and pink, and the Holy Ghost from the Ukraine would storm in from the next class and roar at the peacock priest, and the two of them would communicate through handwritten messages passed by pupils for the following week.

'We'll all be soot by Saturday, Mattie,' Shylock said when we reached my house. 'You might as well know about fucking.'

'What about it?' I said, but my body thudded, because it was Shylock who had told me about Santa and the gas chambers. I got up on the granite gatepost of our house and twisted the sign for the Chester Beatty library so that it faced the right way down the bald trees of the avenue. Cornerboys from the hill were always turning it round towards our drive. Once, two Japanese men in transparent plastic raincoats knocked on our door when my blind-folded father was listening to his *Reader's Digest* collection of clas-sics; and I wondered where they had buried their uniforms and their samurai swords on the day that Father Bruno survived the light at Hiroshima.

'Fuck is short for For Unlawful Carnal Knowledge,' I said. 'It is no big deal, really.'

He thought about this for a while as he swung by his arms from the signpost. Then he dropped to the ground without making a fret with his feet. He was a born saboteur.

'Seriously,' he said, 'If we're all going to go up in smoke like granny and granddad, I'll set the white mink free.'

Then I realized for the first time that Cuba must be very close to Ireland and not far away at all as I had thought. When I did my homework under the anglepoise that evening, I did not write AMDG at the top of the page in my exercise copybooks. Instead I wrote out the whole motto in ink that glinted for an instant before dwindling and drying.

Ad Maiorem Dei Gloriam. Tuesday 23rd October, Anno Domini 1962.

—

'Kitty's in the kitchen,' said my mother. 'Go and get some dinner. I can hear your gastric juices.' She did not like it when I sat and studied her, but that was her fault. Other mothers blew ciga-rette smoke out of their mouths up towards the ceiling roses. My mother blew it out of her nose down towards the floating parquet floor, as if she were a member of the Resistance. My father, on the other hand, would swallow his smoke with a bitter and intellectual expression as though he had an ulcer in his oesophagus.

'That's a tautology,' he said to me. 'The kitchen is Kitty's domain. Kitty is the chatelaine of the kitchen. To say that Kitty's in the kitchen is, therefore, a …?'

'Tautology,' I said, staring at the ghost in the television and dipping the rabbit ears like a water diviner to clarify the image. That was my job.

'Good man,' said my dad. 'And to say that your mother is in the kitchen would be …?'

'A bit strange,' I said.

'An oxymoron,' he said. 'You know when people call you a moron?'

'I know,' I said.

'Think of moron with 'oxy' in front of it,' my father said. 'An oxymoron is a contradiction in terms.'

'Think of food,' said my mother. 'Think of Kitty. Go, eat. The Africans are coming.'

'You make it sound like the whole continent is on the march,' my father said. 'You have five Nigerian students. Incidentally, they have Commonwealth passports, which is more than you do.'

'Niger is the Latin for black,' I said. 'To denigrate is to blacken.'

He touched my cheek with his hand. It was ice-cold from his gin and tonic. He had sent me to the shop for a lemon and I had come home with a grapefruit.

'I'm not denigrating anyone, Harry,' said my mother. 'But to be teaching half-a-dozen lads from Lagos the *Briathar Saor* and the *Módh Coinníollach* is a bit much. It isn't what Daddy had in mind when he cycled round the midlands on his *rothar* giving classes free, gratis and for nothing.'

'We colonials should stand together,' my dad said. 'Is that Kennedy?'

'No,' I said, peering at the ghost in the television as it misted and melted. 'It's Khrushchev.'

'So it is,' he said. 'Middle stump, Mattie.'

'Khrushchev,' said my mother. 'We'll all look like that by the weekend.'

—

Kitty was cutting out Chinese lanterns for the Hallowe'en party. She had been sewing cinctures and shrouds at the Charity orphanage since she was five. Her handiwork was only beautiful. She said it herself.

'Whatever happens tonight or tomorrow,' she said, 'there'll be a Flash bar in your lunchbox, same as always.'

She opened a tin of fruit cocktail and poured in a glass of cooking sherry. The automatic timer was ringing the Angelus in the belfry up the road, but Kitty could not be bothered. If there was no bell-ringer, there was no bell rung.

'Eat that up, pet,' she said. 'I can hear your chest again. Your mother cares more about her smoke than your wheeze.'

'Kitty,' I said, 'will everybody die?'

'Only if they're alive,' she said. 'Amn't I an awful eejit to have saved up all that money for my funeral? I've been saving sixpence a week from the time I came here, and that was a month before my seventeenth birthday. How many weeks is eight years?'

'Loads,' I said. 'Enough for a military escort, maybe.'

'I should have gone to the Isle of Man with the girls,' she said, 'or flown off in a Viscount to Lourdes.'

'If we die,' I said, 'you'll see your mother and father. You won't be alone anymore.'

The peaches and pears burned my throat like the altar wine I had shared with Shylock.

'I'm not alone,' she said, and she kissed me between my eyebrows. 'I have you.'

Through the dumb waiter I could hear the black Africans practising their Irish for the Bar Library entrance exam under the drifting jellyfish of the dining-room chandelier.

> *Tiocfaidh mé*
> *Tiocfaidh tú*
> *Tiocfaidh sé nó sí*
> *Tiocfaimid*
> *Tiocfaidh sibh*
> *Tiocfaidh siad*

—

Father Bruno stood in his vestments in the sacristy and smoked another Sweet Afton. His cigarette finger was all orange. I would have loved to suck it.

'My parents said the rosary last night,' I told him. 'They said a sorrowful mystery after "Opportunity Knocks".'

'Prayer is a complete waste of time,' said Father Bruno. 'That's what makes it so interesting.'

He handed me a fistful of Communion wafers and I filled my pockets with them.

'I don't want you fainting,' he said. 'The thing is ridiculous. Jesus didn't starve people. He fed them.'

'Could Jesus get us out of this?' I said. 'Out of Cuba, I mean?'

'Jesus wasn't a helicopter,' Father Bruno said. 'He was a man. He is a man who reached down so far into his own humanity that he discovered it was grounded in God.'

I was munching softly on the hosts to overhear anyone coming. He gave me a mouthful of wine to help them go down, but I wasn't sure if it came from the plyboard press or from the chalice that his mother's wedding ring had been melted into during the Battle of Britain.

'When the bomb exploded in Hiroshima,' Father Bruno said, 'I didn't know if I was alive or dead; and I still don't. Perhaps I've been cremated since that moment, and perhaps not. At times I have a feeling that I roamed for hours among carbon forms that moaned and moved. It was Ash Wednesday in the world. Then I became tired and thirsty and hungry. Actually, I became peckish. Selfishness of that order is a sign of life. Or is it?'

He handed me the butt of his fag to dampen under a thread of tapwater.

'Can we put Shylock's name on the altar list of the dead for All Souls?' I said. 'Along with Kitty's ancestors.'

He wrote it down beneath my great grandparents' patronymics and their sixteen stillbirths out of twenty-one pregnancies, with only the first four stillbirths given a name by my great-granny Agnes or Mary Agnes or Mary something.

'*Sacerdoti*,' said Father Bruno. 'That's the Latin for a priest. Yitzhak is a Cohen. He is descended from Aaron, the brother of Moses. That beats Melchizedek.'

'Father Bruno,' I said. 'My dad says that even the end of the world wouldn't be the end of the world.'

'Perhaps we'll put the telephone directory on the altar beside the altar list of the dead on the feast of All Souls, if there is an altar and if there is a feast and if there is a soul,' he said.

—

When the old lady rang at the hall door, I thought that she imagined she was at the Chester Beatty Library; but she was a former domestic who had been in service with a family all her life, and had no home to go to. So I walked with her round the side of the house to the kitchen hatch where the messenger boys would open the tinfoil caps on the milk bottles for the birds.

'Come in, ma'am,' Kitty said, and she went out through the back to bring her in. She took the old lady's shoes and put them on the hot pipe in the pantry. Then she set up the card table where my mother kept her pills, and dressed it with a white tablecloth that was twice too large.

'Isn't it terrible about Cuba?' I said to the old lady. She smelled like a bus, a sad smell but a nice one.

'It is,' she said. 'God help you.'

I laid the card table from my parents' anniversary canteen, soup spoons and dessert spoons, fish knives and fish forks, settings for the main course, settings for starters, little silver scoops for the sorbet in between, and a napkin in my napkin ring.

'Thank you, sir,' she said.

Kitty brought in soup and homemade brown bread. Her eyes had filled up, and she kept her head straight and a bit back to stop them dribbling. I could hear the Africans at it in the dining room, murmuring, memorizing, mesmerizing, as if the Pentagon and the Politbureau would postpone apocalypse for the *Tearmaí Dlíthe*.

S'é do bheatha Mhuire
Tá lán do ghrásta
Tá an Tiarna leat.

When they had finished the half of it, and I could hear my mother's voice drilling them over the hiss of the gas fire in the grate, the old lady looked at her upside-down face in the soup spoon. She had gone through the brown bread like a tomboy.

'*Sancta Maria, mater Dei, ora pro nobis peccatoribus nunc et in hora mortis nostri,*' she said.

'Amen,' I said.

Kitty poured my father's Oloroso sherry silently from the ship's decanter down the scintillating tilt of a crystal glass into its cut and concave facets.

'Milk, ma'am,' she said.

———

'Shylock! Shylock!'

The chant became a commotion, and the Holy Ghost from the Ukraine threw the door open and walked in. Father Bruno and he began to wrestle each other at the teacher's podium, but it was almost as if they were embracing, like a man and a woman should. The classroom was so quiet you could hear the nail heads in their boots grate on the dry floorboards as they twisted, and their brief, baffled breathing. From the hole for the inkwell on the sloping lid of Shylock's school desk the albino snout of the mouse thrust through, twitching.

'Get out of my class, you,' said Father Bruno to the Ukrainian. 'I tell you, get out.'

'You're mad,' the Holy Ghost said as he left. 'A madman. What you need is electricity.'

When the bell rang and the class ended and the classroom emptied, Shylock put on his wicket-keeper's gloves and carried the lean vanilla animal across to the window. We looked down three floors to the gravel shortcut to the bomb shelter where they kept the cricket nets.

'Forty weeks in the womb; forty years in the desert,' Shylock said. 'That's my father's religion.'

'My dad says it began with the hydrogen atom and it ends with the hydrogen bomb,' I told him. 'My mum says it was somebody else who said it, but my dad said it was him. He said it first.'

Shylock dropped the mink at arm's length, and we watched it fall as soft as a stole to the gravel path. For a while it lay there like a streak of whitewash from the boundary marker. Then it stretched and sidled off, but slowly, as if its spine had been wrenched, or its little foetal paw.

'It had to be handicapped,' Shylock said. 'Same as a horse. A mink could kill a fox. It goes for the jugular.'

The creature went north. He or she reached the pond where Father Bruno stored the goldfish he had saved from certain death along the college avenue when they were thrown from car windows after the garden fêtes. Paused, and passed on.

Actually, he was veering in the direction of the mink factory.

—

On Saturday, at the party, the house was full of elderly females with blonde hair. My mother could only desire the people who resented her. Men and women who had voted against the Treaty entrenched themselves in the drawing room; those who had voted for it mobilized in the study. Those in the middle who had fought in the Royal Air Force during the Second World war occupied the dining room and the veranda. The Africans stood in the hall talking to the Holy Ghost from the Ukraine. Everybody was miserable. No one danced to the new Cliff Richard album.

Kitty, however, was radiant.

'I knew it'd be a washout,' she said. 'I would have said it if anyone asked me. We should all be in the church, praying.'

A middle-aged woman wandered into the kitchen. She walked over to Kitty and kissed her on both cheeks. That was the mulled wine I had been stirring and serving with a stone ladle.

'Kitty,' she said, 'I'm sorry to be asking you this so late in the day, so late in the Doomsday. How are you?'

'I'm well, Mrs Montague,' Kitty said.

'You were in an orphanage, Kitty,' the woman said. 'Was it awful?'

'It was grand,' said Kitty. 'Thank God.'

'Have you siblings?' said the woman. 'I mean, have you brothers and sisters?'

'She has me,' I said.

'Ah,' the woman said, looking at me through her eyelashes. 'Can a man serve two mistresses?'

When she had gone, Kitty turned the wireless up again. One man was saying miss-ill and another was saying miss-isle.

'My father's name was Morgan,' she said to me. 'He was a Methodist. Pleurisy was what he had, not tuberculosis. My mother adored him. She kept his gloves until she died. Now you know, pet.'

———

The floating parquet floor was being mutilated by the guests' stilettos. My father trotted two fingers down my mother's buttoned back as she stooped to study the cuts.

'Don't do that, Harry,' she said. 'One of these marks is a cigarette burn. Who would stub a cigarette on a parquet floor?'

'Well, I wouldn't want to denigrate anyone,' my father said, and he handed me his cigar by the sodden end. 'That's the best Cuban kind, Mattie. It's my shot at gallantry. Take a puff or two. It's a nice vice.'

'That's an oxymoron,' I said. I did not want to taste my father's saliva, but I loved the glasshouse heat in my mouth when I sucked.

'Actually,' he said, smiling at me, the way he did sometimes, 'I think it's more of a tautology.'

The Holy Ghost from the Ukraine was standing at the television, watching bishops in the bonnets of the priests of Jupiter being blown into St Peter's by a gale-force wind.

'A Second Vatican council?' he said. 'The first one is only over.'

'Too little, too late,' said a fighter pilot's wife. In fact, he had flown Hurricanes and not Spitfires.

'Well,' said my mother, 'I can truly say that for the first time in my life I am grateful to have only one child.'

Men in bow ties and women in gowns were sitting on the stairs to half way up the house. I made my way among them, stepping over drinks and dinner plates, and spying at the freckled shoulders and the old throats of the girls as they munched with their mouths open. They had been born so long ago they did not even have vaccination scars.

'Boy coming, boy coming!' one of them shouted. But I passed on.

When I reached my own room, the door was ajar. The anglepoise had been placed on the carpet, its hood flush with the floor so that the low light was horizontal. And a woman of an age somewhere between Kitty and my actual mother was sitting on my bed, reading a book from my bookshelf.

'I hope you don't mind,' she said. 'You have so many books. It's like the Chester Beatty Library in here.'

'You're welcome,' I said. There was a whiff of something in the room, not a spray or a slipstream but a slight scent, a sour, saline, shoreline odour.

'I have a little boy who loves *Moonfleet* too,' she said, 'and all the books by Roger Lancelyn Green. He's in boarding school. I wish he weren't. I wish he were here now.'

'I know,' I said.

She ran the tips of her fingers over her brown bouffant to stabilize it, a bit like Father Bruno. Beautiful black hair glittered in her armpits.

'I couldn't stay downstairs,' she said. 'The conversation was neither from the heart nor from the head. All the predators are pretending to be prey.'

'I know,' I said. 'Would you like to rest here for a while?'

'Yes, please,' she said. 'Thank you.'

I closed the door as quietly as the lid of my music box. You could not hear the tongue ease into the groove.

———

The breeze carried Glenn Miller dance music far to the east towards the West Country. At the bottom of the garden among old broken beehives and the wall fallen sandpit, there was only the grating of the trowel. I dug quickly and quietly. The light was still on in my bedroom. The bitch Labrador would be sleeping in a scullery, the stencil of the harness still on her fur, with her whining litter rifled; and the paralyzed mink might have stripped a chicken in the run at Milltown, I would not lead a black Chevrolet cortege for Kitty to the cemetery gates at the close of the twentieth century. I would not wake the dead, nor would I waken them. Yet it was better this way for Shylock, who would otherwise be bowing and blowing kisses all his life to those who united against him; and better as well for Father Bruno, who was as radioactive as any meteorite; and better even for the sacked old lady, urinating in her underpants in a confession box when the churches closed at night.

I settled the music box into the hole I had made. I put in my birth certificate and my last school report, along with a photograph of Kitty and myself at the snake house in the zoo on my first Holy Communion day, with a heavy, hot constrictor looping its tyres around my neck. Then I added three Victorian pennies, each with a different image of the Queen: as maidenly, and middle-aged, and matronly. I had got them all in change from the same chewing-gum dispenser.

How strange that the names of the two presidents both began with the letter K. It was like Achilles and Agamemnon. It was like Romulus and Remus.

Now there was only my grandfather's speech against the Treaty, in illegible longhand, and four surviving wafers from the last light collation with Father Bruno. I bedded them in the foolscap sheets. The archaeologists would not be able to tell if they were consecrated. That would be their mystery in the museum.

Kennedy and Khrushchev. Khrushchev and Kennedy. The names belonged together as if each needed the other in order to be fully itself.

I reached down so far into my sadness that I discovered it was grounded in joy. I was an adult because an adult is a child without parents.

I looked back at my home for the last time. The Africans were singing *acapella*. Shadows smoked at the windows.

'*Ad Maiorem Dei Gloriam*,' I said.

WAKING A JEW

Then he realized that he was not dreaming and that the hammering was happening at his own front door. The other, browner beat was the sound of his heart in hiding, the sound of its startled darting. Where had it been all this time? It was broken, yet it worked. He put his right hand over it, in under the eiderdown duvet, as if it were a baby whose breastfeeding would betray everybody.

'Wake up,' a voice was crying from out in the one-way street; and the voice was a woman's. But why were they using a woman? They had never used women before.

'Wake up,' she was calling. 'Wake up.'

So he lay still and inhaled through his mouth to listen, listen closely, listen carefully, because of the bluebottle noise of his sinuses. And if he lived, if he survived, if he went on existing, he would have them yanked out straightaway, those polyps in his nose, under local anaesthetic in the day-care clinic on the coast road, where there was no mortuary with a fake plaque saying Hospital

Administration. Because it was not fair to be always stifled, always suffocated. He had never smoked. He was the only boy in the building who didn't scavenge for fag ends. Yesterday he had traded tobacco for aspirin, brilliantine for biscuits, and brought them home in his underpants to his mother who had kissed him on the forehead like an important corpse and told him, her Solomon, her sweet King Solomon, that he was responsible.

'It's time,' the woman was yelling. 'Are you in the land of the living?'

Am I? he thought. Am I responsible? Lord, rescue my soul from their destructions, my darling from the lions. I have a right to breathe easy in my seventies, for Christ's sake. I am tired of all this shit.

'Bring out your dead. Bring out your dead.'

That was not her, the woman. She was down at the door by the wooden washtub where crocus bulbs grew upside down among the winter pansies and where he had buried the last of the dollars in oilskin when the border closed. The baritone whoops had come from the corner, the house with the trellis. But the house with the trellis was Christian, a cross in the toilet.

'Say if you're there,' she implored him. 'I'll take No for an answer.'

By now they would have blocked both ends of the road, the lane to the grass courts of the tennis club and the alley in which a eucalyptus was patiently uprooting the hydrant. He could hear the trucks clearing their throats, gunning the motors to blot out boots and shouting, the garbage chucked like children into the stainless steel of the pig's snout. Yet no one would look out; no one would look up. They would stare instead at the softly boiling eggs as they evened the nooses of their neckties and their wives slipped studs with gold initials through the apertures in their shirt cuffs. Mass bells should be pealing too, cassettes of a carillon spooling beside the tannoys in the church tower. That would be heaven.

Solomon sat up. He sat upright. He was a man who knew what day of the week it was. It was Friday, and Friday was bin day. One thing followed from another if you let it. Had he put out the bins? Had he bins to put out? Come to that, had he bins? He had a black bag. Perhaps he had two black bags. You never could tell what you might stumble upon in your own back yard. That was what it meant to be a widower, to be a man without a woman. For the first time in forty-two years, you found out when the rubbish was collected.

'Mr Blatt.' It was Number Seven, his next-door neighbour, the indefatigable one. 'You asked me last night to rouse you this morning. Rouse me early tomorrow, you said. Well, it's early, and it's tomorrow.'

Thunder of the knocker, lightning of the bell; and after the din of its bitter dentistry, fists on the frosted pane, first gloves, then gauntlets. There was an order to everything, even to urgency. But was it night or day? The blind he had drawn was the colour of morning. Its black had begun to go grey in the face. That was a plus. That was a surplus.

'Rosen, it's me. It's Tess. Tess of the Dodder Valley. I'm in my dressing gown.'

Wait, he thought, wait a minute, you bloody woman. Wait until my heart stops; wait till I find where my eyes are. And he went searching behind him, roaming the hill of paperbacks on what had been Melanie's side, the window side, the white east of the bed, and frisking finally the tinfoil jackets of the antacid tablets he received on the tongue like a Catholic between killings.

'Don't break my door down,' he said. 'The novelty has worn off that one.'

His glasses were hidden in Jane Austen, at the page where he had stopped when the Judy Garland midnight-movie season started at ten to the hour with the star in blackface for Harry Rapf's 'Everybody Sing'; and when he put them on, the room arrayed itself around him, tidy and detailed, like the way it had looked when their good granddaughter spring-cleaned at the childminder's rate because she was saving for slacks and a scooter. Now he knew where he was and who he was. He could leave the why to the rabbi and the how to the interns; but he would take great care to be buried with his tortoiseshells. He had been right as well to leave in Melanie's contact lenses. After all, they had not removed her aluminium hip. They had not hacked at her bridgework with mechanic's pliers.

'Mrs Cassidy,' he said, as he came down the stairs, one by one, to the hall. 'Mrs Cassidy, you would wake the dead. Do you know that?'

'I have a hard enough time waking the living,' she said back. Her hand was in through the hairy letterbox, wagging at him. Where were her rings gone?

'I was in the shower,' he said, and he sat himself down on the bottom step, beside the pampas grass, where he had levered out a carpet rod to stow beneath his bed in case of burglars. He was not about to open the door in a pair of Boxer shorts and a scar from a duodenal ulcer.

'You were in the shower?' she said, and her shadow blew its nose at the glass. 'Be careful in the shower, Mr Blatt. You could do yourself an injury. Where would I be then?'

His breasts were soft and spacious. He could write on them, like vellum, with a ballpoint pen, smiling at the sink of the nib in the spring of the skin; and she had studied the letters, upside down of course, with a double chin from straining, saying: Solomon, Solomon, Solomon Rosenblatt. My solemn man, my happy man, my roses and blather. What are you doing to my breast? What are you doing to my heart?

It was the first and last time he had writtten the Lord's name in Hebrew.

'I can't let you in, Mrs Cassidy,' he said. 'I am more or less in the image and likeness of God. It is no fit state to be seen in.'

Four phones rang at once. Rang in the hall, rang in the kitchen, rang in the bedroom, rang in the bathroom. The klaxon in the bathroom was for strokes, falls you could not rise to. A bathroom was a breeding ground for embolisms, thromboses, cardiovascular gnashing; for clots, vomit, stoppages, prayer, incontinence, embraces, choking, piss. Where there were taps and tiles, the Red Sea would not part, the Jordan would not ford. Sand would flow from the faucets.

'Are you not driven demented?' said his next-door neighbour.

He reached out. Lifted the handset like the dressing on a wound.

'I don't mean dementia,' said Mrs Cassidy's shadow. 'I mean annoyed, like.'

'How did you get my number?' he said. 'I am ex-directory.'

'This is your wake-up call,' said the phone in an English voice. 'Thank you for using the service.'

'Thank you very much,' he said to the English voice. He had tugged a plume of pampas grass across the brown of his breasts. The indefatigable one might be seventy-odd, but her corneas came from a long line of snipers.

'I hope you did not think I said dementia,' said Mrs Cassidy's shadow. 'Did you think I said dementia?'

'This is your wake-up call,' the phone said, but the voice was only pretending to be English. 'Thank you for using the service.'

'Anyway,' the shadow called. 'Happy anniversary.'

'Thank you very much,' he said. 'I can hear you. I heard you the first time.'

'How many years would you be married?' said the shadow at the door.

'It is not that sort of anniversary,' he said. 'It is more history.'

'Everything's history now,' the shadow said. 'Look at me.'

'This is your wake-up call,' the phone said. It was English all right, but lower middle-class, West Midlands, putting on posh. 'Thank you for using the service.'

He swung the receiver down like a club on the cradle. Then, after a moment, hoisted it to hear again. Had he broken the bloody thing? But the distant air-raid siren of the dial tone was there still, still low and clear.

'Hello?' said Mrs Cassidy. 'Hello?'

And he had thought at the time it was strange for a Soviet soldier to say that, as if he were a Yankee, as if he were Johnny Weissmuller meeting the first Europeans; but the man had gone on saying it from the doorway of the hut, hello, hello, hello; and Solomon had said the only Russian word that he could remember. He had said da; he had said da, da, like a baby dragging itself behind the corduroys of its father. And the soldier spreadeagled himself at the door frame to protect his boots while forty papery corpses watched his breakfast of yoghurt and coffee steam in a parallelogram of January sunlight.

'Are you all right for bread and milk?'

'I am all right for bread and milk,' he said. 'Are you all right for bread and wine?'

'You're a terrible man.'

She was right. He had come from a malodorous drop. He would have to change. There was no two ways about it. His shorts were stale. He could smell his penis. If he had a coronary on the dual carriageway and they saw the state of his underpants in the morgue, he would die a thousand deaths. So he would strip off, stand in the shower, and soap himself. He might even sing the Shema. Why not? Every man was a tenor in his own toilet. As long as he said Adoschem instead of Adonai, what harm could there be? Hadn't Melanie sung Kiddush at the ironing board like a second Sophie Kurtzer? Besides, his granddaughter danced with the Torah at a feminist minyat in a Tel Aviv sportshall, and she dwelleth in Israel even unto this day; she had not been smitten in the knees, and in the legs, with a sore botch. To be sure, her convertible had been daubed with acrylic paint from a spray can early one Saturday, but that was the old people for you nowadays. In the dormitory suburbs of Zion the just did not sleep. They kept vigil. They were vigilantes.

'I am going to Mass now,' Mrs Cassidy called.

'I am going to wash now,' he told her. 'In ten minutes I will be a new man.'

'You could be talking about baptism,' she said.

'No,' he said. 'I am not talking about baptism. All baptism is baptism by fire. I am talking about sprinklers.'

'Shalom, Rosen,' she said. The shadow lifted; left. Blue brightened at the mortice lock.

'And also with you, Tess,' said Solomon Rosenblatt.

———

When they had come back from the hospital, Melanie went upstairs to the bedroom and lay down. He made her a cup of tea with a teabag, but there was no liner in the pedal bin, and he stood there in the middle of the kitchen, not knowing what to do, while the bag burned his fingers.

In the maternity hospitals they would give you the X-rays. They would give you a parcelled miscarriage, even. They would not file the breaking wave of your torso in a plain brown envelope, like a frothy calendar. They would not incinerate the ruin of a breast that had fed the mouths of her children, the hands of their father, a breast that had grown with its quiet sister through the early nineteen-thirties while the sun danced in the sky. And when Jean Harlow's knitted bathing suit scampered across the screen behind the Yiddish subtitles, he had pressed his calf against her in the turreted church pews of the neighbourhood cinema and asked her was she saving her milk for her honey?

'I am saving my milk for my son,' she said to him, 'and my honey for my beloved.'

He had knocked and gone in.

'Room service,' he said.

'Why did you knock?' She had taken off her shoes and her ear-rings. She lay on the bed with her bare feet side by side as if she was at the chiropodist's.

'I don't know,' he said. 'I don't know where I am.'

'The door,' said Melanie. 'The door into the room; the door out of it.'

She had opened the window too. The long lace curtains blew like a bride's train.

'You're not going to see anything you haven't seen before,' she said. 'There is no mystery left. Come in.'

The radio was on, but it was low down, whispering about orgasms. Orgasms are a shared responsibility. What sort of shit was that to be airing when the children were fresh home from school, spelling the morning's words for their mother, lamp, ramp, camp, and cutting out pictures in the *National Geographic* for their project on Tutankhamun?

'I should have thought of a biscuit,' he said. 'I never thought.'

'The tea is grand.'

'You like the biscuit with the sombrero on the wrapper.'

'I went off it,' she said. 'It was too noisy.'

He sat on her stool at the dressing table and looked into the three of him in the mirrors. They were not the three men of Mamre, those flickering triplets in replica button downs, and he, he was not Abraham. Neither was Abraham, either. My Lord, he thought, if now I have found favour in thy sight, pass not away, I pray thee, from thy servant. Do not let them gut her like a halibut. Her breast is a kitchen. Dynasties victual there.

'Do you know what?'

'I don't know anything anymore,' he said. 'I know zero.'

Why did he not have cancer of the prostate? Every male child of a certain age was supposed to, and he was certain of nothing on earth except his age. He had been born in the twentieth century, in the waiting room of another millennium, and he had drunk cocoa there until the station master made them stand on the platform in the train's incense: so he was at least a thousand years old, if not already posthumous. Yet his prostate, whatever it was, was still working away at whatever it was meant to. He might even outlive the criminals in the Kremlin and the scented Vatican fat cats, though by then the kids in the cul-de-sac where he lived would skedaddle when they spotted him, a gangster gone gaga. His mother had settled as soot on the branch of a birch tree, but her son was a perfect specimen. The genito-urinary girl had written it down, and the cardiologist fellow had written it up. He could dress now.

'You can dress now, Doctor,' he had said. 'My girlfriend would kill for those braces. They are very in.'

'I am not a doctor,' Solomon said. 'Everybody doctors me.'

'Being a patient doesn't stop you being a doctor,' said the heart specialist.

'I am not a patient, either,' Solomon had said. 'I am neither animal nor vegetable.'

'There is nothing else to be except a patient or a doctor,' the doctor said patiently, 'unless you believe in the communion of saints. Do you believe in the communion of saints?'

'When I close my eyes,' Solomon said, 'I can hear the sounds inside my mother's stomach.'

Then he was so confused that he put his vest on back to front, and paid with Visa instead of Amex. In the car, in the rush-hour traffic, in the red lights flaring their fireballs out of the darkness and the downpour, the neck of the singlet chafed his Adam's apple like the gloved finger of a hand tracing his throat.

'One. Four, one, five. Two, one, two,' she said.

He stared at her now in the vanity mirrors. They had taken off their watches and their glasses and gone to bed together, back to back, night after night, year in, year out, since the time the scientists sent monkeys and dogs into space to see if there was any hope of escape; but the capuchins and the poodles had brought no olive branch back to the ark, and, year in, year out, night after night, back to back, they had gone to bed together, shut out the light and practised dying, while their watches crawled like insects over the carpet and the tortoiseshell spectacles folded their wings and waited.

Eternity was a waste of time. He had wasted so much time he might be eternal.

'That's the code,' she said. 'Ring Joseph. Why don't you?'

'I am not in the mood to confess to a beard,' he said.

'He's not a beard; he's a shoulder.'

'A cold shoulder,' Solomon said. 'An older, colder one.'

'But a brother, first and foremost. He doesn't stop being a brother because he's a psychiatrist.'

'No,' said Solomon. 'He is always and everywhere a beard.'

'He is not a very good beard,' she said. 'Be fair to him.'

The radio was gossiping about a celebrity who had autographed her panties for Rwanda. Each knicker weighed in at a king's ransom: the bottom line was a round figure, a cool K. Also, some chaplain at a Mickey Mouse technical college would shave half of his head for five hundred smackers. If pensioners could twist like Chubby Checker in the plaza of a multiplex, so could anyone. The Third World depended upon us. Do it now. Do it this instant.

'What time is it?'

'I don't know,' she said. 'I am never sure about America. I think they are just waking up.'

Her feet had never been barer. Ancient varnish dirtied a few toes. That was from when she had worn the espadrilles; but when had that been? He wanted to turn round, go back to her, to hold them in his lap, heavy and hard as candles, the parts of her that he had never pet-named. But it would shame him. He hadn't held her hand since the last photograph; and when had that been? How could he hold her feet? Yet he had followed her footprints through deserts and dust bowls. Where there was sand in his life, there was sight of her steps, two by two and side and side, the unoffending Bedouin house shoes.

'Listen,' she said.

Outside in the garden, the wicket gate whistled on its hinges. He had oiled them once, and lost the advantage of ten extra seconds.

'It's Number Seven,' he said. 'It's Citizen Tess.'

'Pretend we're dead.'

They were Mrs Cassidy's blows as well, a Beethoven's Fifth at the hall door. The woman had militia in her blood.

'Don't,' Melanie said. 'Pretend we're dying.'

'Jesus was a Jew,' said Solomon.

'She told you too?'

'She told me too.'

'What did you say?'

'I told her I thought he was a Roman Catholic.'

They listened for the gravel and the gate; for her gate and her gravel. Then there was only the wind.

'She has hair from a saint,' Melanie said. She had drawn the duvet over her, but her feet were not hidden. They leaned like tennis shoes she had whitened and left on a ledge to dry. The bin men would pick them out and shake off the eggshell.

'You put the hair under your pillow,' she said. 'You sleep on it.'

Powdered milk would be provided by fourth-class pupils from a primary school. The girls were line-dancing in relays until the cows came home; and word was in that drag queen Gloria Mundi, appearing in cabaret nightly plus Sundays at the Enigma, would contribute the blouse off his back.

'If there's a miracle, you place an advertisement in the saint's magazine. It does not have to be a huge big one. It can be a little small one. "Thank you for your wonderful work on my melanoma.

You're a saint. Love to all the dead"; and you put your initials at the bottom and the postal district.'

Then he did get up and go over to her, and he did kneel down and gather her feet into his arms like stove wood. He had seen it happen in the old proscenium picture houses and on video cassettes. Now it was happening here: to him, to her, but not to both of them. Rain on the high electrified fence made slick sounds like the flint of cigarette lighters. Brown drool from the bunk above him dripped on his navel; but his sunken umbilicus was a faraway place. It was at least a day's journey from the waterhole of his nipples across an impossible wasteland where even the bacteria had evaporated. He would run out this minute to where the dachshunds were patrolling and throw himself on the children's high-voltage climbing frame.

Calls would be answered before midnight, the radio was announcing. After midnight it would be too late. Pledge what you can while you can. Principles won't be worth pumpkins when the clock strikes twelve. Think crystal balls, not glass slippers. If you want to be in with the smell of a chance or, in the case of those celebrity unmentionables, the chance of a smell, ring-a-ling-ling instanter. People were waiting to hear from you now.

'My parents should have called me Sarah,' she said from the bed behind him. 'I am dying of my own name.'

His tears ran down his nose onto the twenty-six bones of her foot.

———

'Then he told me, this black American soldier, to choose a pair of spectacles from the mountain. Well, at first I was afraid to. I was afraid I might start a landslide around me, and be buried forever under the downward drifting mass of a million prescription lenses, a great, glittering ice-cap of glasses. There were glasses for reading

Victor Hugo and glasses for walking a punctured bicycle, glasses for baking what hadn't been bottled, glasses for watching Westerns when the whole parterre hurrahed if they saw their misspelled surnames in the end titles of the Hollywood shorts: best boy, key grip, bravo! But better, best of all, there were glasses for boys to take off before kissing their girlfriends, and glasses for girls to put on before teasing their boyfriends with: I thought you came here to stare at Jeanette MacDonald.'

"Jesus Christ,' said the soldier, 'you are worse than a woman choosing a hat."

Then I reached up to my own height, you see, and I stretched out my hand, and I pulled a pair of eyes from the glacier. Very gently, very gingerly, in case the hill would flinch and avalanche.

"Hosanna in the highest," the soldier said.

Their frame was tortoiseshell, which you cannot buy now for love or money because it is too inhuman to the tortoise, and the wings were made of thin wire with flexible grips. The previous occupant had padded the left grip by winding a tiny strip of bandage around it. I imagined he had an ulcer on that ear; but why not on both? Why not on both at the same time?

"Can you see with them?" the soldier said.

I breathed on the lenses and his fingerprints appeared.

"Well?" said the soldier.

They were like the markings on an aerial photograph of a lost archaeological site.

'I can see everything clearly,' I said.

"You haven't put them on," said the soldier. You must understand he was American. "Put them on," he said.

'I can see everything,' I said. 'I can see.'

"Jesus Christ," he said, "you couldn't see the writing on the wall when you walked into it."

It came to me, there and then, out of the blue, why the person had padded the grip. He had leaned his head on his left hand while he wrote with his right. He was tired, you see. He's been studying for his last examination. His father hides the sherry in a bookshelf behind *Diseases of the Breast*. His mother notices nicotine stains on the moons of his fingernails. His sweetheart will open her mouth, open wide, open wider, her tongue slippy with strawberry ice-cream, so he can spot the new filling, a dull pellet of silver where the gum bristles with stitches. And he leans his head on his left hand and he writes her a letter with his right.

I can see him fifty years ago through the peephole of his glasses. Through the magnification of his lens I saw him today, this Friday, the twenty-seventh of January in the year of our Lord, Five Thousand, Seven Hundred and Fifty-Five.'

Solomon stared at the students and the students peered back at him. Some of them squinted through the cage of their hands. Children had scratched at the whitewash on the inside of the windows of the tram with the compasses from their geometry sets, and sometimes he had seen their pupils at the slits as the car shuddered through the forbidden district. After that, the authorities had coated the outside of the windows with a dark preservative.

'Fifty minutes,' said the teacher whose perfume smelled like aftershave. 'That was beautifully judged, Dr Rosenblatt. We have time for a couple of questions.'

The children were so tall. They could all be basketball players, Ethiopians leaping about. The desks were designed for old-fashioned humans. Where had these femurs been cultured? Was it diet or hormones? The girls were budding and bleeding in rooms full of dolls with real hair that thanked you when you truncheoned their mechanical stomachs, and the boys woke at night to the pool of the serum of their sperm, a water mark of tree rings radiating outward, ripples that stretched and sank and ceased like the last creases in the freshly laundered bed sheet. They in their light years, he in his heavy, what had either to say to the other? The time of their life was not the life of his times. He was a widowed man with the pong of old age and a few cranky anecdotes. They were Isaac and Rebekah, lifting up their eyes in a field in a far country.

Solomon peered at the students and the students stared back at him.

'Anyway,' he said. 'Enough of Bindermichl Displaced Persons' Camp in Linz. All of us lived happily ever after, once upon a time.'

They gave him a glowing ovation, some of them standing, the desks like bin lids, more of them now, feet on the floor, all of them then, until it became a prank, and the teacher beat on the table with the duster, and the chalk dust made Solomon want to sneeze, but he stifled it. His polyps would punish him later, his sinuses start up their horseflies in a lampshade.

'Thank you,' she said. 'Thanks very much. I won't forget this.'

'Not at all,' he said; but she had been talking to the students, so he worked his other hand deep into his pocket to tug at the tight elastication of his togs. They had been biting into his scrotum since he arrived at the school, but what alternative had he had? There wasn't a clean pair of underpants in the house, not even in the laundry bin. He had had to make do with his swimming trunks.

'On behalf of us all, I would like to thank Dr Rosenblatt for sharing his life story with Three B today. We're very privileged. We're mindful too, Geraldine O'Connell, that this isn't any ordinary day, and not because it's Friday, no, I heard that loud and clear, but because it is of course the fiftieth anniversary of the liberation of Auschwitz by the Allies.'

'The Russians,' Solomon said. 'I am not actually a doctor, you know.'

'I'm terribly sorry,' she said. Her poor cuff was streaked with pink chalk. She had made it worse by dabbing at it. That was from writing on the blackboard while he spoke. The names of his family and his friends were listed in columns behind him, under the crucifix with a missing shoulder, and the names of two of them had been spelled correctly: David and Joseph. She had not had so much luck with Mordechai and Moishele, with Yossele and Zavel, in their pale-red approximations.

'You were thinking of my brother. He had that effect on women, actually. He is still a doctor, but he's no Doctor Kildare.'

'Doctor who?' she said.

'Absolutely,' said Solomon. 'He is the living image of Doctor Who.'

Their eyes met for a moment. Then the tramcar sparked, swerved, moved on. As he crossed the tracks, with the four Arrowroot biscuits in one pocket and the three stamped analgesic tablets in the other, the breeze carried a slipstream of eau-de-toilette from the passengers on their way to the Easter ceremonies.

'Jordan has a question,' the teacher said. 'Haven't you, Jordan?'

The lad had written it out. He smoothed the page with the side of his banana.

'Can you find it in your heart to forgive?'

'I would,' said Solomon, 'if I could find my heart, but I cannot remember where I left it the last time. They have given me a cardiac muscle to replace it, with a pump-action component that is all Greek to me. It does a grand job.'

He ought not to have talked at such length about his family. He had been invited to discuss Hitler and the Holocaust. What had Hitler and the Holocaust to do with smelly Esther, a cot death in the spring offensive? What had Zindel's autograph book for stellar signatories to do with the statutory guarantees of minority rights in multiculturalist polities? Jack Haley, Ray Bolger and Bert Lahr meant no more to these third-year teenagers than the names of the patriarchs. Yet Hitler and the Holocaust was the sum of all these subtractions.

'Deborah,' said the teacher. 'You have a question.'

The child had beautiful, bare arms, like the missing limbs of the Venus de Milo. Her mouth and her eyes were the same age exactly: there was not a day between them. She had been born by

Caesarean section. He was sure of it. Caesar babies were cherubs. The smiles had not been wiped from their faces in the dumb maul of the birth canal.

'Would you like to be an Israelite?' she said.

'What a wonderful question,' Solomon said. 'Thank you for asking it. Yes, I would love to have been an Israelite. I would like to have been with Joshua at Jericho. That was before King Solomon, you see, and so I would not have had to endure the comparison all my life. My name has been the source of some not inconsiderable unpleasantness.'

'I'm sure that Deborah means Israeli. Don't you mean Israeli, Deborah?'

'Yes,' said the Venus de Milo. She stuck out her lip and blew her fringe from her forehead. 'That's what I meant. Sorry. Would you like to go there, to Israel? Is it your fatherland, sort of?'

He thought about this while he groped at his groin. They must have shrunk in the sea. He would buy a dozen or so shorts on his way home through town; that would do for a month. Anything was better than asking Citizen Cassidy to kick start the washing machine; and drying them in the microwave had not been fruitful.

'My fatherland is Mother Earth,' he said to the cherub, 'and my motherland is Father Time.'

'Is that Kahlil Gibran?' the child said.

'No,' he said, 'it isn't. I would have thought it was a bit beyond Kahlil Gibran. It is something my father used to say when people talked politics at the dinner table.'

Who was the boy at the back of the class, leaning his head on his hand and toying with a ballpoint? And the old, ordinary woman frowning at the state of his fingertips: who was she? The light was against him. He closed his eyes to see, but her bulky housecoat hid her. He could not be sure if her breast had been butchered and burnt like a plum pudding with a blue halo of brandy.

Now the class was turning round to look as well, and the boy at the back made a face at his friends in the front; but he sat straight, twirling his pen like a baton and beaming interest. He was another of God's incognitoes.

'John Paul has a question, which John Paul is too shy to share,' the teacher said. 'I shall ask it for him, and Martin Brennan will give it his undivided attention. Shall I ask it for you, John Paul?'

The boy bowed his head.

'Don't make it too hard,' said Solomon Rosenblatt. 'I am no Einstein; I am barely an Ein. Once or twice I have been able to say Amen in my life. Once or twice I have been able to say Amen to it. Alleluia is another matter; alleluia is a long shot. *Dum spiro, spero.*'

'I know what that means,' said the cherub.

'I know you do,' he said. 'It's a call to arms.'

'John Paul's question is this,' the teacher said. Really, she stank like a bouncer. 'What is the last thing –'

But the bell was ringing suddenly its oriental, ululating all-clear call, the kids were rising up in their places, striking their breasts like baboons, jostling, rejoiced; and the teacher made a bullhorn of her hands to be heard in the hubbub.

'Quick march, one, two, three. Quietly, quietly, quietly, please.'

Basketball candidates stooped over him for a handshake. Their palms were as clammy as his from the cotton pockets of their trousers, from juggling lunch money and testicles while the addled granddad wisecracked through his Western History module. 'Shalom,' they said to him, 'shalom,' as if he were a Christian charismatic at a prayer-in, as if he were a folk singer with an ukelele strumming the psalms of David to an air from *Oklahoma*. 'Shalom.'

'Goodbye,' he said. 'Goodbye.'

A plaster-cast leg lurched at him from the left-hand corner of his field of vision. He autographed it with a flo-pen, block letters in burgundy, while the invalid dispatched cheese sticks between the herpes on his lips. On the far side of the cripple, at the head of her handmaids, Praxiteles's masterpiece smiled slyly.

'Goodbye,' she said. Her face tilted to interpret his upside-down signs on the plastercast mould.

'Shalom,' he said. 'Shalom.'

Boots thawed on a radiator. Windcheaters slithered with a noise like nylons from the bentwood backs of chairs. On the loud industrial floor among woodshavings and cycle helmets, tupperware cylinders bewildered him. He had drilled a rival's initals in the desk lid with a corkscrew and filled the borings with blue octopus ink. The cantor from Krakow unstrapped his arbutus leg and hopped from the changing room. Somebody had abandoned a pair of tortoiseshell glasses on the window ledge. They angled like the discs of a desert observatory at the dead masses drifting in space.

'Coffee,' said the teacher. 'Coffee and a ciggie. That is, if the secret police don't come to take me away, ha ha.'

She had rolled up the ivory sleeves of her blouse and was slowly effacing the names on the blackboard. Mordechai was missing, Leib and Lorelei, Tadeusz the arriviste who preferred to be Tadeo, and Zavel who married out, gave up the synagogue for the tenor sax, and wore a yellow star cut from a sheet of watered silk. He covered his nose and mouth with kitchen paper so as not to trigger catarrh, so as not to breathe the smell of their chalk-dust.

'Happy enough?' she said. She wiped her hands elaborately. The board was pitch black with a small swirl of gas in the upper atmosphere. Megaphones in the corridor summoned assembly. Ash settled on his shoulders; pollen from a pine wood clouded his watch face.

'Happy as Larry,' he said.

'God,' she said, 'you have the lingo.'

'Amn't I living here for years?' he said to her. 'Since before they launched the ape in a spaceship.'

'Go way,' she said, and she steered him through a labyrinth, lockers and lights, left, right, left again, towards the land of caffeine, the coast of mocha, where the substitute teachers would be dunking their wholegrain ration in polystyrene cups while the veterans broke soluble codeine tablets from blister foils like discount Communion hosts. For he had discovered the same staffroom and classroom the world over. Only the corridors were different; and even then, if there were light and time enough and no official was dragging him by the elbow through the milling children, he could still identify each boyhood friend behind a Bunsen burner from the streaming faces of the swimming squad in the coloured photographs among the college trophies.

'Out into the firmament,' Solomon said. 'I am telling you the truth. He came back a better beast, a much more manly mammal, with backbone in his spine. Only, his spine was lighter. His skeleton was lighter. The bones of his foot were lighter. You would expect the opposite, of course; but that would be a great mistake. The greatest mistake of all is to expect the opposite.'

'I'm afraid it was all before my time,' she told him.

'You're right to be afraid,' he said. 'Everything that was before your time is before you now. Sooner or later, you will be old before your time.'

'This way,' said the teacher. 'This way is quicker. The stairwell at break is just bodies. You'd never get through them. It's Dante's Inferno.'

She stopped for a moment to smile at him; so he stopped and smiled back. Somebody should speak to her about the aftershave. She was a nice individual.

'Between ourselves,' she said, 'I am so relieved. I was terrified they would start asking about the Palestinians. One of the religion teachers was winding them up. All last week he was at it. I put my foot down fast. Take it from me. But they're at the age when they love to embarrass you. Plus there's this boy who is black, very black-is-beautiful, black is the be-all and end-all, the only black in the school, in fact, so obviously we're delighted to have him, but. I thought he'd start his thing about the twelve million slaves, etcetera. Then his sister rang today to say he had hepatitis, thank God.'

'I understand,' Solomon said.

'We did Anne Frank for starters. They loved that. The girls did. Half of the girls are writing diaries. The things you find out about the families. Dear Jesus. Anyway. Then we saw the film. You know the one. For the life of me I cannot remember the title. I don't know whether it's amnesia or what. Maybe it's Alzheimer's.'

'I understand,' Solomon said. He was beginning to sound like a beard.

'I don't seem to be able to remember anything anymore,' she said. 'Zero. Isn't that terrible?'

He had seen too many films in which stout and stocky gentiles played the stinking inmates shrinking to italics in the middle distance; too many films in which the final credits assured an exiting audience that no Alsatian had been abused in the making of this motion picture. His early twenties could only be imagined because they had never been photographed.

'I don't know what to tell you,' he said to her.' I don't know which is worse: to forget our memories or to remember our forgetfulness. I don't know which is better. You should talk to my brother. Once he looked like Jesus Christ. Now he's God the Father. His ultimate goal is to be an American.'

'Ditto the delinquents here,' she said, 'but I don't want them to be American. I want them to be European. You know.'

'Know what?' he said, 'What do I know?'

'I try to be positive,' she said. 'You know, to be proactive. But.'

'As far as I can see,' said Solomon, 'the only aim of education is to teach people to read silently.'

'*On y va,*' she said. 'Open, Sesame. Welcome to our safe house.' And she held the door for him as he passed on into the sniggering, gregarious staffroom. 'Or at least it was our safe house until the secret police decided to stamp on the civil rights of smokers.'

'That's all right,' he said. 'I don't smoke.'

'It's all wrong,' said the teacher. 'I do. You can't say a cross word about homosexuals nowadays, but if you light a cigarette you're a Nazi war criminal.'

'Actually,' he said, 'most of them didn't smoke, either.'

She sat him at a table full of open exercise copies with jolted, slantwise writing down the wide margins. Lists on grey graph paper scrolled at his feet. Mugs over many weeks and months had printed noughts in profusion wherever he rested his wrists. His coat hairs snagged in stickiness, in circles within circles, cells in metastasis. He put his hands on his knees and played Chopsticks.

'Coffee in a momento,' she said. 'Then, with your kind permission, I'm going to disappear for two minutes and twenty seconds. It is not to powder my nose, etcetera; it is to perform some rudimentary breathing exercises in the disabled toilet, which is more like a torture chamber than a restroom, to be honest, but the alternative is to puff in the carpark.'

And she was gone before he could tell her, sugar and milk. Because of his accent she would bring him black, bitter coffee; because of his faith she would be afraid to offer him food, milk or meat, in case he went stalking off like a sulky Ezekiel. It was no wonder he'd lost weight since he started the lectures. Even his hands had shrunk back. Now the ring on his finger moved up and down as if it had grown more gold.

'I never heard such shit,' said the man beside him, the man who was twisting straws from a fruit-juice carton round his finger. 'Even when you meet them, you know who they are. I mean, they don't have to be togged out. You can almost smell them. The way they talk, they way they move, the way they shake your hand. The way they shake your hand would make you sick at times.'

'The point is,' the girl beside him said, 'you wouldn't leave a dog with a baby, would you? I don't care if it's the nicest dog in the world, even a Labrador, say, that someone who was visually impaired would adore. No, you'd have more nous. So the same thing applies with children. I wouldn't leave a seven-year-old, any seven-year-old, boy or girl, alone or on their own with one of them for five minutes. Listen, I wouldn't leave Justin, and he's seventeen, almost.'

Her hand had not stopped marking the botched copies in front of her, X after X in a brilliant, blood-red ink, like the dye his mother had pricked into letters on long johns and on pillowcases lest they be mislaid in the place where the train was to take them.

'I don't know,' said a third man. 'I'm not sure.' He pried the last of the raisins out of his scone and began to butter the halves while his colleagues ogled the ceiling in a show of outrage at the imbecile's dithering; but the bread was soft, the margarine hard, and the nine fresh raisins by themselves would be convertible currency. How could he roll them in his fingers like balls of mucus? For nine fresh raisins there were women on the landing above who would let you feel them all over with their clothes on, and one of them was pregnant, with a craving for mint.

'Listen,' the man beside him said. 'Not a million miles from where we're sitting now, there is somebody we are all agreed upon.'

'Who?' said the man with the raisins.

'You know who he is, that's who,' the woman said. 'Someone whose name begins with an S. Someone who thinks he's God's anointed.'

And his teacher appeared out of nowhere, out of a puff of smoke, with a matching cup and saucer in her hand. She set it down unsteadily, the black, bitter coffee and the small seedless grapes on a stalk.

'This is not "So Long, Farewell",' she said. 'It's more *Auf Wiedersehen*. Back in a jif.'

He sweetened his mouth with the grapes to brace himself for the other.

'What about God's anointed?' said the man with his mouth full of scone.

'He's always bringing girls into the audio-visual room, that's what,' the woman said. She had stacked the copies to one side and was drawing lines through names on a list.

'Pastoral care,' the scone said.

'Pastoral fare,' said the man with the straws.

'Well,' the woman said, 'I hope he uses a pastoral letter.'

Solomon leaned over. The coffee had made his eyes water.

'Excuse me,' he said. 'What are you talking about?'

He had darkened his accent a fraction. That impressed people. Often it made all the difference. Restaurants without room in them rearranged tables. Shows that were block-booked found seats in the circle. Even motorists at parking metres had awarded honorary degrees to the elderly German gentleman who could not reverse so readily in a right-hand model, Volkswagen or no. He had been amused by it, bemused by it, beholden to it. He had accepted the space, the seat, the table, with good grace and the odd guttural. Besides, to be taken by strangers for a German was proof, if any proof were needed, that God is not near-eastern but far-eastern, a Zen master, a smile and not a scowl, the Buddha of the ludicrous. That, at any rate, was what his brother had been saying for forty years in five remaindered ebullitions.

'What are we talking about?' said the straws. 'Do you ever read a newspaper? We're talking about parasites, about perverts. About Roman Catholic priests. Men who dress as women and prey on children.'

'I understand,' said Solomon Rosenblatt. 'I was confused. I could have sworn you were talking about Jews.'

—

'Melanie. Is that you?'

'Speaking. Is that who I think?'

'Who else?'

'How are you?'

'I don't know. I'm here.'

'You'll have to speak up,' she said. 'You're very far away.'

It was like a language lesson. He was learning English again from the *Beano* and the Bible. His tutor was a Tommy who had been seconded with shingles.

'What time is it where you are, Melanie?'

'Israel is two hours ahead. If your clock has gone back for day-light-saving, then we're three hours ahead.'

'So it's what?'

'Late. Dark. It doesn't matter.'

He listened to his niece breathing in a house in Tel Aviv. Cars sounded their horns behind her, below her apartment balcony; but it could not be a wedding. It must be the traffic lights again.

'Are you not at the Sabbath service?'

'I am,' she said. 'This is a pre-recorded interactive answering machine with mail drop.'

'What about your feminist prayer group?'

'I am going through a heterosexual phase at the moment. His name is Benjamin.'

How could she suffer the horns? They were worse than ambu-lances. It was where she lived, of course, among Yemeni riff-raff.

'Benjamin is all right,' he said. 'Benjamin agrees with Melanie.'

'Yes,' she said. 'He goes down very well in certain quarters.'

She breathed like a mystic. Her lungs were so light. And he would dip his fingers down into the cot to make sure, to be certain, to feel her swift, silent exhaling on his hands like a twitching cricket in the wickerwork lantern of his bones.

'Melanie,' he said.

'I'm here.'

'She's in hospital.'

'Good. That's good. That's as it should be.'

'She's on her own. She doesn't have to share. It's private.'

'I know. I know. I understand.'

'She watches television.'

'Nothing changes.'

'She likes the children's television.'

'I remember.'

'They've brought back programmes from thirty years ago. You'd recognize them.'

'Of course I would.'

'Off the top of my head I would not be able to tell you the names of the programmes, but they have given her so much morphine that now she is a morphine addict.'

'I know, I know. I'm here, I'm holding you here in my sitting room in Tel Aviv. I'm hugging you. Can you feel me hugging you? Can you?'

Silence streamed from the satellites like the seraphim. Their cries went up to Heaven and came down again, at the international rate.

'She walked ahead of me through the twentieth century,' Solomon said. 'Like a pelican of the wilderness, an owl of the desert. Now she watches cartoons. She waits for her morphine. The houseman injects her and the hippo sings the alphabet. Zee is what they say now, not Zed. X, Y, Zee.'

It had taken him an eternity to master the subjunctive. The Tommy with the shingles had mouthed it for him as he sat on the floor with the other fellows in a half-moon round the teacher's tea chest.

'It should not be,' he said. 'It should not be.'

'Sshhh,' said the Tommy. 'Sshhh.' And he made a Caruso pout while the class nibbled with their nails at the lice in their armpits. 'Sshhhould.'

'It's for the best,' she told him. 'Sick people should be in hospital. They feel better there.'

'They don't get better there,' he said. 'In among the conifers is a block called 'Hospital Administration'. It has nothing to do with either. It's a make-believe; it's a morgue.'

'You're healthy. Healthy people hate hospitals.'

Her breathing could not blur the snarled allegro of the traffic. It was hell on earth. Benjamin would want to be Cary Grant to keep her happy in that grubby Babel; and she would need to be Audrey Hepburn to stoke his snap, crackle and pop. He had seen the sabras windsurf on the lake of Galilee with their army walkie-talkies dangling from the strings of their bikinis and the men watching like Zulus in under the parasols.

'Hello?'

They smoked in the shade and drank out of reach of the terrible ultraviolet. They were healthy folk who hated hospitals. Because hospitals were for sports injuries and abortions, for the donor queues in the plasma unit when the sandbags were being filled. What could the topless centrefolds in their comics make of a mammograph? It is clouds descending and the birth of stars.

'Hello?'

Let them stick to the shoreline. Let them clean out their face masks while the Christians write postcards. There is a time for being profoundly ignorant; and if there isn't, there is at least a time for being ignorant of your own profundity.

'Hello?'

'Melanie hates hospitals,' he said, 'and she's dying.'

It was the first time he had said it. At any rate, it was the first time he had said it in English. So he sat for a moment, thinking about his thoughts; and the Lilliputian lanes of downtown Tel Aviv seeped from the handset onto the eiderdown.

'Are you there? Can you hear me?'

'I can hear you. I can hear the Circus Maximus too. It's like Ben Hur over there.'

'Dearest,' she said, 'have you been drinking?'

'No. That's my sinuses.'

'You must be strong,' she said. 'I know it was never one of your weaknesses.'

'I am strong. I'll survive.'

'Survival is not strength. Survival is length. Length is no yardstick.'

'Melanie,' he said, 'are you growing a beard?'

'I'm growing impatient, that's what. Your wife is more anxious about your laundry than about her lymph glands, and you're sitting on your bottom feeling autobiographical.'

'You get it from my aunt,' he said. 'Nettle and dock in the same sentence.'

'I have to be hard. If I'm not hard, I'll cry. If I cry, I'll wreck my make-up and I've just put it on to go out.'

'You're too young to wear make-up. Brush your teeth and you're a beauty.'

'Except for my forehead.'

'High forehead, high intelligence. The fringe hides it.'

Above and beyond them, a hundred miles out, in the blue-black stillness of space, the satellite waited for word. Green tendrils of silence climbed like the limbs of a vine; twirled, twined; and quivered toward the world again, while the circuits worshipped.

'How does Benjamin feel about family?'

'Please don't talk about offspring. You know I don't want offspring. I want children.'

'At my age, it amounts to the same thing.'

'Then you're a knave as well as a fool.'

'First Hitler and now the contraceptive pill. The Ashkenazi will be like the Amish. The tourists will pester them with their Polaroids.'

'What is wrong with being Sephardic? Tell me.'

'They're not the people of Einstein, the people of Kafka, the people of Freud, the people who recreated the world in seven decades. All the visionaries are gone. Only the opticians are alive.'

'What do you know about Einstein? Bugger all. That's what you know about Einstein. Kafka and Freud, my kidneys. You know about Betty Grable. You knew about her before and you knew about her behind.'

'Arse,' said the Tommy. He tapped Betty's bottom in the life-size pin-up, and the hunkering students hooted lewdly, even the two who had passed blood in their stools.

'Arse,' they said. 'Arrsse.'

'I know what it is,' she said. 'You're giving those lectures again.'

'The odd one,' he said.

'They're all odd. They're all pathological.'

'Tit,' the Tommy said. 'Tit or boob.' The tip of the billiard cue bobbed at the Victory sign of the starlet's cleavage.

'Tit,' said the man with the frostbitten foot, the few teeth, the pelvis-like antlers. 'Tit. Orboob; orboob.'

'Why do you do it?' Melanie said. 'Why?'

'I want them to remember,' said Solomon.

'You don't remember,' she said. 'You repeat what you read in books.'

'The veil of the Temple,' said the soldier with the shingles. 'A bit of all right.' His stick triangulated the vaginal region: up, down, across; and across, down, up again, as if he was sketching a Star of David.

'I'd better go,' she said. 'This must be costing you a fortune.'

'You'll get what's left. You'll get what's right. I hate to think of you wasting it on blazers for boyfriends.'

'Briefs,' she said. 'When will you call me?'

'You don't mind?'

'Of course I don't mind. I love you.'

'I love you too,' he said. 'So at least we can agree on one thing.'

'Cunt,' said the class. 'Box, snatch, hole.'

'You see,' he said, 'there's no one else I can say Melanie to.'

'You say that to all the women.'

'I do,' he said. 'I am not able to say it to a man.'

And when the tutorial was finished Solomon had gone out into the camp, into the grey sea of its choppy canvas, burlap and tarpaulin, the breeze-block walls, the executed shirts on the guy strings of the windbreaks, the waterbarrels staring at the salt stains in the sky. Flies flew, birds landed, men stood to urinate, and women crouched in trench coats to lick soup bowls like a lover's genitals.

'Have a child,' he said. 'A child has twice as many bones as an adult. Did you know that? Did you? There are a hundred and one reasons to have a child.'

'Sshhh,' she said. 'Sshhh. I'll have a hundred-and-one children. Sleep well.'

All over Europe, Europe was all over. People were pitching tents in their own country.

'Goodbye, Melanie,' he said.

'Goodnight, Solomon, roses and blather. Goodnight.'

But he held the phone to his ear when she hung up, although the beau Benjamin would be ringing through his battle plan for a secular sabbath, free sex with expensive wine, and although the automatic exchange would continue to bill him in its deadpan, digital way if she lifted it off the hook for the late-night picture-show or a bath and beauty-sleep or a bottle of pills, perhaps, that would start in pins and needles and end in sutures and stitches.

The satellite was moving in a blue daze over the face of the deep.

———

The way home brought him past the hospital to the docks, and in the dead centre of that diameter, between the chlorine of the ward and the iodine of the estuary, he could go no farther. The road ahead was blocked at the level crossing.

'Shittim,' he said. 'Shittae, shittae, shitta.'

He slowed in second, the engine stalled, and the presentation plant he had been given by the aftershave angel at the school fell forward from the front-passenger seat onto the floor. Clumps of compost stuck into the soaking carpet square. Now he would have to stop at a service station and pay the boy a pound to valet the mess. Manure was still manure by any other name, nitrate or stardust. He should have stayed in bed, behind his eyelids, when Tess Cassidy called.

'Christian dignitaries will also be attending the memorial service,' said the medium wave to the knuckles on the knob of the gearstick, 'among them the Polish primate and the Papal nuncio.'

Cars had been driven onto the sleepers of the railway track. That was the long and the short of it. He could see by stretching the skin at the corners of his eyes. People were gathered in groups at the barriers, clapping and chanting. He could not hear their palms or their mouths, but the motorists around him were turning off their dims, and so did he. Had there been an accident? He did not wish to witness another fatality. On the other hand, there was no reversing. The traffic was bumper to bumper. In the rear-view mirror above him he could see the rear-view mirror behind him, and a woman's angled gape as she flossed briskly; behind her, a sudden, incongruous cortege; and beyond it all, at the back of everything, the floodlit towers of the hospital he had come from.

'Back again, sir?' the porter had said. 'What can I do you for this time?'

Because he had left that night when she died, not taken the elevator, gone down the stairs, the cold flights, one Madonna, two Madonnas, three Madonnas, more, and out the hall, avoiding the chaplain with the budgerigar, standing at the payphones till the priest had passed, watching the workman frost the windows of the kiosk for Christmas, and then the last heave, pushing the revolves of the door over the stiff, resisting horsehair, to find himself surrounded by the smokers on the steps, by duffle coats and dressing gowns, their fragile incensations, the breath of a body going up in smoke to a sky without stars.

'You too,' they said to him, smiling. 'Aren't we terrible creatures?'

'Communists,' the announcer said, 'defectives, gypsies, homosexual persons, Jews, Muslims, pacifists, prisoners of war, Quakers, Christian Scientists, and a large part of the indigenous German transvestite community whose sufferings have never been acknowledged adequately by our polarized, either-or Euroculture in the post-war world.'

The man's voice on the car radio was a kindly counter-tenor's, though the atmospheric interference hissed and booed him until his blurting was a ruined aria, shouts on acetate, shrieks pelted by sleet; and when the neighbours had carried their armchairs and antimacassars into the very best room in the house, the room that was always empty, always aired, the room where his father had told him about love and the uterus, then his sister would serve sodas and spa water, and the whole street would sit and listen to the clarinet concerto on the valve wireless; sit and listen and breathe through their mouths while the elderly relatives shut their eyes and held their heads as still as if they were nudes being painted in a life class.

'Sshhh,' said his father. 'Please.'

His leg would fatten and fall asleep from his criss-cross boy-scout crouch in the forest of sideboards, but he could still applaud at the close of each movement like the costly, cushioned front row of the theatre a hundred miles away where they were clearing their throats now, the regional oligarchy, and the men were using the programme notes to fan their moustaches and the women were picking fibres of wool from their gloves off the stone in their engagement rings.

'Sshhh,' said his mother. 'Sshhh.' But she was speaking to her lap, to the strange stomach noises that squabbled inside her like a radio being tuned.

'She won't stand in a line and let a doctor look at her,' said his father. 'It would be worse than death.'

'The line or the look?' said a voice in German, and his father sighed back at it in Esperanto. So his grandfather must have been present, prickly and elongated, a public statue with a prayer shawl of pigeon droppings and a place in his heart for Lillian Gish; the tubercular shofar-blower who had gargled violet phlegm for the first time on Rosh Hashanah; that bigot of a bookworm with his agitator's bulletins and his rainbow rhetoric of a new life in a new land, *yarmulkas* in Kenya, *Echt Deutsch* in an African yeshiva.

'Shittas, shittarum,' Solomon said. 'Shittis, shittis.'

If a suicide had been guillotined by a commuter train, drivers would have sprinted from the booths of their cars to inspect the deceased. Bystanders would have chattered among themselves as if they had been on Christian name terms all their lives. He would have seen starbursts, flashes of light, and a debonair photographer handing his fedora to a detective as he draped the black hood of his camera over his inflammable hairdo. Then the onlookers would have scattered and sped home, settling the children earlier than usual – the bedtime story, the night prayer, the light on the landing – to make love at last in a new endearment, an altered tenderness, grace beyond faces, the landscape of their flesh without a name to it, a space to be held and handled and handed on, the place of all pasture.

'My waters are breaking,' she had said, but that was the morphine. He bobbed his head at the oxygen tent and the nurse made him a cup of tea with a tea bag in it.

No one had blinked; no one had budged. Nobody raised an eyebrow, raised a hand, raised the matter, raised the dead. In the lanes to left and right, the incoming, the outgoing, overgrown adults aged at a standstill in the sashes of their safety belts. Even the toddler in the car ahead of him had tired of trying to exasperate Fatty Arbuckle with his plasticine grimaces, and the girl in the rear-view mirror had given up grooming her gums.

So he fumbled at the tufts of hair behind her ear in the way that she had liked him to, and he left the oxygen tent, the tent of meeting, the airy, prayerful tabernacle; but he had come back again, stepping in his stockings lest his parents look up at him from the oil lamp in the pantry, to tweak the pleats of the muslin cone over the cot where his new brother was smelling of cloves and privies. It had been his own idea, the enormous wedding-cake cover, to ward off greenfly in the hot months.

'Hello, bareface,' he had said. 'Hi, buddy. Hello, hello, hello.'

'And the European Parliament observed a minute's silence at midday,' the radio said to the handbrake, to the hairs that were hers in the space between the seats, to his four relenting fingers, the ringworm years, the years of worn rings, a white wedge in under the wedding band, a weal, really, almost a lesion, before he gave them both up, sugar and starch on the same day, at the shame of the sight of his eighteen-carat coil split open like a seal on a bottle of medicine.

'I'm not the lady with the lamp,' the motor mechanic had said. 'In case it goes and ulcerates, you should see a doctor. I don't know about seeing your wife. She might ulcerate you more.'

Then he put away his pocket pliers, the long-haired boy in overalls, and they stood in the smell of surgical spirits at a ramp where iron chains hung from a cross-beam.

'You know where to come,' said the motor mechanic, 'if you ever want your fillings out.'

And his mother had been so embarrassed that she excused herself, stood up and walked out as the first phrases of the adagio lifted the parlour like a row boat; and he, he had slipped out after her, round the back of the barley-screw stools and the lowered, listening heads, holding his pockets with his fists to hush them, the chinking nickel change, the cigarette cards of the great aviators, glycerine sweets in the shape of comets, and a damaged stylus he had played in a garden on the grooves of his own thumbprint.

'If she wanted to join her cousin in Canada, she'd have to strip to the bone and let a stranger inspect her,' said his father. 'That's not public health; that's veterinary medicine.'

'Sshhh,' said his father's father. 'Sshhh. Let me listen.'

The music rose and fell, Rosenblatt, rose and fell.

When they came for him, he went with them quietly. The budgie flew in front of him along the corridor. At the end of the room the tent had been taken down. She lay with a look of astonishment on her face. He breathed through his mouth so as not to disturb her.

'Would you like to say a prayer?' the nurse said.

Her feet had fallen apart like a ballerina. Between the big toe and the second toe he could see the pressure mark of her flip-flop from the odysseys of a suburb.

'Pardon,' he said.

'A prayer,' said the nurse. 'But only if you'd like to.'

The only prayer he could think of was the prayer for orphans. His mind must be going. He was starting to wander, like his father before him, his mother before him, and Melanie now, now Melanie, before him in the flesh.

'I said a prayer,' he told the nurse. 'My prayer has been answered. At least, there has been a reply.'

Where were her contact lenses? He could not imagine where her contact lenses might be. If she lost them again late at night, in the small hours, in a power cut, she would have to bump down the staircase on her bottom, trudging the carpet with her buttocks and heels like a stalled tobogganist who has cleanser on his face and a surgical cavity in his nightgown. Yet if she left them in for too long, she would destroy her corneas. She would be blind, and where would he be if he were blind, hunting for the string of the light switch in the toilet, urinating on his ankles in the darkness? Because she could never have a guide dog. She was afraid of Alsatians.

'I'll leave you alone now,' the nurse said, and he stared at her, stared at the holes in her ears where the drop earrings would hang for her first date, her boyfriend, her lover, her husband, her helpmate; but she would take them off, her earrings and her shoes, when she went upstairs to the bedroom to lie down, to free her swollen breast and nurse a baby, because a child would be thrilled by the sight of it, the beautiful brightness at her throat, tick-tocking glimpses, and he would reach up to touch it, yes, to tug it, no, to tear it, stop, from the soft droop of her lobe.

'Sshhh,' he said, stroking her hand, the fingers and bone, not the soggy blue of the bruise where the drip had been leaking. 'Sshhh.'

Two beds down, they were pitching the tent again.

'Clear skies and stars galore for any armchair astronomer,' said the wavering medium in the stalled cabin, 'but ground frost and black ice on the back roads, so my advice to you plural is: lock up, lie low, and avoid all unnecessary journeys.'

Yet he had followed his mother out of the chamber music on the public-address system in the hospital and into the car park, her Solomon, her sweet King Solomon, and he had sat there, such a running board, picking grime from the steering wheel, such an automobile, grime that might have been sweat or dead skin or soot from the leavings of the city.

'Isaiah, 43,' the chaplain said, and the budgie ran up and down his shoulder. "I have called you by name and you are my own. I have engraved your names on the palms of my hands.'"

'They called us by number,' Solomon said. 'They tattooed the wrists of our arms. Auschwitz, '43.'

Then he slept.

She had not died in her own language, Yiddish of the areola, pidgin of bibs and milk. Yet the paperback he had studied said that she might. He would write to the thanatologist on a point of information. He would tell him to his beard that she had brought his booklet on bereavement into their home and left it for him in a plain brown wrapper on the west side of the bed at the luminous hands of his clock.

Why had she done that? Why had she done that to him?

There were no answers at the back of the book. There was only an advertisement for another work by the same chat-show celebrity on post-natal depression. Still, Solomon had read it from the end to the very beginning, from the appendix to the acknowledgments, as if he were back at the brand-new classroom radiator, cribbing mnemonics in a Hebrew primer, and the eight-year-olds were rowing like frogs, face down on the rafts of their school-desks, practising the breaststroke for a visit to the baths.

'All aboard for Berlin,' the teacher had said. 'We haven't won a medal since the fifth century.'

'But thou art he that took me out of the womb,' the boy wrote in the slow, stiff, matchstick letters he had never mastered; 'thou didst make me hope when I was upon my mother's breasts.' Would the teacher return the confiscated copy of *Hollywood Heights, Hollywood Lows*? And he watched the letters dry, the page discolour, the wood disintegrate, until he was far removed from a room where radicals had scheduled typing skills and Talmud Torah on the same curriculum because they were dying, all the women in trousers, all the men in open-neck shirts, to be part of the new order of life.

He knew what he was dying of. He was dying of a pain in the breast, of a place called Melanie. He was dying of a growth that had brightened inside him and gone on brightening until he could not look at it through his tortoiseshell glasses. It would show in an X-ray of his chest as the birth of a nebula, gases and gravity, a seven-day wonder; but it would not show the star at its right-hand side. It would not show a seat in a bus in North London where a woman from the east of his life does not get up as usual and gather her groceries and walk to the step well, though her stop is near, is next, is now; and yet she's still sitting, and her stop dwindles behind her, smaller and smaller like the letters on a wall chart in a doctor's surgery, but she hardly looks, she hardly looks back. For the first time in ten years, almost ten years, nine years and seven months, she can feel the slightest seepage in her, ooze of a freshet from her, blood stencilling her lips as a period starts.

'Are you all right?' said the man.

But Solomon could not lower the window. It had been jammed for weeks. So he opened the door a fraction. The radio had been right about ground frost.

Coldness felt for his skeleton like a housewife frisking a chicken.

'It's not my fault,' he said. 'I can't go back.'

'Animal rights,' the man said. 'They're blocking a train.'

'Animal rights?' said Solomon. 'I'm an animal. I have rights. I have the right to go home.'

'Don't look at me,' the man said. When he spoke, you could not see his face. The words were mist and fog. 'I thought you were dying. I thought you were dead.'

'I couldn't be both,' Solomon said. 'Dying is the opposite of death.'

He must have drowsed; he may have dozed. Half of his leg had gone to sleep in his shoe, in the pins and needles of amputation, and his waistcoat buttons were still twitching in time to the blows inside his body. Perhaps his heart would steal a march on his prostate. That would be perfect. Then they could tow him to the ties, and have done.

'I was daydreaming,' he said.

'Thanks be to Jesus,' said the man. 'I like my mouth-to-mouth a little later on a Friday evening. Beer before bubbly.'

Air from his nostrils steamed and smoked in the moisture of beasts, the venting of cattle. How could an Eskimo suffer the sight of it, this heat-haze from his ribcage, a pent-up, panted thing, the ghost of his bloodstream going before him through the seventy words for wasteland? It was something else he would have to ask Melanie, because he did not know any Inuit or Aleut, though he had seen one in the zoo photographing a waxwork of a hunter with a harpoon; so he must jot the question down among the other queries on the sheet with the Roman numerals, like the checklist that he drafted before phoning his brother the beard in the promised land of Palo Alto, California. Otherwise he would be speechless when he woke in the morning to find her up before him, and gone before him, to find that he was lost, and then to lose what he had found, a tiny corkscrew hair in the ransacked hollow of her half of the bed.

'Who are they?' Solomon said. 'Over there, at the railway tracks.'

'Right animals,' said the man. 'That's who.'

'You are a voice speaking out of a cloud,' said Solomon. 'Do you know that?'

But the man was walking away from the crank in the car, shaking his skull at the dusk, at the hocus-pocus of people and the hardened arteries of the city around him. His hands swayed sky-high in the sign of surrender, but no one looked up and no one looked out. They were mouthing contentedly the chorus line from the same rock song on every wireless; on every radio set the same amplified slogan at a rally in a stadium. Some of them skimmed through the evening editions, speed-reading advertisements for attic insulation and articles that downsized the estimates of yesterday's massacres, while their children's fingers quickmarched along the headrests. Outside, in the wind, upended toddlers pissed against a tree trunk.

'It was only a dream,' Solomon said to the steering wheel. 'You do not wake from a nightmare.'

He felt his face, the new growth, stubble like stitches in a hospital. At night, each night since nineteen-thirty-six, his skin had bristled. The hairs had stood up.

'Please,' she would say. 'I can't close my eyes with the light on.'

He had not petted her breasts for ten years; but would he have felt it, the stone in the apricot?

'The girl in the physio said she'd walk on my spine if I wanted,' he told her.

'People have walked all over you for years,' she said. 'Why pay for it?'

'It was probably my accent,' he said. 'Of course we'd end up sleeping together.'

'You'll end up sleeping on a plank,' she said. 'The same as you started.'

Pillars of salt had soared around him. The overhead halogen lights whitewashed the car park, the perimeter fences, the igloo of the morgue where the attendant would incinerate empysemic lungs or the entrails of a stillbirth. All the watercolours of cholera matted the huts and outhouses, the radiography ramp, the smoke-stack, the shingle roof of the cell-count clinic; and beyond the square of shadowless sodium, its terrible detergent glare, he could imagine the fringe of the forest, glints of tinfoil from a picnic, the pine trees waiting for the solstice when the Christians would come with their hacksaws and their hatchbacks and their hands smelling of resin like toilet freshener.

'I will survive this,' he thought. 'I will go on from here to be married for more or less forty-two years; for forty-two years I will go on from here to be more or less married. But I will change the names on all the forms at all the frontiers. I will call her Sarah, though she was not a Sarah, really, and neither was Sarah herself; but at least it does not rhyme with anything awful in the seventh edition of *The Home Guide to Good Health*; and I will call myself something other than Solomon, since I am not majestically wise or majestically well off, even if I do on occasion allow myself to believe that I am the shakings of both, the delusion of brains, the illusion of cash. The majesty I abdicate to the son who drowned in my semen.'

Birds that had lost their bearings sang for seconds in the blind-ing rectangle, and gave up. Pylons loomed to left and right. A field-grey sleeve threw down a filter cigarette that fell three feet inside the line they could not cross, dropped there between the wire and the walk way, landed and lay a yard outside the boundary; and the sleeve waited then, high above them at the clapboard parapet, its buttons on the belt feed.

'Amen,' said Solomon Rosenblatt. 'Alleluia.'

When he stood out of the car, he had as many shadows as a soccer player. They walked him like bodyguards across the quick-dry tarmac of the overflow corral to the hospital's red revolving entrance. Ashes and butts festooned the horsehair mats, but the smokers had disappeared.

'I'm sorry,' he said.

'Sorry?' said the porter; and he turned down his Walkman.

'I need change to get out of the car park.'

'The barrier's up,' the porter said. 'The borders are not closed. As well as that, it's free after midnight. Even the coffee is free after midnight. Everything's free after midnight. Did you not see the signs?'

His thumbnail was already fumbling at the volume control.

———

'Give us an N; give us an O!'

The wind from central Europe shifted a hair's breadth, a compass point, and Solomon heard their outcries gust into earshot. Under the signal box by the turnstile, men and women stamped their desert boots on the chippings to stay warm. Children peered from a thicket of ski pants, the muted, queuing kids in their kindergarten gabardines, their mittens made from ankle socks, the balaclavas blazing out of loose ends and leftovers: and his mother had told him, this, this is amber from a bonnet; indigo from a prayer shawl, that; and there, in the cut-off caterpillar colours, is burgundy from your grandmother's ovengloves. Now you know three things more.

'Give us an A; give us an H!'

For a moment he imagined they were throwing their arms to heaven, the children wading in their parents' Wellingtons, the roly-poly tot with the seven sweaters for asthma, and the boys' cauliflower ears taped back for the bar-mitzvah studio portrait; but they were only hauling helium balloons down out of danger from the high overhead wires, the skull-and-lightning legend, and snagging the strings in the picket's cardboard placards that he couldn't, for the life of him, decipher.

'N.O.A.H. What do you have? Noah!'

German was breaking through the English on the radio like the stalagmite of a tooth through a cheap enamel shell. He leaned towards it, listened for it, his lips parting, his mouth opening to block the rumpus of his nostrils although the cold air quickly sketched the chink in his bridge and the scald on his tongue from the bolted coffee. In a high-fidelity studio somewhere in Hamburg, the calm, contralto tones of a woman with headphones guided through the blizzard of a bad transistor his language of special occasions: of weddings, of erotic novellas, of the telephone. So he shut his eyes and everything went red, the amniotic pastels of blindness, and then he could almost make out the little obliterated letters on the tongues of leather shoes, names that had melted into sweat stains, lips that the snow had smeared like ice-cream.

'No! No! No! No! No!'

He was homesick for the worst years of his life. When he had been sick at heart, he had been single-minded; when he was sick unto death, his hopelessness had passed almost for peace of mind. Without these things, without his unhappiness, man is a beast of the field.

'Yes! Yes! Yes!'

He was a sentry in a cemetery. At night he pushed a dustcart among the beehive headstones, tucking hot-water bottles in the blankets of gravel.

The voice in Hamburg welled and swivelled like a warp on vinyl, a backing track to the singalong on the home service. Yet she was right to be righteous: the supermodels had indeed behaved splendidly when they hurled their rabbit stoles, their fox furs and their ocelot leggings, on the charity bonfire in aid of all threatened species. They had stood up; they had been accountable. Perhaps they had not yet given their life's blood in a bloodbath, but they were donors already, with Pelican pins in their lapels.

> 'From the adder to the zebra,
> They were all in Noah's Ark;
> The A to Zee of you and me
> Does not exclude the shark.'

They had printed the lyrics of the hymn on banners and sandwich boards. Small children tapped on the passenger window, gesticulating wildly at the message on their chests; and the crowd hooted and honked around him, waving their fists and flashing their lights in hail-fellowship with the funny juniors. Yet the soldier who had stood in the doorway of the hut, the Soviet who had said hello, hello, hello, to the silence, the stillness, the woodwind of their pleurisy, covered his mouth with a cloth from his pocket, with linen from the lost kingdom of napkins, from the ruined empire of the handkerchief. He was not a Jain out of India, afraid of inhaling house-dust mites lest he swallow the molecules of Elohim. He was a Russian. He was afraid of inhaling.

He stood at the door of a place that began with A and ended with Z, and his tears ran down his nose onto the twenty-six letters of the alphabet.

'Who is the dumbest of the animals?' a woman called as she roamed among the cars with pamphlets, petitions. Her enormous earrings were Spanish question marks; her vanilla buttocks abounded. He worked his wipers to be invisible, squirting the last spurts of Melanie's washing-up liquid onto his windscreen. Now

nobody would notice him. Now he could yank at his swimming
-trunks where they gnawed at the fold of his flesh.

Now he could wait.

First the photographers; then the policemen. You would
expect the opposite, but that would be a mistake. Whoever they
were, these demonstrators, liberals or Jehovah's Witnesses, the
toyboys of Utopia or the gigolos of Eden, they knew which level-
crossing was closest to the television station. Ecstatic protesters
would preach to camera, and call their au pairs on a cellular phone
to video the newscast. None of them had understood that only the
virtues which ruin us are real: the rest is history.

Why were they playing the 'Chorus of the Hebrew Slaves' on
his radio? Was it a tribute? They should be playing Sirota. They
should have sent Sirota's Edison cylinders up into the firmament
instead of man's best friend or his first cousin. Then the Lord
would have come out of hiding, like a Jew from the raftered ark
of an attic after a pogrom, and been seen face to face for the first
time since the death of Moses. A satellite in outer space would be
his footstool, the international calls occur as love cries, and the
universe declare to the world of earth that this was the promised
hour, the sabbath rest, the feast of day fourteen.

'Back in your cars. Stay in your cars.'

But the Hebrew slaves had been hired out as decoys in a thirty-
second commercial for life insurance. The hewers of wood and the
drawers of water were lilting Pharoah's Lullaby. Solomon's hand
reached out and switched them off all by itself, the undertakers
and their siren from Egypt.

'Stay where you are. Go back, go back.'

How tall and stately the policemen were, stately and tall. You
would know from the way that they walked that they had driven
cows to a milking shed when they were only boys, when they were
barely breastfed, batting the spattered flanks with tennis racquets
as the foreigners stood up out of their sunroofs, adjusting the light

metres on their cameras; and you would know from their boots and their batons that they were not accustomed to lowering their voices at a car window or to raising their heads at the visitor's hatch in their headquarters. Yet nothing had prepared Solomon for the smell of grapefruit on the gauntlets of the motorcycle escort, for the sting of citric acid on his lip and the sight of himself in the convex visor of the helmet, an obese and bulbous medallion, neither image nor likeness but a billboard caricature; and he had made the sign of the Cross in front of them, the three militia pistols, made it deliberately, elaborately, up, down, across, like the patriarch in Petersburg blessing the bayonets of his conscript uncles from the Pale of Settlement, while the whole patrol chortled in the style of the silent movies.

'Here's a Yid who thinks he's Euclid.'

Now they were lifting the vegetarian joggers at the level crossing, shifting the cars that had been left there, until he could see again the dull apron of tar and arrows where the railway tracks thinned into tramlines.

'Maybe he thinks he's Archimedes. Do you think he thinks he's Archimedes?'

Yet the veterans of the ashram went on chanting mantras in their saffron parkas with the luminous armbands, and his mother passed him on the other side of the street, not watching, not wanting to watch, studying the longitude of the footpath, stepping with care, cautiously even, as if she had found herself among many snails mating, the pained antennae on the crazy paving, their lonely, foaming unions.

'What is the sum of the squares in the Star of David? Can you tell me that?'

'Move it, move it. Keep it moving. We all want to be home for the *Late Late Show*.'

'The sum of the squares in the Star of David is shit. That is what it is.'

What would the child with the glitter on her face do now? Her balloon was sinking without trace in the depths of the sky. She would have to look for a smaller child with a bigger balloon to browbeat; and she already was.

'Move,' I said. 'Are you deaf?'

This time Solomon remembered. He opened the door wide.

'Don't be aggressive with me,' the policeman said. 'Are you one of those troublemakers?'

'I'm sorry,' Solomon said. 'It's the window. The window is kaput.'

Why had he said that? Why had he said that word? It had come out of nowhere.

'What's the name?' said the policeman.

Capo, yes. He had once said capo, but that was different. That was about Italy, about baksheesh or blackmail. He had never said the other.

'I asked you your name. Do you know your own name?'

The waiting was over. He was almost at one.

'Rosenblatt,' he said. 'Solomon.'

The policeman angled his torch at the windscreen, at the paper disc with its stamp, its small print, its star. Solomon looked up to him, the curt and vertical deputy whose feet would overshoot the bars of the bunks in the guardhouse. With a diver's leaded shoe on his good foot, he could kick you to death in twelve seconds. Twelve seconds had been the record. Nowadays, of course, the divers wore flippers. The contestants would have to cast about for an ice skate.

'Well, Mr Solomon,' the policeman said, 'do you realize you've been a bad boy?'

'Yes, I do,' said Solomon. 'I have lived long enough to learn that I am the greatest problem in my own life.'

'I mean,' the policeman said, 'you have not been paying your proper car tax.'

'My wife does all the paperwork,' he said. 'She is wonderful at paperworking. You should see her. It is lovely just to watch.'

'Tell her to wake up and get a move on,' said the policeman, 'or we'll be knocking on your door one of these days.'

'I will talk to her tonight when I see her,' Solomon said. 'When I talk to her tonight I will see her immediately.'

'Are you all right?' said the policeman, but he did not shine the torch in Solomon's face in the way that he should have, really.

'If the truth be told,' Solomon said, 'I am not myself.'

Yet his sinuses had cleared. He could breathe carbon monoxide, fumes from the diesel buses, and the saturated bark of the birch tree at the barrier.

'I think I'll have to bring you home with me,' the policeman said.

'Pardon?'

Out of the nightfall, out of the street lights, he could sense it now, shape it now, the immense, intended, uneventful thing.

'Listen,' he said.

'You listen to me,' the policeman said.

Listen for the low bronchitis of the locomotive, for the slow arousal of its breathing; listen for the shorter, swifter gasps, the respiratory spasm in the lungs. Hear this, O Israel. For a moment he caught sight of her on the station platform; but the steam became mist, and the mist became a cloud, and he could no longer make out the hatbox with the sanitary towels and the bottle of syrup for her stomach noises.

'Home is where you should be,' the policeman said.

They had walked away without looking back, the two parents, the two grandparents. Side by side and two by two, they had gone along the gangplank into the hull of the dark. The trainspotters had watched it from the embankment while they sharpened their pencils with their marvellous Swiss knives.

'I've been to the market to buy a fat pig,' the policeman said.

And the panting, pent-up wagons begin to trundle past, the shackled stockyard boxcars clattering on the rivets of the tracks.

Even the pedestrian with the Mickey Mouse headphones covers his temples at the sound of their wailing, at the rocking, clock-work length of a whole train howling up out of blackness and back gardens and blackberry bushes and a shortcut to the Jesuit church. The campus cyclists are wheeling away their racers while the bolted carriages shudder through, all chalk and creosote and the locked smell of sheds, solid with livestock silent as the tomb, the speechless, shitting cattle in the fog of their lungs and the children grinding their faces into their mothers' genitals.

'What?' he said. 'What are you telling me? What?'

It was gone. The barrier was lifting. Urine glittered on the sleepers.

'Home again, home again,' said the policeman. 'Jiggedy jig.'

THE SEVEN AFFIDAVITS OF
SAINT-ARTAUD

The tortured man becomes for the whole world the recognized one,
the revealed one —Antonin Artaud

1. A PRIEST

Whatever I say will make no difference.

You have it plotted already. The beastly priest in one corner
and the suffering Son of God in the other. The double-crossing
cleric and the cross-addicted writer. Antonin Artaud versus the
sinister Jesuit. It's a binary system. I can't escape it. After all, it's
the essence of theatre. He could have told me that. Perhaps he did
tell me. But I should have known. Amn't I a theatre man myself?
Didn't I serve as chaplain to the Holy Family Amateur Drama
League, for God's sake? Wasn't I at the Abbey the same night I met
him, watching from the wings? Betty Chancellor was on as Juno,
or was it Shelagh Richards? Both beautiful, one an adulteress. The

same bounder was married to each of them at some stage. But a good production of the play. Only sniggers now where there used to be catcalls. That's progress.

Anyhow, it was that far back. That long ago. The room I live in at the Milltown Institute was larger then. The tree outside it was smaller. I was about the same size, give or take. We'd ordain thirty men every twelve months on the Feast of Saint Ignatius Loyola. Now we do one in a leap year. The photographs in the long corridor get littler and littler. From grey to black-and-white, from black-and-white to colour, from colour to instant Polaroid pictures, and from instant Polaroid pictures to the fire extinguisher.

Actually, I blame the Stations of the Cross. The political and religious authorities – Pilate, Caiaphas, the crowd – come out of the Passion narratives badly. Everything is seen from the point of view of the poor unfortunate culprit or casualty or whatever you want to call him. Anyone else is cast as part of the firing squad. It's not the injustice I object to. It's the simplification, the sentimentality. Sentimentality is just cruelty in a good mood. You know that I appear in two films as the SJ who won't open the door to the visionary poet? Then I call the police. They beat him up, of course, with rubber truncheons, Keystone-Cops style, and put the sounds in afterwards. Mercifully, one of the versions or perversions was Arts Council and the other was arthouse, so nobody saw either.

As well as that, they got my name wrong. M-A-C, it said, though I wrote it out in block letters, upper-case M, lower-case C, in the 'Please Write Clearly' permissions column. Chap with a ponytail and a pirate earring took it from me. Turned out he'd been to Clongowes. Had the accent but not the aptitude. Father Anthony he kept calling me, instead of Father McMahon. I suppose I should be grateful he didn't me call Tony.

Actually, it had been the most beautiful evening. You know Artaud was certain sure the world would end in November of that same year? Which was only what, six, seven weeks from the time we met, on an evening that turned out, circles within circles, to be his birthday; or so he said. His fortieth year in the desert, though I found out afterwards he was forty-one in fact. Looked eighty, mind you. But the Biblical fib is a theatre thing, and so was the end of the world. Not that the end of the world would be the end of the world, at least from his point of view, if you follow me. Told me so himself in the station cell. The stench of cold urine and warm chlorine from the cleaning woman's bucket. God forgive me.

November the something, 1937, by which time he was in a straitjacket. Round about All Saints, All Souls. Of course he was terribly Catholic in spite of himself. After all, you make the wine of your adult life from the grapes of your first six or seven years. Well, there was no sign of Armageddon in the streets with the shop-front awnings down for sun and not for showers. I'd cycled into town through the clear-headed horizontal light that makes Dublin so three-dimensional in a mild September. The schools had started up again so the streets were full of bicycles. I was reading my office on the handlebars. *In the day of my distress I sought the Lord: my hands were raised at night without ceasing.* It was that fine.

Sometimes you feel so happy and so wistful at the same time that you wonder should you see a doctor. September does that sort of thing to people. Did it to Artaud, for that matter, or it may have. Nowadays, of course, they say it can be seasonal. On the other hand, if anyone else finances a film on his trip to Ireland, let the weather be at least reasonable and not Lear-on-the-heath, for God's sake. One of the hand-held things I saw had sleet and hailstones, and he bunks in a bin out the back. At the ramp outside the refectory where scholastics in the kitchen were on duty round the clock as a virtual dumb waiter for the walking wounded. In those days every religious house had a farm attached. There was one fellow looked like John the Baptist from his time in the trenches, and he'd lie down in the car park where the field used to be and the bomb shelter beside it, and he'd drink straight from the cow. I kid you not. Life was better for bums in those days. They were the major-domos of the high road. Nowadays they're post-traumatics. Then they were tinkers, and you stood to windward when they gave the soup bowl back.

Point of fact, the day after they arrested Artaud, I was waiting in the orchard for my altar servers to give them apples. They swung from the branches in their shirt sleeves while I corrected their Latin exercises. *The queen praised the soldiers who had fought bravely in the Forum.* So he wouldn't have been sleeping rough, you see. He would have been sleeping smooth. In the thirties and later on, even in the war years, especially in the war years, I used to sleep as late as Hallowe'en without wearing the jacket of my pajamas.

It was while I was getting ready for bed that the doorbell rang. Then he started the pummelling. I put my stock back on, went out, and looked over the banisters. He had his hand in through the horse-hair guard of the brass letterbox as far as the wrist. Beautiful hand, too; has to be said. Strong, sallow, feminine. Middle-class fingernails. Moons. Do you know that the continents are parting at the same speed at which our fingernails grow? That's the kind of thing he would have said himself, of course. If you listen to the tapes, where he isn't just choking on these strange jugular ululations, it's all apocalyptic. When I went to see him, two days after the arrest, in the barracks, in the cell – the door was open, it wasn't locked, those wretched films! - he told me that, when he was an infant, somewhere in the Eastern Mediterranean, Syria, Smyrna – where by the way his grandmothers were sisters, say no more – his hands had been splinted in a kind of wooden mitten like a mousetrap, to stretch and separate the bones so he'd have more room for them to range on a keyboard. His mother wanted him to be a concert pianist. She wanted him to play Debussy, Satie, Ravel. This in a man who needed forty different rituals to get him from the door to the window, and who thought that his tears smelled like semen and his semen like tears.

I shouldn't be putting ideas in your head. Ho

What do you want? I said. I wasn't going to put t

chain in case he tore through it. I've seen psychosis.

strength. I've seen a mother lift a Swastika Laundry-\

dying child in the middle of Westmoreland Street. *I wan*

priest, he told me. *I'm not a priest,* I said, which was true. I \

been ordained. I was only a deacon at the time. I said that to the
fellow with the ponytail and the pirate earring too. Hadn't a notion
what I was talking about.

Please go away, I said. *Go on away home now like a good man.*

He had the hand in through the door still, and I was staring
at it, where it drooped down towards a little wicker lattice thing
that the post would drop into each morning and afternoon. And
every morning and afternoon, if I was in the house, I'd save the
best foreign stamps for the boys in Rudiments as prizes for a table
quiz of the memory work. They were all philatelists in lederhosen,
of course. All dreaming of the Cape of Good Hope and the Penny
Black, or is it the Penny Red?

Or is it a penny dreadful? The mind ... goes. Comes and goes.

The first If is, if I hadn't touched him. That's a gene from my
mother, now. She was always touching a person here and there. I
held the tips of his fingers in the tips of mine, and that was the
Michelangelo moment, as my first Provincial used to say. There
was no turning back then, there was no more *modestia*. I opened
the door on the chain, and a gust of his scent caught me like the
smell of Africa when you step off a plane in brightness onto the
apron. It was the body odour of fear that I knew from boarding
school and not the tang of rage. To an experienced nostril there is
a difference; and my olfactory system is still spot on after the four-
score years, I never smoked in my life. Once a cheroot. A cheroot
the day I buried my father.

Who are you? I said. And that's the second If, I suppose, because
if he'd been beery and obesely bloated, I would have rung the

ds down below in Donnybrook sooner than I did. But he was a beautiful man, sitting there on the lead grid of the boot-scraper with a bright shoelace in a dark shoe, and a face like Our Lord in the porch light. He was the best looking male human being I ever laid eyes on, and that's over fifty years ago. I've taught boys who'd break a girl's heart just by looking at them. I've taught boys who'd break a man's heart just by looking at them. I'm long enough a man in the world to be a man of the world. But Antonin Artaud left them standing. Not that he was a matinee idol. He wasn't Metro-Goldwyn-Meyer. He wasn't American at all. He was European. He was Eastern Mediterranean. He was as handsome as a woman, in a manly way. You could have put his face on a coin worth real money instead of all those farm animals.

Who are you at all? I said to him. To this day I can't tell you if he answered me in French or English. Sometimes I think he said it in the Greek of the New Testament.

I am Legion, he said, *because we are many.*

2. A CLEANING WOMAN

I had my Mongol with me because they wouldn't take her in the national school on account of her wetting and the tempers, although she'd a brother in every year they could have called to pacify her. My neighbour, now, who kept an eye on her whenever I was cleaning in the church or down the barracks, a very nice Protestant lady called Mrs Henry, had TB at the time. Pleurisy she called it, of course, but I knew what she meant. Before that, she'd let Grace Mary run in and out the whole time and wash her mongrel in the sink with real soap, if you don't mind. I tell you, that dog was the cleanest person in the street. She was half terrier and half I don't know what, and forever licking her nipples on the doorstep.

There were those in my own family who told me to put the child in with Mrs Henry while she was infectious. Because the coughing you'd hear coming through the wall was desperate altogether, like the whooping cough of the sealions across in the zoo. You'd hear the sputum splat in the chamber pot at night. There was a woman I knew had a bad spina bifida boy, and she brought him to the sanatorium every week, and the granddad would wheeze into his face for the whole visit. The little lad died in Cherry Orchard before he turned twelve. The bishop came and confirmed him there in the bed. But I couldn't do that to my Grace Mary. One of my sisters said I should do or I'd have her on my hands till she was fifteen or sixteen. That was when their tubes went, usually, not like today. You see them middle-aged now, if they're not caught in time on the hospital scan. Then they do the D and C. Oh, it wasn't all sodalities back then, either, sir. Don't mind what they tell you on those stupid singalong programmes on the wireless about the good old days. I was alive in them.

The thing is, Mister A. adored my Grace Mary. She was after making her first Holy Communion the same year, so she had the dress on still and the veil and the pearly purse. I think she thought she was a fairy princess instead of an angel. Mrs Henry went and got her a wand and all, even, though she made me wash it in the sink first and steep it in boiling water before I gave it to the child.

Then again, the wand was for the hair, really. I had to shave her hair the night before her Holy Communion because she had ringworm. Then I had to paint her skull with the Jensen Violet. Of course I told her that was because she was special, like, and the teacher went along with it. She was no bother, Grace Mary. Never once.

So.

I had with her me when I was doing the floors in the station. Red tiles they were, all broken with the guards' boots and the anthracite sacks at the Aga, and Mister A. went down on his knees at the sight of her, there in the cell, and he asked her for a blessing. He told her she was closer to the Lord than anyone he knew on account of her innocence, because the good bread had dedicated her to God, and she was pure. His English was a bit astray, but I knew what he meant. And Grace Mary knew what he meant, is more important. She put her hand in through the dirty bars and she blessed him like a priest would. *In the name of the Father and of the Son and of the Holy Ghost*, she said. Very serious, almost solemn. After a while, Mister A. said *Ah-men*. He said it that way: *Ah-men* instead of *Aye-men*. And that's the way I say it myself ever since, long before it became popular and profitable, like, in the long-haired masses that you go to now, where the celebrant asks you to pray for the girlfriend he used to have before he joined, or the fiancée, maybe.

I'm not saying he wasn't touched. He was a bit mad, and who isn't? If he hadn't have been ill, he wouldn't have been locked up in a cell, would he? Although the station sergeant left the door wide open after the first day, same as if he was a woman in with her children for the night to get away from the husband. My own cousin slept in a glasshouse in Phibsboro while her old fellow was home one time from six months deep-sea in the Panama Canal. I grew up beside the Gorman, and I can tell you this for nothing, sir. They used to lock up homosexuals and women at the change, and there was nothing wrong with them apart from that. Sure there were priests in a special wing where you had to be a nun to be a nurse, and there were Latin passwords, like *Kyrie Eleison* and *Hosanna in Excelsis* to get in and out of the service lifts. Word of a lie.

Wait till I tell you something.

Would I be a good father? That's what Mister A. said to me the night before they shipped him back to France to the asylum there, and then it was years before they let him out again. Is it any wonder the Lord sweated blood in the garden? It was after the War was over, when they were shaving the women's heads for having babies with the German lads. Grace Mary was dead herself then, though the hair had grown back a different colour by then, sort of Titian, and she was buried in the nuns' plot as a mark of respect. They took her into care, you see, after she kept Communion in the pocket of her smock and gave it to the mongrel; but they doted on her, they did. *The Carmelites have the Little Flower,* Sister Joseph told me, *but we have Grace Mary.* And they used to hang her white patent-leather shoe on the Christmas tree in the classroom for years until somebody nicked it for the half-a-pair and dyed it dark brown for her own daughter, the creature.

Would I be a good father, Mrs Heritage? He was fascinated by my name as well, and how I cleaned everything in the church, the toilet as well as the tabernacle, and how the priests would walk through the wet on the floor when I'd just done it, and not look up from their breviaries. *Would I be a good father?* In my whole life he was the only man who ever asked me that, my own included. *Mister A.,* I said to him, *you would be a beautiful father because the man who can ask that question has gone and answered it.* Then he showed me a photograph of a tiny wee baby, still scrunched and soggy after the birth, like, and wrapped in the most beautiful lace christening shawl, a real family heirloom, and he told me, this Rudolph Valentino filmstar of a fellow who could look like Methuselah, right enough, from not eating and sleeping: *That is my mother, Mrs Heritage. That is the body that made my body. You are a part of the body of Christ, but I am a part of the body of crisis.* Now that's something you wouldn't hear everyday on the 46A. Oh, you could tell straight off he came from a lovely family. He was quality. He would have made a beautiful priest now that they've turned the altars round. Sure the men would be looking at him as well as the women. They would too.

The last time we saw him, he drew a face on his knee with one of those special pens they have to mark initials on cuffs and collars in the convents. It would stay on your hands for years, that dye, like a tattoo. When he rolled up his trouser and stretched his leg straight out, the face on his knee was the face of a sad man; then, when he bent his leg in under him, the face turned into a smiley fellow. Well, you can imagine. Grace Mary was in pure paradise. I saw the very same expression on her face later on, during the Emergency, when I took her to the zoo for the monkeys' tea party, the time they shot all the deer in the Phoenix Park and sold them for meat to them that could afford it. That was World War II for you.

The peacock came scuttling over as if he was going to attack her, but, just as she was clutching on to my good coat, didn't he stop and stand there in front of the two of us, and then he opens all his feathers into a fan with all the colours of a stained-glass window, like, all emerald and indigo and turquoise and words I never said before or after, as if he was saluting her. And I thought of the sad man and the smiley man, and I wondered did the face wash off in the lunatic asylum from all the steam baths and the seaweed baths they gave mad people back then, or did he still have them when he died and his friends that you were telling me about kept a vigil round the corpse for three nights to stop the mice from having a go at his soft places, the tongue and the lips, God bless him, and his privates too that gave him no peace of mind in his lifetime.

So that's that.

Do you know that in Japan they call their Mongols English? Mister A. told me that, and I knew what he meant. *You're English*, he says to Grace Mary. *You're an English lady. Am I, Mammy?* she says to me in her veil and all, with her mouth gone golden from ice pop. *Maybe in Mongolia*, he said, which I never thought was a real place, same as Timbuktu, but it is, apparently, *maybe they call them Irish on the other side of the world.*

3. AN INTERPRETER

Sanest man I ever met. He had total insight. Total insight into his world; the interior, I mean, of his terror. Total insight into the world at large, the external nightmare. But you have to understand that the expression of that insight was semitic, not Anglo-Saxon. Take the baculus. Everybody has their tuppence ha'penny to say on the subject of the baculus. Everybody's embarrassed about

— 144 —

the baculus. The shillelagh, if you like. Call a spade a spade and not an agricultural implement. I mean the magic stick he came in search of. That's what brought him to the Aran Islands in the first place – basically to find this phallic appurtenance that Saint Patrick had supposedly provided himself with, as a prophylactic against ... excitation. Does anyone seriously imagine that a man of Artaud's total insight would peregrinate across Ireland in pursuit of a fetish you might find in the British Museum? Of course not. No more than Our Blessed Lord intended his disciples to take him at his word and excise their genitals when he spoke of severing any member that obstructed the progress of piety. Our Lord had the very same ... semitic intensity.

What Artaud meant to convey by means of metaphor was the depth of his regard for Irish chasteness. What he sought in his visit to this country was the imitation, the *imitatio* of that chasteness in his own life. After all, he'd had a lot of bother with the sixth com-mandment, and no wonder – Paris was full of the most hourglass Russian émigrées at the time, and he was an enigmatic beauty into the bargain. It was a great test of his mettle.

Of course it was Paris that provided our common ground. I'd been at the Irish College before the War when I was training for the regular clergy. That's another story, which I serialized, incidentally, in a parish newsletter over several years. If you'd told me then that I'd end up in the discalced Carmelites, I'd have laughed. I even had a licence to hear confessions in French, and, by golly, did I hear some strange ones. I don't believe there are English terms for some of the stuff I heard, or, if there are, they're in Greek and Latin.

Then I was at the Somme after that, first and second battle, and, not to state the obvious, it appears that I survived them both in some shape or form. When I came home to my first curacy in a district that included the British military brothels in the so-called Monto in the middle of Dublin, all right, I had two housekeep-ers and a top hat for ecclesiastical corteges. But I could never fill a churchwarden pipe - what my parish priest called a Protestant pipe – I could never fill one in my own parlour without hearing teenagers in no-man's land calling out to their mums in all the Indo-European languages as they lay dying. *Mamma, Mama, Mother, Muti, Madre, Mammy, Ma*; on one occasion, I even imagined I heard '*A mhamaí*', but I must admit it might have been a 'damn' at the moment of death. All you could see from the periscope in the trenches was the boys' breath rising and the steam from their urine when their bladders burst. Only a man who's dying lets himself do that. When the bowels go, they give up the ghost. Sure if we can't control our genitals, what's the point?

Which brings us back to the saintly maestro. Because you don't want to hear about the war to beat all wars. The funny thing is, though, they were my very best years. I was happy in my nappy. Simple as that. In the sense of being filled and fulfilled. Between ourselves, there's very little BS on a battlefield. No-man's land is where you meet real men.

No, no, you want to hear about Art. Which, when I think of it, would be a good title for you. Not as in work of art, I don't mean that, but as in Art, short for Artaud. Like we say Art for Arthur. That's very Dublin. You could call your programme *Art in Ireland*. Hmm? Plus you'd have the pun.

Did I tell you that in seven years and six months as a seminarian at the Irish College, I never once climbed to the top of the Eiffel Tower. And neither did he. Artaud. Art. Whatever. He told me that in the cell where, and I stress this, he was being looked after by Sergeant Something McHenry, a decent Presbyterian who, incidentally, met the Pope on his honeymoon. Life, as they say, is stranger than Art.

We had a good laugh, the two of us, over the Eiffel Tower. There was a dentist I attended in the rue Sebastien Bottin who used to eat his meals in the birdcage café at the top of the tower because it was the only place in Paris where he didn't have to look at it. People felt very strongly about Eiffel back then, one way or the other. Always quarrelling about him, even when they were playing chess. They'd stop the clock, and bicker. You have to remember that in those days one in every five or six people had lived through the Commune. That's how far I go back.

Tell the truth, we had a lot in common, myself and himself. We'd even been to the same barber, as a matter of fact, only a stone's throw from Notre Dame, where you wouldn't find a barber now, and where, incidentally, I served the Archbishop's Mass more than once. In the cathedral, I mean, at the high altar, not the barber's. But that's another story, which I'll omit. Tourists couldn't just wander round during the services in those days. It was either pray or out. There was sacred life and there was street life, and there was a bit of in-between, like the Orientals doing their T'ai Chi in the Luxembourg Gardens. I used to watch the wily old gentlemen at it; and he did too. Artaud. Come to think of it, we might even have been watching them at the same time. Only God knows.

Of course we spoke in French, Art and I, and not in Hiberno-English. The French language has been my only concession to femininity in a celibate life. It requires one to make such unlikely configurations of the lips. Perhaps for that reason my most memorable conversations in the language of Péguy, great poet, forgotten but not gone, have taken place in the confessional, where director and client are at right angles and in restful darkness. Hmm? Not that I visited Art as a priest. I was there only as an interpreter for the authorities, at least until I was sidelined by a chatty, very asthmatic Breton from the French legation, which is a paradox, I suppose. If he'd shut up, he wouldn't have been so breathless. He had good Irish too, now that I think of it. I was doing perfectly well until he arrived.

Priest and interpreter share the same Latin root, of course. You probably know that. You're old enough to have done the classics. In the days before the paperback Penguin Library, God help us.

Not that I wasn't shy meeting him. Is that a double negative? I have gone and committed a double negative. My first today. I was shy meeting him, is what I mean. The stubble, no braces, no shoe-laces. It's the norm now, it's detention procedure, but, back then, you didn't go to church if you hadn't a clean collar. The poor had their pride. As well as that, I'd seen him in two of his films at Father Burke Savage's ciné society over in Manresa out by Dollymount. I saw him as Savonarola in one film – flick, as we used to say, the flicks, because they flickered – and as a chaplain to the maid in *The Passion of Joan of Arc,* by somebody famous.

I'll think of it in a minute.

He was quite chuffed when I told him. I think I pretended I'd been to more than I had. Even in calamity, compliments are welcome; perhaps especially in calamity, they provide a sort of welfare. Man does not live by bread alone, but by bread and circuses.

What was that name at all? I had it in my head when I went over everything. They say it's just an electrical storm, the memory.

I told you on the phone what happened after I was ordained in Paris. I was offered indecent postcards by a man with a Wilhelmine moustache at the west door of Notre Dame. That must have been during the War because I was in uniform. I daresay he thought I was English. I kicked him until he lay on the pavement, shrieking. Two women clapped me as I gave him my full attention. His cards were strewn on the street for all to see. Serrated picture postcards. I didn't stop until a gendarme shouted at me. You can put that in if you want to. Depth is detail, basically.

Art knew that he was not his body or the totality of its contor-tions. In itself, that's a general perception. But he also knew that he was not his consciousness, either. His brain had a mind of its own, which he observed intermittently as … an alien mental entity. You follow? He was a third term in between the two possibilities. He was divided, like Caesar's Gaul, into three parts, and the third part was pain. That's why he wrote to the Pope. I posted the letter myself on the day of his deportation. Indeed, I wrote a full address on the envelope: Il Papa, Citta del Vaticano, and then Italy instead of Italia, because Art had only written the Holy Father's title, *Le Pape*, in copperplate calligraphy, and there was a reputable barrister in Dublin at the time whose briefs were often dispatched to the Bar Library under the same designation, The Pope, and the sorters in the GPO knew where it was meant for. It was meant for the Pope O'Mahony, Senior Counsel, or maybe he was K.C., King's Counsel.

Total insight. It comes to us all at the point of death but in his case, it arrived early and escorted him all his born days. I have it myself, but I'm over eighty. He was half that. Did I mention that I'm dying of cancer of the rectum? I thought it was haemorrhoids when my stools started to spot. I always assumed it would be the aorta, same as my father and his before him, but there you are. I don't want a private room when I go to the hospice. I want to be in an ordinary ward where the post-Christians can watch me dying the way a priest should. I shall, here it comes again, I shall *interpret* their death for them.

Admittedly my motives are near enough a vanity to be venial. I want my dying to be an ethical action and not just a biochemical interaction. Something I can put with pride on my curriculum vitae. Art, Artaud would have been the very same. Total insight. He was buried, you know, without benefit of clergy. A liturgist without a church. Of course he lived among freaks and freemasons, not to mention unmentionable *Menschen*. Nod and a wink to a deaf man, or is it a blind man? It's a miracle he stayed sane to the end.

A student from Nanterre – that's the college you go to if you can't get into the Sorbonne – buttonholed me once about my meeting with Artaud. Brought a small cassette recorder that kept stopping, and he said *Scheisse*, which is German, of course, and not French. He thought that suffering meant you must be very spiritual, and that Art was therefore a saint. If only it were that complicated. He was a very young student, mind you. The next ten years will tone him down. He seemed to think Artaud was a mystic by virtue of his predictions – the violence that unfolded, the victimization across Europe, the Eucharist of the cockroach as I called it once in the pulpit. I used to put a lot of effort into the old sermons.

What about *Art in Dublin: The Eucharist of the Cockroach*? Has a certain *je ne sais quoi*, as the man said.

But anyone could have seen they were going to wipe out the Jews. That didn't take a prophetic retina. I'd read a French edition of *Mein Kampf* ten years before the Austrian corporal came to power. During Art's Hibernian escapade, shall we call it, Poland was in negotiation with the proper authorities for the speedy purchase of Madagascar as a permanent population centre for their Jews, or for their indigenous Jewish communities as the anti-semites prefer to describe them. The anti-semites always have to go the long way round, in public at least.

Would you like me to talk about our friend for a few minutes in French? *Belle époque* French, for that matter. The nineteenth century only ended in 1914, and the twentieth century won't end until the Soviet Union is called Russia again. I'll see that from upstairs.

Dreyer. That was the name. Carl Theodor Dreyer. The batteries are still working.

4. A PHOTOGRAPHER

It was Sergeant Alexander McHenry, a DMP man down in Pearse Street who went sick during the Lockout so he wouldn't have to baton nobody, that asked me to come in and have a look at this foreigner fellow with no papers to speak of and three days in the cell already on a charge of breach of the peace. The sergeant took it into his head he might be Jewish because of the long hair and the rings on his fingers, if you don't mind. So he meets me at the Pillar one weekday morning, and he says: *Mendel, there's one of your crowd below in the station, and I never thought I'd see myself saying a sentence like that.* Which was his shot at a compliment because we had the name for not being scofflaws at all. Look it, they didn't even patrol the South Circular Road until Daiken the butcher's was done one night in '43 for a brace of jugged rabbits in the window. The kids used to love pulling off the fur like stockings.

So I told the sergeant, Yes, I'd go down and parley-vous when I could, but business first. I was doing the backside of a wedding breakfast out of the Gresham Hotel, the bride and groom were just leaving for the first train from Kingsbridge, and the guests were doing a conga across the tramlines. Swear to God. I had a new Leica with me, a lovely camera, hand it to the Germans, and I was Flash Gordon away. They're more likely to take the card from you if you snap them after the toasts instead of before, tell you that for nothing, and these were flush folk, all hats and high heels, the girls with cigarette holders and the old ladies wrapped in dead ferrets. The spondulics were on show, surely.

I had a bit of everything in those days, Dutch and Deutsch on my mother's side, Lord have mercy, though the radiologist in Mercer's Hospital tells me, every time I do go to the fibroids clinic, that I'll die speechifying in Yiddish because that was my breast and bib, and every last thing, he says, comes full circle sooner or later. I didn't tell him my dad collapsed singing along with an old spitting acetate of Gilbert and Sullivan, doing the three little maids as a parlour piece at Purim.

Do you know what? I can hear him this minute.

The sound waves never stop, you know. Travelling and ravelling and unravelling for all time, all eternity. Five-hundred-and-thirty-seven miles an hour is the speed of sound. And if you got ahead of it, if you went at five-hundred-and-thirty-eight miles an hour, you'd hear everything that had passed away passing away again, the way you hear the cheer of the crowd in Croke Park on the wireless before you hear it on the wind. You could hear Moses Maimonides at the height of his powers, if you knew where to listen in the galaxy Andromeda. You could hear the great rabbis in their gentlemen's agreements and disagreements. Rabbi Joshua ben Hananiah and Rabbi Nehunya ben Hakanah and Rabbi Simeon ben Azzai. You could hear my little sister that died of peritonitis in Jervis Street, and she reading the list of messages out loud at four years of age before she took it to Wassky's Fruiterers and Victuallers on the corner.

Jaysus, you'd be like Yuri Gagarin or the Yankee after him, what was his name? Ah, the semi-finalists is always anonymous. Swear to God.

The sergeant used to call me Pontifex Maximus, which is what they call the Pope amongst other things you could mention. *A builder of bridges is what it means, Mendel.* This is the sergeant talking, as if I didn't know. I can hear him too. And why did he call me that? He called me that because O'Connell Bridge was my pitch from the time I had pimples, and I fought for it. Fisticuffs isn't the word. Cold as Copenhagen in a crosswind, your breath going up in smoke. You'd be wearing three cardigans under the one coat, but you'd get the courting couples there, that was the whole thing, on their way to the Royal or the Capitol, and they were good for a set of three-loose-for-a florin, that was two bob, or a four-inch-mount-for-one-and three. If the girl had gloves on, you had to bet on the diamond, but I'd be right nine times out of ten. There's a glow for the first few months. When you say *Dickey Bird, Dickey Bird,* and they walk past you, you know they're married. But the arm-in-arms kept me in decent rooms over the minyat in Lennox Street for as long as I liked. So I was on that bridge when it was Sackville Street, I was there when they called it Sráid O'Connell, and I thought I'd live to see it magic into De Valera Avenue, but there you are. They'll wait until he dies now, if he dies at all.

First Holy Communions, yes. Confirmations was a waste of time. People never took it seriously, and it's their bar mitzvah if you think about it. Hurling and football finals, fantastic trade. The bit of booze. And the Easter parades with the Spitfire flypast, all grand out. St Patrick's Day, of course; Lá le Pádraig as the Gaeilge. The college graduations, though the Trinity porters, the skips, they'd chase you out of Front Square if you didn't have the permit. You had to be double quick, scouting for one of your own would order a framed full-size with the mortarboard and proud parents. I did them all, every one of them, and the National at Earlsfort Terrace for the nouveau riche. Then, when my niece Esther went and graduated as a medical doctor, I was in them myself with a camel-hair coat from Kingston's and a Kodak instamatic, posh at the time. December the eighth was a grand day for me too, when the culchies came up for the Christmas shopping. That was nifty. But the Eucharistic Congress was my best ever, and I did the Protestant Bishops in the Mansion House on the same day. So there. I done ten rolls before the Mass started, even, because these nuns – they used to call them Mickeydodgers – they all wanted singles with the bunting as well as the group shot. I had a sherry in the Shelbourne after that, which was strong liquor for me. An *al fresco* practice, but, as Harry Kernoff used to say as he passed me with the *Herald* or *Press* sticking out of his pocket: *You're an artist, Mendel, same as myself. Never forget that. Jaysus, there's two of us in it, anyhow.*

From the way your man was talking, down in the station, I knew he wasn't Jewish. He went on and on about physical things and the affliction of the body. Affliction? What's affliction about it? We don't talk like that at all. Between you, me, and the four walls, that now is Christian carry-on, no offence. The scrupulous, sinful, shameful sort of talk that gets nobody nowhere. I knew a Jesuit whipped himself. Admittedly not very hard, but still. That's not civilized. Or privates. What kind of a word is privates? Generals is more like. But the Irish are not the worst. Look at the Germans. What do Germans call the vestment of a woman's breasts, fair play to her? They call it a *Büstenhalter*.

We're different. We're supposed to make love on the Sabbath, for God's sake. Because that continues the Creation, don't you see?

But he had a grand face, that fellow, lots of little declivities and crevices, and I shot him from every angle in lovely half light. Natural sepia down in the cells. He must have cried on cue, because I remember the black tears on the negatives. I got two goes out of the same picture, too. Swear to God. Sold it once as the prophet Jeremiah for a missal card in the Dominican shop in Parnell Square, and the second time it paid me a golden guinea as St Joseph the Worker for the frontispiece in the *Capuchin Annual* in 1947, the worst winter ever. I thought the river would freeze. But I was Flash Gordon, for all that. There was a snowman at the GPO took a week to melt into a dead sheep.

I met the sergeant at the cinema that same weekend, and we were heading up the balustraded staircase that was built in Belfast for the *Titanic* and then sold South on account of the wrong measurements that some Shinner had put in. Any time we went up it together, McHenry'd say to me: *Mendel, we're ascending to the ballroom balcony of the ship God couldn't sink* - there was RMS stamped on the stanchions underneath the spiral, where they kept the ice-cream tubs — *and, by the living Lord Jesus, we're getting off it as fast as our feet'll take us* — and I'd laugh back because a copper's jokes are always clever, and then we'd settle in for the programme, and I'd start to feel my hands again, with Nelson Eddy and Jeanette MacDonald swooning on the screen in front of us. During the newsreels the sergeant asked me: Well, is he Jewish? And I told him, Not a blind bit, because there was no point telling him that, as I closed the cell door behind me, for privacy, like, and walked away, I heard him. I thought I heard him. Singing. I thought I heard him singing the Shema.

5. A SERGEANT

Antonaki. That was his name. Antonaki. I remember it because of the Aki. It's Os and Macs and the odd Fitz in my line. And I'm good on names. I'm even better on old names. Brunswick Street is still Brunswick Street, no matter who's in charge. Rutland Square is still Rutland Square. I always try to call a man by his Christian name, unless he's a complete cornerboy or he's above me. Then I call him Doctor or Sir or Judge. Priests I call Padre. They don't always like it. But the Christian name is like a nipple to a newborn. They just gape at you, all dozy, and the hands go down. Then you give them the Chinese burn. Call them by their Christian name and the black sheep turns into a lamb of god. The red rag becomes a white flag.

The strong voice is from the tinnitus. I have terrible tinnitus. Same as all the boxers in the Garda Club. Tinnitus or the trembles. My ears go from the noise of tinfoil to the din of carillons. Bennie the Bush had it, too. He was a featherweight and a pigeon fancier. The same with Con Flanagan, whose brother shot himself in the married quarters because he'd been writing literary fiction in the station diary about his patrols. And it wasn't Volume I either. That queered the widow's pension, until the coroner's court said it was an accidental discharge. Then he got the Last Post and the arms reversed, and the top brass walked in the cortege, but we had to dig the grave ourselves because the IRA had frightened off the undertakers. They had a Sopwith Camel circling over the church-yard, on recce for an ambush. That was because the Volunteers had better marksmen. Most of them had been demobbed from the British army after the Armistice. Some of them had the DSO or the disability entitlements from the Legion, along with the Irish pensions. But the police in the honour guard were all Catholics, apart from yours truly, and one of them was a Blasket Islander. The only trench they'd ever seen was a pit-and-pile outdoor toilet at the bottom of an allotment.

Ask Willie Blackwell. Willie's alive, in the Incurables in Donnybrook. We went to Rome together for the pilgrimage in 1928 with the Commissioner. Commissioner Eoin O'Duffy. Now they say he was a Fascist. They say he was a queer. He's dead, of course, or they wouldn't dare. But he toured the country in an open car, each Kill and Cull of it, places so dark at night the constables used the rungs of a ladder to keep them in line. I got to know him on the pilgrimage. I took his picture in the Coliseum. I was the only Protestant there. Smells and bells is right. Sure there isn't even candlesticks where I go on a Sunday. When they built it, the church in Irishtown was on a spit of land surrounded by water. My great-grandfather rowed across to the services, three times a day. Matins, Holy Communion, and Vespers; and they say the RCs are the pious crowd. We raised the roof with the singing. Now you'd need a gramophone player. And the boats are gone, and the water is gone, and you can't read the headstones, hardly. It's all tarmacadam and traffic lights where there used to be moorings.

Teeth tell you a lot. Your man had good strong teeth, so I knew he was respectable. You can always tell a gurrier by his teeth, even if he's a mickey-dazzler in the rig-out. And I treated our friend accordingly. Didn't twist his arm, even. Nobody ever fell upstairs on my watch. I gave the odd hooligan a good hiding, but I didn't put them through the courts afterwards. That way, they'd have the private tuition but no criminal record. Because even a week in jail is a life sentence in a small country. No, I've nothing on my conscience. When Bertie Shinkwin died, and he gave a great many tutorials in his time, the travellers came from all over with the most beautiful plastic bouquets. And it was his wife Nora who frisked all the women during the house raids. She was in full uniform too, doing it. The same Nora petitioned the Privy Council for clemency for the lad who laid a mine at her father's arboretum. That's why they mention women on the DMP plaque in Westminster Abbey, not too far from Alfred Lord Tennyson. *Into the valley of death rode the six hundred.* There was more than six hundred of six rode into it. I could tell you some of the names. But you won't read them off any entablature in this godforsaken half of a country.

Now.

The beating. The famous beating. There was no beating. I shaved the man. I shaved Antonaki. I shaved him with soap and a strop razor, same as I'd shave myself. I might even put the one blade to my own cheek. Because I don't care where you are or who you are or how you are, even the fucking demoniac feels better after a close shave. You let your appearance go, you've let your whole morality and morale vamoose. You might as well sleep in your clothes. You might as well sleep without clothes. Sure we even shave the shadow off a corpse before we lock the lid. I rest my case.

I shaved him in the cell. He was stripped to the waist. There was an old scar on the small of his back. Somebody had stabbed him. More a shallow stab than a slash. I ran the nit comb through his hair for the eggs. I could see them stirring. That's long hair, of course. All the arty sorts are crawling. I would have deloused him too. Delousing a fellow always made me feel sleepy. Peacable, like. You have to pay attention. You have to be alert. You can't think of your problems. Of course, you need the nails for it as well. Not so short that you can't hear the creak when the louse breaks and the two bits bisect between the enamels; not so long that they wiggle away with a backflip. Some of these smart alecs can do a triple somersault, if you let them. Regulation length is best. They can't cope with the pincers. A brick of jelly is your best man for strong nails. Women know that. It's to do with the gelatine. Gelatine for the nails, gelatine for the gums, gelatine for the deep roots of the scalp.

I was … sifting his hair. That'd be the right word. I was sifting his hair for the eggs when a Johnny-come-lately out of Limerick, a lad of twenty-two with a centre crease in his hair, a real spiv of a sleveen-type, came round the turn of the stairs.

That was the start and finish of it.

You see I knew the type. He'd make a toilet roll of an inno-cent gesture. I'd be the disciple Jesus loved inside an hour in every station in the state. I'd seen him, when he should have been on indoor duty, orderly chores, reading the lists of the banned books in the Prohibited Publications Ledger. *Sweets of Sin, Sweat of Sodom, Switch of Miss Whiplash*. The little greedy eyes. I had him sized up, like a master tailor. I knew which way he folded, all right. But he'd be at the garda retreat in the Pro-Cathedral the week after, and going to the altar twice in a day because he saw the Super in the line for Communion.

I lost it. One and only time. Very few, anyway. Very, very few. Twice, three times in the forty years, which is a good batting average. There are those who wouldn't mind that class of thing. It'd be like the first cigarette of the day. But not me. Not me. I was coming up the quays one time, late now, very late, sometime in the small hours, and this woman walked out of the river mist in front of me. An old, bald-headed woman, God bless her. *Sergeant McHenry,* she said, *Thank God it's only you.* I didn't know her from Adam, or from Eve, is it? But I thought it wasn't the worst thing you could say about a man with forty years' service in two forces.

Is this like Confession, I suppose? No wonder they keep the Hoovers in the boxes now.

Afterwards, when the colour in the piss pot was kind of pink, I thought I might have gone too hard on the kidneys. That's when I called the doctor. He was lying on the floor like a foetus. I said to him: *Talk to me, will you? Talk to me, Antonaki.*

6. A DOCTOR

Antoneo.

There was a time when I knew the names of all the institutions he ended up in. It was more than a list. It was a litany. A star turn at a party, almost. I had them organized alphabetically in my head, you see. Same as the feis ceoil when I was small. Brother Cornelius set 'St Patrick's Breastplate' to a simple sort of tune, and I sang it, no bother, into the violet footlights of the college hall. The parents

were out there somewhere, watching, my father twisting the programme in his hands until it was as tight as a pipe cleaner, and my
big brother sitting up on the wooden horse with the other prefects
to see me do it.

> Christ before me,
> Christ behind me,
> Christ above me,
> Christ below me.

Christ with every preposition I can think of. Over, under, after,
before, beneath, beside, beyond. Beyond the beyond.

As it happens, I had a patient a few years ago, round the time
of the Kennedy visit, because President Kennedy RIP got blended
into his delusions then, his ideas of reference, his obsessional fears,
and he used to recite them, all the prayers and petitions in 'St
Patrick's Breastplate': *Christ this, Christ that, Christ the other*, as a
sort of charm against the demons in his poor demented intelligence. An exorcism, like. A rite of exorcism. Do you know, I think
it helped him too? Don't quote me, though.

Sainte-Anne was one. One of the asylums Antoneo was in. St
Anne, the mother of Mary. The grandmother of God, I suppose.
And Saint-Dizier. There was Lafoux-les-Bains. There was Divonne-
les-Bains. And, later on, another Les-something-else. Quatre-
Mares, Ville-Evrard. You could sing them if you had a tune, if you
had Brother Cornelius and his button melodeon. At the end of
the day, of course, came the fall of night. The nightmare. Rodez,
which I mispronounced for years. The thought of it still tortures
me. And the priest, the monk who knew him, who'd translated for
him, said it back to me the same way at the bunfight in the Alliance
Francaise one Quatorze. Rodeth, he said, and I could never decide
whether that was courtesy or contempt, or a bit of both. Because
you sound the zed, you see, like a cricket's staccato.

Rodez.

Where he had to put up with the poseur Jacques Lacan looking after him. That must have been worse than the insulin injections. Worse than the enemas. Worse than the restraints. Lacan and R.D. Laing. The pair of them in it. The Grimm Brothers. Laing said to me, it was this time last year, he said: *If you strike the word therapist, it breaks down into a criminal category.* It becomes: the rapist. Quick as a flash, I said back to him: *Pharmakos is the Greek for poison and for remedy.* I tell you, I wasn't born yesterday.

Wasn't that a good one?

Villejuif. Another asylum. If you gave me a minute I'd remember a dozen or so. It's from all the mnemonics you learn as a medical student. Finetunes the faculties. Of course, when I was a registrar, they called them sanatoria. Or clinics. Clinics was a great favourite. Sometimes it'd be the spa, even. You'd think it was Baden-Baden and not bedlam; you'd think it was TB and not manic depression. That was the whole point. The new one is bipolarity, by the way. Bipolarity, how are you.

He didn't mind the drugs. He was narcotized from the word go. In fact, and this is interesting, he had written, carved, inscribed, the letters L-A-U-D on the wall of the cell, with what? Knife and fork? Miraculous medal? There was no plastic cutlery in those days for the self-harming. If you self-harmed you got stitched with the biggest needle, the strongest thread and no anaesthetic. You wouldn't do it again in a hurry. No mousak; no medicine trolleys; no tennis courts. Just the four cemented walls, like a handball-court upended.

The writing on the wall. What he wrote was L-A-U-D. Laud. The Latin for praise. And the janitor or the janitress, she was there with her Down's Syndrome child, and her BO; I shouldn't, I won't. She knew the word as well as I did. Which goes to prove that, back in those days, the poorest of the poor had a huge vocabulary, really. Compared to now. On the other hand, it might have been the first half of 'laudanum'. Because laudanum was his mother's milk. You didn't have to be a doctor. The tremor, the pinpoint pupils, the festination. He had the heebie-jeebies all right. That was long before the days of the detox protocols.

Four drugs good, two drugs bad. But the ECT was another matter. For every year of his life an electroconvulsive course. It left a foul taste in the mouth, afterwards. I mean that, literally. So he dreaded it. Because somehow or other, he found out, they're fierce cunning that way, the psychotics, he found out that they learned about it from slaughtering pigs, from stunning pigs before bleeding them. Cerletti, Ugo Cerletti, the Italian who started the procedure round the same time, the late thirties, he was absolutely frank about it. He'd seen it done, and thought: why not? Of course in Antoneo's mind this cross-pollinated immediately with what? With the demoniac. The madman in the scriptures, the gentile Legion, and Jesus sends the evil spirits out of him into the herd of swine, and they rush into the sea or the Sea of Galilee. And drown.

Once a Catholic. Half, two-thirds of my patients over the forty years, Catholics. Of course it's a Catholic psychiatric hospital. The separated brethren all go, or went, to St Pat's. Except for Beckett. I have a notion now that Beckett came here. Around the same time, I think. Middle thirties. Of course you're not meant to know that. If it's true, that's in lodge. Very hush-hush. When they do declassify the files, though, they'll have to rewrite the history books. Ministers. Prime Ministers. Cardinals. The odd psychiatrist. The very odd psychiatrist, I should say. The roll-call continues. Every apple loves an orchard.

Maybe you'd better leave Beckett out of it. Isn't he still alive?

Names reminds me. Antoneo came out with all these names of friends he had in France. In Paris. I wasn't arty, amn't arty now, the wife goes for lunch in the Gallery, but I knew some of them. Coco Chanel, Pablo Picasso, Jean Cocteau. Isadora Duncan, the one who was strangled by her motorbike. Anaïs Nin, the naughty novelist. Not that I ever peeked. I thought he was completely florid, but no.

He knew them. Intimately. They were his bosom buddies. So you never know, do you?

And I was scooting out the whole time, from the cell downstairs to the hatch at the front desk where I could check to see my brand-new, open-top, red-laminate Riley sports motor car with the doors opening the way they do now, which was new then, a complete novelty, with leather upholstery and a walnut dashboard. I was terrified someone would steal it. The irony is, it spent most of the War in the garage, of course, with no petrol except for the odd fill-up from an old low-grade schizophrenic I knew in Lobitos, and it was gone when we came back from a holiday in Parknasilla during the D-Day landings.

Well.

When I went back down to Antoneo, his mouth kept moving, but no words now. It was like a silent film. It was maddening, really. The way, if you were watching one of the old black-and-white reels, you'd want to bring in somebody deaf and dumb to lip-read what exactly Charlie Chaplin is saying. Is he saying the exact words that appear in print on the screen straight after the shot or is he saying something completely and utterly different, like *Do you think we'll get this done before it rains?*

Come back to me when you want to know about Charlie Chaplin. I met Charlie Chaplin. I've met him many times in the Butler Arms hotel in Waterville. And he doesn't look a bit like himself in reality.

The thing is, about suffering. It can deepen you; it can diminish you. You can pray to be deepened, not to be diminished. That's all you can pray for. Anything else, praying for it not to rain on sports day, that sort of thing, that's voodoo. My brother had a Coca-Cola venture. Import Coke and sit back. That was the plan. But the publicans, you see, they weren't going to buy fridges in 1935. They didn't even have electricity. Then, during the War, Coca-Cola went and distributed a free bottle of Coke per diem per G.I. for the duration. That was marketing. My brother had to take his three boys out of St Mary's and send them to the Brothers. He went into P.J. Carroll's to sell cigarettes. So he was a salesman, so he had to smoke them. You can imagine. Then my wife lost, we both lost, our first child. At birth. A gynaecological blunder. She was post-partum for two years. Staring at her hands in her lap, no nail varnish, need I add, like she was reading a book. But if I'd sued, I'd never have built a practice. I would have been shunned. Besides, the obstetrician who botched the whole business had proposed me for the Stephen's Green Club.

To this day, she doesn't understand that. Three sons and three daughters later. Doesn't. Won't. Can't. It can deepen you; it can diminish you.

I had a student here from somewhere in America. Not the top ten. Not the Ivy League. Not in any league. Told me himself he was bipolar. So he knew, you see, he knew that madness is the opposite of imagination. He knew that much. He could see through the whole tormented genius lark. The high achievers, they're all breakfast, lunch and dinner sorts, and lights out at ten. Disciplined daily life. Daily life is discipline. Daily life is ... the deed.

He gave me doodles, you know. A good few. At least the sergeant did, the DMP man who was minding him. Our friend did dozens of sketches during the six days, seven days he was in for. Arrested on the first, rested on the seventh. Cartoons, you could call them, cartoons on paper napkins. Not scatological, but saucy, and then a bit. Bizarre on top of that. Well, he had this notion, pure delusional overdrive this, that governments would open sperm banks for the military so that they could replenish their losses as they went along. You'd be doing your bit for the war effort twice over. Enough said. And he tried to ... illustrate the idea.

I told him about *Snow White and the Seven Dwarves*, which was showing at the time. He said he'd heard about it. He said he'd love to see it. Maybe he did, eventually.

Cartoons were all the rage. The vogue.

I wish now I'd kept those doodles. You wouldn't have wiped your nose with one of them in Dublin in the 1940s. They used to lower the blinds to change the clothes on the tailor's dummies. But the drawings might have paid the mortgage for a while on my daughter's place in Stepaside. There's no point in having regrets, though, is there? You end up regretting everything, even the future before it's happened. You'd end up like Lot's wife, the pillar of salt, the saline deposit of all the tears you ever let show.

Don't forget to take out the bit about Beckett.

7. A PRIEST

It always comes down to sex in the end. Always.

Neddie Redmond was a curate in Westland Row in 1916, in the days of the two pulpits and the theological tennis matches between the preacher and the devil's advocate. They gave it up because the devil always won. Anyhow, Neddie knew before anyone else what was going to happen. On the day, on Easter Monday, hundreds of men turned up for Confession after the 7 am morning Mass. Half of them would lose their young lives during Easter Week, and what were they confessing to Neddie, with the pistols in their pockets? Little sexual trespasses, and masturbation. Half a century later, forty ... six years, 1962, the Cuban Missile Crisis. Queues for confession out the church. What's on everyone mind as the American ultimatum to Khrushchev goes tick-tock, tick-tock, tick-tock, toward twelve o'clock midnight? Little sexual trespasses, and masturbation. Neddie was in the box, weeping.

I taught for forty years in the hot stink of boy in a Belvedere classroom. Damp shoes drying on the radiator. Greek breathings on the blackboard. The rough and the smooth. Or the Caighdeán. Slender with slender, broad with broad, and the lads tittering. Chalk rotting my nails. When the past pupils come back, they ask about Brother Tuck who ran the sweetshop.

You don't know whether to weep or what. 'Jesus wept' is the shortest verse in scripture; or is it? What about 'Rejoice exceedingly'? That's in there too.

The day they extradited him, the ship leaving Cobh passed another one coming in, and the two honked each other out of good manners. The dear deported was in the brig on the ferry to France, and Laurel and Hardy were in the state rooms on the liner from Manhattan. They played the Adelphi for two weeks, and a matinée Wednesdays as well as Saturdays for the schools. I saw them myself. I think I told you I was always a theatre man. Watched them from the wings. Funnier in the films. One of the priests in Cobh had played their signature tune on the cathedral bells as they disembarked, and the bishop transferred him straight out to the Styx. Somewhere called Fivemiletown or Sixmilebridge.

Water under the bridge. Bridges under water.

That was the saddest thing about Antonin Artaud. Nobody would ever call him Tony. He could never assume flesh. He could never rise to the body. Because the body is a great challenge. A greater challenge than the mind. Its sanity has nothing to do with cleanness, and its sanity takes practice. The soul is simple but the body is hard. It takes shape slowly, like an idea. It takes time, takes a life's time. And its atonement is hard won.

Artaud. The body of his work; the work of his body. Eighteen ninety something. Nineteen forty what?

Pity the poor beast that kept him standing as long as he let it.

A WOMAN FROM WALKINSTOWN

My name is Mary.

Frank says I should say instead: I am Mary; I am Frank's wife, like in the *Reader's Digest* articles about our kidneys and our ovaries and what they do to us. There was a whole series in the seventies that started: I am Paddy Joe's prostate or I am John Paul's pancreas. You would feel the place in your body where the thing was, and know.

Mind you, the PJs are as ancient now. They would be having their prostates checked every twelve months for prostate cancer. Even the JPs are getting new titanium knees to play mixed doubles under lights, and they were mostly born between the Mass by the Pope in the Phoenix Park and the day he was shot at his own front door in the Vatican Square.

Which is why Frank says I am his backbone in a spine-chilling world; but not everybody reads the *Reader's Digest* anymore. You never see it in waiting rooms these days or in casualty. You see *Hello* from a year ago with some German princess who's had twins at fifty-two by IVF or a Hollywood funeral of an anorexic starlet in a casket, and the parents probably got a million for the rights.

There was no Mary born in the whole of Ireland in 1992. I don't know about the North. I don't care about the North. Not a single one was born here. There was Miriam, Maureen, Maggies galore, but not Mary. You could go through the Rolla in the girls' school, in Guardian Angels, go through all the M's, and not find her. Except as a middle name or a middle initial or a Confirmation name, maybe, in sixth class.

Not one Christian name Mary.

Confirmation names mean nothing, of course. I can't remember my own. It was either Moninne or Movinne. But, sure, Confirmation means nothing. Nobody knows what to wear for it. Holy Communion is what matters, and baptism. Baptism and Holy Communion is all you need in this world.

Holy Communion and baptism are more important even than the Mass, actually.

I christen thee Mary. Thou art Mary. You could do a module of grammar sometime with the transition years and start off with Thou and Thee. Thou and Thee and the difference between Thy and Thine. My and Mine and Mine own. Nobody knows these differences. They are dying in France and Germany too, the French and German teachers tell me. Everybody is on first-name terms, even people who hate each other at the employment tribunal in Liberty Hall, the principal saying through her implants to the solicitor: I cherish Mary as part of the school's diversity; yet.

Yet. Not but. Yet. Whatever yet means, it is more dangerous.

I was doing cell division and I asked the Junior Certs, the A stream it was, when I had the A stream, about the three Marys. They hadn't a notion. They'd never heard of keening. In a table quiz today, nobody under fifty would know the four Marys. Mary Redmond, Mary Cotter, Mary Field, and one other Mary. That was the *Bunty* stage. The stage before that was the *Princess Tina* stage with the light-up tiara, and the stage after that was the Brontë sisters and sanitary towels, unless you were a trollop and wore tampons.

Mary Raleigh it was. Mary Raleigh. She was the jaggedy blonde.

Mary the First, Mary the Second, Mary the Third. Bloody Mary, the queen and not the drink; Mary who thought her tumour was a pregnancy.

You would have thought now because of Mary Robinson, but no. The big name in 1992 was Hannah.

My Fr PJ says if Mary goes, Jesus can't be far behind. He seems quite pleased about that. He puts on his collar every day, and his varifocals, and he sits in the visitors' room. Always has a Penguin Classics paperback in his pocket or a rolled-up *Irish Independent*. He wants people to think he's a chaplain and not a psychiatric patient. But the real chaplain wears T-shirts and goes around with a parrot that says: Now and at the hour of our birth.

Actually, the chaplain never goes near Fr. PJ. Ordinary priests don't like Jesuits that much. Jesuits are forever saying mysterious things that could mean anything at all to an ordinary priest, let alone an ordinary person. If they were to say to you: I am still waiting, Mary, you wouldn't know what they're waiting for. It could be feta cheese, it could be the 46A; it could be the fullness of time. There is a tremor around their words.

They might even be *awaiting*, instead. Awaiting is more than waiting, obviously. Waiting is for waiters and waitresses, but await-ing is more than balancing upright on your two legs. If you are awaiting, it is probably Christmas that is coming or the Feast of the Annunciation that is round the corner. You can do that kind of waiting on your knees or on your back, even. You can do it lying down.

In the maternity, the time the Pope was shot, half the nurses were called Mary. Mary this and Mary that. Mary from Ballinasloe, Mary from Tubercurry. It was still Ireland then. When they came back from the weekend at home, they'd say Aye instead of Yes for all of Monday, because they'd been back to the breast and bib, back to the cattle grid and the Aga.

The midwife, though, was just pretending. She said 'idear' instead of 'idea' because she'd trained somewhere in England. She was called Imogen, and she was pretty ugly, God help her. You couldn't imagine how ugly she was, with this huge, ugly jaw. If I had have been her, I would have changed my name to something more forgettable, like Ann or Jane. It just drew attention to her ugliness. Parents run a terrible risk when they name their baby. They should stop and think. They should think twice.

These days, I suppose, you could go to the Blackrock Clinic and have it done in day care, the big policeman chin on her thinned and tapered. But she'd be sixty now, Imogen would, and when you're sixty, you don't give a damn.

'Do you have a denture?' the nurse says, when you're signing the consent form for the ECT, and they say it in a whisper like it was something disgusting. I couldn't care less.

I couldn't care less.

'When were you born?' they ask you. They ask you that before they do anything else in the A and E too. Before they do stitches, bandages, anti-tetanus, cup of tea. 'What is the date of your birth, Mary?' they ask, as if it were all astrology, as if once they knew that, everything would make total sense because you were a Capricorn or a Virgo.

Imogen didn't ask me my date of birth when the Pope was shot. First she said I was an elderly primigravida, when I was only twenty-eight-and-three-quarters. Afterwards, she said I'd have loads more. She said, please God, she'd see me howling on a trolley in nine months' time. She said the killer's name was Mehmet Ali or Mehmet Allah or something Muslimy, and the Pope would be dead on arrival from the internal bleeding.

'I was going to call her Mary,' I said. 'I'm going to baptize her and call her Mary still. I don't care if she's dead.'

'That's a lovely idear, dear,' Imogen said. She'd been standing in the Vatican front square only six years before, in 1975, and she remembered saying to her mother, turning to her and saying: 'Do you think would they ever shoot the Pope?', although she meant another, Paul VI, the one the Italians called Pope Hamlet because he was always thinking, thinking, thinking with his mouth open.

I christened her with my tears and some snotty stuff from my nose. I am 90 per cent water anyway. I know that from teaching biology. I am 90 per cent at sea in myself. Imogen had gone and taken the afterbirth away with her to be turned into make-up removal in a factory in Switzerland.

A nun came in and started praying for the Pope out loud, and everybody joined in the responses, even the woman who wouldn't lie down because she wanted to squat with her boobs out and her husband watching. It was headless-chicken time, people listening to the radio and to new Walkman thingies with headphones, or charging down the corridor to the colour TV set in the men's waiting room.

Somebody thought that Popes should wear bullet-proof vests under their vestments. Somebody thought that, if he lived, John Paul might have a colostomy and be in a coma and need a deputy Pope. It was like JFK all over again. Where were you exactly when the Pope was shot?

I was exactly having my in-between sewn up by a registrar who looked like Omar Sharif and who said that the assassin had disgraced Islam and that he must have been a Shia and not a Sunni because Shias were like that, fanatical.

I was holding on. I was holding onto her. I was holding on for dear life. Frank was going to dust the soles of her feet with golden glitter to keep in his wallet, but he had to go and buy Marlboro cigarettes first. He'd been off them all through the pregnancy, the Marlboros in particular, in case he died when she was only at university or in transition year, but the whole world had changed forever, and the kiosk in the hospital didn't sell cigarettes. It was brand-new hospital policy from the first of January that year, the year of the Pope being shot.

Fr PJ says that all deaths are equal, but some deaths are more equal than others. The chaplain says, have I not read *Animal Farm*? The chaplain says that PJ's paperback in his pocket is probably George Orwell; that he's reading and digesting and passing somebody else when he thinks he's being original. He is only breaking down somebody else's proteins, really. He is not being brilliant; he is just being bacterial.

Babies are born without bacteria in their tummies. They're born without *helicobacter pylori*, the tiniest little living thing you can think of. Finding it there alive and well and kicking in all that awful hydrochloride in our bowels, softening our stools for us, our breakfasts and our lunches and our light collations and our candle-lit dinners, won somebody Jewish the Nobel prize. But a newborn or a stillborn baby doesn't go off, like people do, when you have to disembowel them before you do their hair again and put their hearts back in. Stillbirths don't get that fridge smell, like Mam did. Five days I had her at home in the crib and she still smelled sweet. She smelled like a chapel, kind of. Candles and stiff, starched cloth.

Out in Walkinstown they call me the John Paul woman. There must be an Elvis Presley woman in the world, too, and a Lockerbie disaster woman. There must be a Chernobyl woman out there somewhere, maybe even in Chernobyl itself, wherever Chernobyl is or was. Women who lost their lambs to flash photography and pandemonium and the faxes shuddering out of the fax machine as the Twin Towers went down or Lord Mountbatten got blown up in the boat in Mullaghmore.

There was a Mary from Mullaghmore, now that I think of it. Or maybe it was Mary from Mountmellick, who used to yank the young doctors' stethoscopes for a laugh.

All the John Pauls are at least in their thirties now. They're older than Jesus was, God help him, which would make Mary what? Forty-five, forty-seven, at the change, all prolapse and pelvic floor, no sleeping pills in Galilee then, no Zimovane or Stilnox or Mogadon, God bless it. When all the rest of the women in Nazareth would have had grandchildren to scrub in their kitchen sinks, she didn't even have a grave to go to. He was one of the disappeared, like in Argentina.

The graves either side of Mary's went gravel and concrete ages ago, but the tulips come up every year in the little street in Deansgrange cemetery where she was buried, the day the people smoking upstairs in the 46A that was stopped outside the turnstile in the wall blessed themselves when they saw through the crowd that the coffin was white. When the tulips come up depends on the weather and how deep down the bulb is in the compost.

Fr PJ says that stillbirths are always still being born, but the chaplain says that is not the exact quotation by whoever actually said it, some famous person in a book, and that he'll think of the name. He'll be thinking of something else all together, he says, and the name will come to him, just like that, out of the blue.

'Mehmet Ali Agca,' I said, the time the whole science department went to the faith healer in Mullingar and we joined the table quiz for spina bifida in the hotel bar.

'Fair play to you, girl,' said the facilitator. 'Where did you have that hidden away in your head?'

'I just did,' I said. 'I just do. Somewhere or other at the back of my mind, there are names you never forget.'

NORTHERN LIGHT

When they left the pub at closing time, it was still as bright as Iceland, and it shouldn't have been. It should have been dark, it should have been drizzling; it should have been Whitechapel weather, all cobble and foghorn and the city fox seen for a second at the cemetery turnstile: Belfast at its worst, the winter solstice. But it wasn't. Because this was more or less midsummer instead, bonfire time in the Irish school in Donegal where she'd learned the conditional mood, the Modh Coinníollach – *I would do it, you would do it, he would do it, she would do it* – on the day the boy from Buncrana slotted his strange, sinuous tongue into her eardrum until he could taste the wax there, so he said; and the side street they were walking down, she and the soldier, had turned so dry from the drought and the dehydration that there was chickweed on the camber, which you might pick in passing for the budgie cage of the child you babysat on every second Thursday when the parents went ballroom dancing, although they said it was always only to see some continental film, a film with subtitles and no story to speak of from start to finish, because the contestants in their swallowtails, with the numbers on their backs like bull's-eyes on a dartboard, were mostly Protestants.

'But more power to them,' the soldier said. 'Isn't that what they say in these parts? More power to them.'

She must be the only woman in the city who was wearing tights, and Wolford tights at that, the costly cashmere semi-opaque ones, during a heatwave. That was because she didn't want him to touch her there, the soldier beside her in his ludicrous burgundy flares with the wrong brown moccasins, the soldier who wasn't even white, after all, which was why his teeth shone the way they did, like a TV toothpaste ad in colour almost, the Colgate ring of confidence, with the bit of bar food, peanut probably, lodged in his front uppers. Hers were yellow always, no matter how mightily she scourged them twice a day at work with a fresh toothbrush every other month. Not canary yellow, obviously; not even lemon yellow, or the thin trace of cream yellow on the fancy cardboard coasters that had piled up on the counter in the pub beside them as they drank beer and Babycham, but not the Procul Harum whiteness that she wanted, the American dazzle. She was that tempted, someday she would try Tipp-Ex. She would try it on her toenails first, of course, just to be safe, just to be certain sure it wasn't poison.

'Weird,' the soldier said. 'Goes without saying. Those newspaper photographs in the gold picture frames, you know. The shots of all the other pubs that got blown up, with the dates at the bottom and the lists of the casualties in the posh handwriting, like Sr Joseph's. A sort of a Fuck you, excuse my French. A sort of a We're still here, we're staying here, so sod off.'

'Sr Joseph?' she said, because she had thought he would have been a Hindu or a Buddhist, maybe, or nothing at all, even, like the Church of England English, with their sales of work and their punnets of chutney and the big Bingo numbers of their military hymns up on a pillar beside the pulpit. At least the Presbyterians put their money where their mouth was, and didn't place bets or play the pools.

'Sr Joseph was a nun who wrote like that,' the soldier said to her. 'Sr Joseph was all organized and alphabetical. No wonder I went into the army.'

She looked at him then, looked at him as he laughed, the bright enamel flash without the least tobacco trace. He might be twenty. He might be twenty-two. But then again, he might be thirty-two. You never knew with Indians or with Japanese or with blacks. The chubby Filipino at the smear test seemed only fifteen, sixteen, yet she had two kids as tall as herself, two boys, and one of them made his Communion already, so he must be what? And the burgundy flares were a glam-rock giveaway. All the teens, down as far as the O levels in St Thomas's on the Whiterock Road, were back in drainpipes since Johnny Rotten and the start of punk, with the spiked hair and the screeching microphones, awful brawling brats that they were. He was somewhere in his twenties, then, give or take; but that was all right. That was the way she wanted it. She wanted to know nothing.

'My name isn't really Charlie,' the soldier said. 'It's Chaaru-chandra. But it got shortened.'

'Chaaruchandra is nice,' she said back. And she wished he hadn't told her. She hadn't asked him. She hadn't told him hers. Instead, she had told him her Confirmation name, Grace, which nobody remembered and which she had never once used, even as an italic, or was it an initial, a capital G with a full stop, between her Christian name and her surname. Why did they have to name names anyway? What had names to do with anything? They were neither here nor there. They had nothing to do with meeting the man, the right man, the right place, the rendezvous, and bringing him back then for a cup of tea or a cup of coffee, a Kimberley Mikado, and him thinking to himself all the way from A to Z how far he could go with a grope. You could do that without names. You could.

'Charlie's fine,' the soldier said. 'Charles is a bit too Prince of Wales for the flats, and I never liked Chas. The only Chas I knew was a shit.'

'Charlie's all right,' she said. 'It's happy-go-lucky, hopalong, kind of. In Irish, it's called Cathal. Cathal's very common here. It's like Tom, Dick, and Harry, actually, except that you never meet a man called Cathal in the streets where Tom, Dick, and Harry live, unless he's working for Blindcraft.'

'There was this guy,' the soldier said, 'who came to Birmingham from Bombay via Mombasa. Opens a store, starts a family. Long story short, he calls his sons Tom, Dick, and Harry. He calls them Tom, Dick, and Harry, because – wait for it – he wants them to blend in.'

She was looking in her bucket bag for the door key. She had opened and closed the door a dozen times in the practice sessions, opening and closing it the way you would do if you were bringing in milk or messages, noticing nothing and not being noticed, and every third time it had jammed, it had wedged from a warp in the wood that should have been planed beforehand; and she had to shove it hard with her shoulder until her shoulder hurt around the vaccination mark. But he was there now and could help her. He could probably break it down if he wanted to, break it down or kick it in if he liked. Breaking down doors and kicking them in was what they were good at. One of them had trampled on a Moses basket in Mrs Muldoon's. Back on the famous 15th of August, in the beginning times, one of them had thrown Mr Gallogly's hearing aid into the outside toilet.

'Let me,' he said. 'Less is always more.'

They were being looked at too. The girl who was passing by, the girl in her bare feet with the pastel platform clogs on either hand, glanced up at them, as she crossed a hopscotch square that was chalked on the pavement, and a man in a cervical collar on the other side of the street swivelled his eyes without turning his head because of the plaster of Paris. Then he shuffled on, eyes front, back rigid.

Let them mind their own. Let them look away. It had taken seven minutes, seven minutes exactly, from the yellow Guinness toucan above the double door of the pub to the Child of Prague in the sooty lunette over the entrance to the terraced house, and that was the same duration as every rehearsal. Down to a T it was.

The door swung open softly, like it was meant to.

———

If she squeezed in behind the cooker, he wouldn't see her doing it from the sitting-room. Besides, he was still fiddling with the portable set, trying to get a picture. Perhaps he was one of the technical types who spent their time in the observation posts on the back-roads of the Border, watching an iron bathtub in some cow field through a pair of binoculars, or a fruit-picker taking a piss at a blackberry bush, and writing down everything, this, that, the whole timeline of the tedium of it, boys with moustaches who weren't allowed sideburns, fellows with headphones and code books and copies of *Mayfair*, crouched in their camouflage jackets in the dreary camouflage landscape of tillage and ditches and the glaring emerald grass over the septic tanks. Or maybe he was fresh in off a transport and more afraid of falling out of the top bunk in the barracks than of losing his bearings in the back alleys of the Beechmount estate when the bin lids started their telltale rat-tat-tatting. Whatever he was, he was no fool when it came to televisions. Not that it mattered, of course. Not that it mattered at all.

'The picture's crystal clear,' he called to her. 'But it's upside down and back to front now. Gary Cooper's head and shoulders are where his legs should be, and the saddle and the spurs are in the sky. It's the horizontal hold. The horizontal hold is your only man. Isn't that what they say in Ireland?'

'That's what they say,' she said. 'But more down in Dublin, really.'

'I know this film,' the soldier said. 'It's the film with the woman who married the millionaire in Monaco. The glacial lady. The ice maiden. The sourpuss.'

'We're not going to watch a film,' she said. 'Not when it's nearly half over when you're just beginning. I hate that.'

'If I got the horizontal hold,' the soldier said, 'I could tell you the missing bits, right up to where we came in. Things are easier to follow if you don't need to understand every single frame in a film.'

She had fetched the sanitary towel out of her bag, and put it inside her pants under the mesh of the Wolford tights. If he dropped the hand, she'd tell him. She'd tell him it was her time, the wrong time. She'd tell him she was having a period. She'd tell him she was having a heavy period. That'd put a stop to his gallop. He'd throw up Carslberg on the carpet. Men were terrified of blood from there, the shrill metal stink of it like an old revolver in a blanket chest or a lick of Brasso on a Christmas candelabrum in the windowsill. They didn't mind the kipper stench of their own stuff, but they shrivelled at a woman's whiff. And she flicked the kettle switch, and came out to him, as if she had flicked the kettle-switch and come out to him a hundred times before, casual, like, without being conscious of being casual, always acting nice and natural. That was the thing.

He was moving round the room with the rabbit ears, pointing them this way and that way, up and down, recceing slowly like a Dalek out of *Dr Who*. He was a Charlie, actually. He was a proper Charlie, when it came to that.

'The day of Churchill's funeral,' he said, 'I was doing this for my dad. By the time the screen stopped snowing, he was asleep in the chair. By then it was almost over, except for the cranes. The big cranes bowing down along the river, all at the same time, all at the same tempo, all the way to Greenwich, because they'd rehearsed it a hundred times, hadn't they, as the coffin passed in a tugboat. My mum came in while my dad was sleeping, and she sprayed the room with her hairspray. That was because my dad had had a colostomy.'

She would forget his name. She would obliterate it completely. Not only would she forget it, she would eventually forget that she had forgotten it. Then she would be safe again, safe again, safe as houses. In fact, she had already forgotten most of it. She remembered only a part of the sound of it, a brief blurt of blue-red colour, like chow or chowder, charcoal, charred, that ended in the taupe of handy, shandy, the lads' hand shandy, God forgive her for thinking of such a thing at such a time. She had done the same when she was fourteen, fifteen, with a name that began with C in the Irish college, and, for the life of her now, she could not honestly be certain, hand on a Bible, if he had been Colm or Conall or Conor or Con or even Colin, though Colin was off the radar except for a mixed marriage or some uppity Teague idiot on the Malone Road who gave his house a name instead of a number and called the Mass a Eucharist.

'I watched *Match of the Day* this way, one time last year,' the soldier said. '*Match of the Day* without the horizontal hold is a pain in the arse, excuse my French, but no *Match of the Day* is worse. The thing is, you can get used to anything, if you have to.'

'You can,' she said, 'You can get used to anything.'

'The thing is', he said again, 'we see everything wrong in the first place. We see everything upside down. Then the brain has to turn what we're looking at right side up. It does it all the time, without thinking.'

And in she came with the tray, the tray with the two lacquered wicker handles and the polished print of Venice, was it, or somewhere at least that was old and flooded. Nice and natural, natural and nice. Put it down on the leather pouffe and pour for two.

'So where are you from yourself?' she said.

He looked at her through the V of the rabbit ears.

'If you were English, you wouldn't have to ask me that,' he said. 'You'd know straight away. You'd know by my accent, wouldn't you? You'd know the exact map coordinates. You'd know the elevation. Square mile, spot on. That's what I like about Ireland. You can be from wherever you decide. "I'm not a Brit," I said to a barmaid in the Beehive. "I'm from West Bengal." "Say something to me in West Bengalian, then, and I'll believe you," she said. Bengalian. Word of a lie. Where do they make them up? So I told her in Bengali that I was born and brought up in Wolverhampton.'

'Wolverhampton?' she said.

'Wolverhampton,' he said. 'Great place; great people. Relegated now, but not for long. Thirty-two years in the first division. Forty-nine caps Ron Flowers got. He did, too. My dad saw George Formby at the Hippodrome. My mum heard Gigli at the Civic Hall. And the chap they hanged, that lummock of a Lord Haw-Haw, he was Irish, lived in Woverhampton. Only thing is, they sold off the trolley buses back in '66. Under a Labour government. That was a scandal. Whenever I think of 1966, I think of three things: I think of Wembley and the Cup, of course; I think of the trolleys taken off, here today, gone tomorrow, just like that; and I think of my mum and dad moving into separate beds.'

She held her fingers in front of her teeth as she smiled, because you could not smile without showing them to the world. That was another mystery, that when you smiled, you snarled, and when you snarled, you smiled. You could not do one without doing the other at the same time. It was a complete contradiction. There were no two ways about it.

'When I think of 1966,' she said, 'I think of something else entirely. It was a year of anniversaries, 1966 was. Anniversaries galore. We celebrated anniversaries for the whole twelve months, January, February, March, April, May, but especially when I was making my first Holy Communion. That's why I was wearing my first Holy Communion dress when I said a poem at the school concert, up on the stage, up in the spotlight, me in the dress, no veil, no gloves. The glare. But I couldn't remember the poem. I was mortified.'

'The boy stood on the burning deck,' the soldier said. 'T'was on the good ship Venus.'

"I see His blood upon the rose", she said. 'That was how it began. That was as far as I got. "I see His blood upon the rose". My parents were down there somewhere in the darkness. My grandparents, the whole three of them, were down there too. In the darkness of the hall behind the glare. I couldn't see in the light. It was blinding me. And a voice, my uncle's voice, he was younger than I was, in the class behind me, Rang a Dó, calling out: "And in the stars. And in the stars". But I tried so hard to remember I forgot everything.'

'Get out of town,' the soldier said.

'Get out of town?' she said. 'What do you mean, get out of town?'

'It's just something I say,' said the soldier. 'It means weird or no way. It means Wow.'

Why was she saying these things? She'd been afraid, so afraid, that she'd have nothing to say to him. She'd been afraid that, in the end, it would have to be the other, the couch, the carpet, the soup bowl full of water in front of the gas heater, month of June or no month of June, red marks on her elbows from the friction of the fabric on the floor, beer on his breath, the long fingernails that a soldier shouldn't have, shouldn't be allowed to have, unless he was some sort of a Spanish guitarist or needed them for a ludicrous brass instrument in the regimental band.

'Sounds like Sr Joseph all over,' he said. 'Sounds like a convent school.'

He was smiling again and his teeth were even whiter, the peanut still protruding; and she thought of the time she had sat into the photo booth in Woolworth's, after they changed to colour, or was it to Polaroids, and she had daubed a dab of her nail varnish on the two incisor tips for the laminated agency ID card, and the taste of it had stayed there for ages, even after the slice of quiche lorraine. She had been stone-cold sober then, and she was stone-cold sober now. There was hardly a tincture of alcohol in a Babycham, and the stomach noises that her body was making, the tiny insect cries, were from runny cheese and the seedless grapes that had turned out to have seeds in every third one of them.

'It was and it wasn't a convent school,' she said. 'One of the nuns had met the Beatles. One of them wore lipstick. One of them had been in Biafra. She wrote their national anthem. It was called 'Biafra Once Again', and they sang it to the air of an Irish song. Then she got deported.'

'I had a priest for metalwork,' he said. 'Face like a fourpence. Frowning. He had this line he was always trotting out. Don't know where he got it. Maybe he just thought it up on his own. "If God gives you salt when you ask for water, that's because God knows more about thirst than you do." That was it. Never knew what it meant, did I? Still don't. But I said it to the padre, a chaplain back from Cyprus with a suntan and a scowl on his face, same as the metalwork man, because it was freezing cold here and his shirt was still short-sleeved, and, I tell you for this nothing, a fried egg in Fort Jericho on the Springfield Road is a far cry from a plate of calamari in a nice little café in Nicosia. Gave him the whole salt, water and thirst thing, and he's really impressed. He looks at me, like. Then, two days later, he puts me down to read a lesson at the service. Must have thought I was deep.'

The room was beginning to condense around them. The surface of the water in the soup bowl shivered like cellophane in the shrill up-current of air from the gas heater, and a film of condensation was forming infinitesimally on the fretwork of the empty plyboard press and the beauty board above the linoleum where the carpet suddenly stopped short, as if ashamed of itself. How damp had a terrace house to be when it was damp in the midsummer, damp in a drought, damp when the drains were choked with chickweed for a budgie cage, and the children ran out screaming to the cardiac ambulance parked on the Iveagh Parade because they thought it was an ice-cream van?

'Still,' he said. 'I do like a red glow. The mother now has the fire going all year round, even in a heat wave. Gives her a focus. Otherwise you're watching rubbish on telly, *The Avengers* or Dick Emery, because you've got to look at something, haven't you? There's more channels on a small fire than a huge set, she says; and she's right. Even the Queen Mum has a two-bar electric in Buckingham Palace when she needs a nightcap. For three books of Green Shield stamps, you can pick up one with all sorts of different settings and a ribbed reflector.'

She looked at him, the fresh, hail-fellow, full-of-himself recruit, cross-legged in the chocolate moccasins, Mr Wolf from Wolverhampton. He had an army-issue condom ready, steady, go, in his inside pocket, probably, wrapped in a greasy foil beside a girlfriend's photograph, and it was not there, pressed against his heart of hearts, to pack explosive putty in a flexible prophylactic for a letter bomb. He was waiting, watching for the signal from her, the least sign, something nice and natural; deliberate, yes, but not dramatic, the hint of a crinkle at the depilated pleat of the mouth, a crease in the arch of the waterproof eyebrow manicure. The coloureds would always wait first for permission. She knew that. Because there was still that memsahib thing about a white woman, even if she was a missionary or a Divis Chrissy, a hint of the top hat and the haughty dressage, the bar of empire bred into the indigenous tribes; and it was worth waiting, well worth it, because there was nobody more naked than a naked white woman. You could be nude if you were black, you could be nude if you were brown; you could be nude if you were yellow, with no breasts to show for it, just the tightly folded tulip they adored for its succinctness; but only a white woman could be stripped of her clothes and her underclothes and her immaculate vanilla unmentionables, and stand before you in the pink, goose pimpled skin of her flesh and blood.

'When this is all over,' he said, 'all this argy-bargy, it'll end up as a boardgame. A Waddington boardgame. Swear to God. People will play it like Monopoly. You buy the Antrim Road. I take the Shankill. Hotel here, hotel there. Roll the dice. So says this Charlie anyway. There'll be a black-cab tourist trail.'

Charlie, she thought. Charles could be Charlie, of course, but how could it ever be Cathal? How did they start with a sound like Charles, the peremptory bark of it, and end with a completely different sound, the quiet throat-clearing cough of Cathal? The thing was ridiculous. No connection existed. It was like the way they had lured the word Phoenix out of Fionn Uisce, soot and ashes out of white-wine water; it was like the way they had coaxed the Falls Road out of Tuath na bhFál, hedgerow country.

'Wait and see,' he said. 'And, in the meantime, keep all your receipts.'

But this was no time to be thinking, to be translating; to be back in a Donegal classroom with its south-facing window from the old sanatorium times, with holes in the lids of school desks that had once been inkwells, and the tutor telling them to raise their fists if they knew the conditional mood. He might be a pronoun becoming a noun becoming a name, the Indian English soldier, but she could swerve straight back into Charlene, charlatan, harvest of barley, shark attack, haversack; and by then, by then it was gone, disappeared into thin air, the short form of the odd oriental mouthful of a Hindu Christian name that was already extinct for ages in her recent memory, let alone the base of her brain.

'Am I hearing my stomach,' the soldier said, 'or am I hearing your stomach? That is the question.'

Was the man with the brown eyes blind? Had he any idea? Had he the sense of sight at all in his God-given face that was peering at her now, probing her now, staring almost? That was the first sign, the second stage, the studied expression. It was the Dr Zhivago gaze of a second-rate Omar Sharif into the muslin lens of the camera, a long, lovely exposure, with glycerine drops from a pipette to trick the tears out of hiding; not blinking nicely and naturally, the way you would do, but the exact opposite of the tic of her boy-scout brother with the Tourette's at the Corpus Christi procession. More like the motionless mason's eye of the white host held up in a monstrance, glaring. But she could play a blinder too.

'Maybe I'm hearing both of us,' the soldier said. 'That's called clicking where I come from.'

'No,' she said. 'It's called Carlsberg and Babycham.'

'Well,' he said. 'Maybe we could mix our drinks.'

It must be time. It must be almost time. It must be creeping towards the time, the hour hand quivering skywards like a magnet, straight as the shortest distance between two points, a petrified spire like the spire of the Methodist chapel where you would never, ever in a thousand years see a beggar begging; and the second-hand lurching from slow station to station, like the man with the metal leg at the last procession, swinging the heavy prosthesis ahead of him, with his whole pelvis twisted like a corkscrew from the strain of the straps that tied him together.

'Do you know,' the soldier said, 'that alcohol is an Arabic word? And they don't even drink. They never swill in their lives.'

First there would be the sound outside, the footfall of the espadrilles; then the brief, bare-knuckle Beethoven's Fifth on the front door, like at the practices, the same six stresses, pause and repeat. Not so much sombrely or seriously, mind you, more as a light-hearted lark, a girlfriend's meet-and-greet, a pal's password, as if to say: *It's me, love.* Then the light, mischievous voice itself, the sing song upward inflection of it, a silly-billy's voice, in fact; some tipsy, twenty-year old feminine nonsense through the tight-lipped letterbox. And you stand up to answer it, the way anyone might, the way anyone would, wiping your mouth, maybe, because you would still be still munching a Kimberley Mikado from the tray with the two lacquered handles and the polished print of Venice or somewhere flooded, and rubbing a knee perhaps, the left patella, just the one and not the both of them, under the thick Wolford tight, because your knee might be asleep at this stage or it might be a bit cramped, like it was from the church bench at the side altar where the kneelers were not padded properly, from genuflecting there for centuries, seemingly, on the new economy carpet at the new economy heater in the front room of a terraced house that had rising damp in a dry spell for far too long to be lived in.

She would do it. She would do it. He would do it too.

'I know that,' he said, 'because I have a degree in pub quizzes, don't I?'

'Get out of town,' she said to the soldier, laughing. 'Get you out.'

———

'When we reached it,' the soldier was saying, 'it turned out to be modern University accommodation. Legoland. It was students who lived in the block, and some foreigners too. But not in dormitories. In single rooms, in separate quarters. Bit of a barracks, really, brighter, of course, and no ramp at reception. Corridors for the men, corridors for the women, if you could call them women. You'd want to see their birth cert before you kissed them. And they're all out in the car park at the assembly point where the bicycles are locked, Raleigh and Rudge and Brompton, old-fashioned bikes with baskets and mudguards like it was Oxford and not Ulster. They're in their dressing gowns and their jumpsuits, slippers with pompoms, terrified we're going to find dope instead of dynamite, and they'll get a criminal record that'll kiss goodbye to their plans for the Napa Valley in California. And there's these

Malaysian medical students, all excited, because they're just in from Malalysia, and they've never seen their breath before. They're blowing out their breath like it was cigarette smoke, and just looking at it then, the mist in front of their faces, and laughing away while the locals get frost-bite.'

That sound outside the door was not the sound of espadrilles, which was a soft sound, the sound of a continental holiday, scooters and crickets in the lemon trees around a basilica. Instead, it was the grating, nail-head sound of a male boot grinding a fag end on the pavement where the hopscotch squares were chalked, and an emphysemic cough at the finish, all growl and no sputum to show for it. They might as well smoke at that stage, of course. By then, it was too late for anything.

'So I checked the rooms I was told to check,' said the soldier, 'and you wouldn't have thought they were going to be dentists and barristers some day, the students out in the car park, because the whole place was a pigsty, pretty much. But there was this one room, a particular room, a girl's room, with a sign on the door that said *Koalas For Twenty Kilometres,* and I went in, I went in, you see.'

There was a name for it in science, a name for the double effect, the Doppler effect, the sound of steps coming closer and closer up the shallow rise of the street, cresting then at the window like the white of a wave, and fading, falling away on the far side of the footsteps, until they dissolved in the light darkness again. But that had been the left-right, left-right lock step of two tarts in a hurry, teens without taxi fare for the crowded flip-down tip seat, their high heels ticking, ticking quickly, like the treadle of a wheel of a Singer sewing machine. Their mother would take out the toasting-fork when they got home, and God help their BTMs then.

'Was the girl there?' she said. 'Was she in bed?' And she thought of the Scot from Fort William, was it, the warrant officer with the eczema in the territorials, who had pissed on a candlewick bedspread, and they had had to go out afterwards, she and her mother and her aunt in sensible sandals, with most of the Christmas money that was in the spaghetti jar, and buy a double duvet in the city centre, no discount asked or offered at the counter, clean sterling five-pound notes without a kink in them for the brand-new bedding with a combination quilt and eiderdown that was warm without the weight of blankets and the washing involved. In the days before the launderettes, in the days before the water cannon, woollens went through the rollers of the mangle and women went through the cubicles of the public baths on the Falls Road, where they had laid out more than a thousand bodies after the German raid during the war, the Catholics on one side and the Protestants on the other, each to his own like the vowel sounds of Donegal Irish, slender with slender and broad with broad.

'It wasn't like that,' he said. 'It was the other way round. It was the exact opposite. She wasn't there, but I could sense her. I could almost see her. She was there in the room. She was as real as you are. She was present the same as you. She was really present. The hood of the anglepoise light over the desk in the corner was down low over a typewriter, an electric golfball with a red-and-black ribbon, and the wood of the desk around it was warm from the heat of the bulb; so I turned the light off, like you would, like anyone would. There was a pencil with a rubber on the end of it in an empty mug for tea or coffee, and you could tell that she was using the pencil to stir her drink, the milk, maybe, or sugar, or the sugar substitutes. Women are mad these days for sugar substitutes and weighing scales under the beds.'

But he said it kindly. He was not angry about anything, really; he was not afraid of anything, either. He was neither angry nor afraid, she thought. Red was the colour of anger and yellow the colour of fear, she remembered, and, if you mixed the two colours together, the red and the yellow, you ended up with orange, because orange was the perfect marriage of fear and anger. Any pound-shop paint-box proved it. But he was a brown man in a brown study. That was the Carlsberg, of course. Five pints and men are all mystics with testicles.

'The rest of the room was spick and span,' he said. 'Even the waste-paper basket was neat and tidy, with toenail clippings on one side and a mandarin with mould on it and teeth marks in the middle, and a damp clump of hair that you'd pull from a sink-hole at the edge of the bin. Not army-style spick-and-span, not a showroom, not a pretend space, all organized and alphabetical, like the set of a play where the whole play is set in one room, start to finish, I hate that, and everything's arranged beforehand. You're looking at the same fucking furniture for three hours, excuse my French, and the more you look at it, the more you realize: nobody lives here. Nobody could live here. Nobody would live here. It's just a set. Just a set-up. And if you don't believe the room, you can't believe the people in it. But this room was so nice. It was so natural. And it had this lovely smell. It had this particular smell, you know, that you wouldn't actually call a smell. You would call it a scent instead. Because scent is gentler, isn't it?'

The boy from Buncrana had done the very same thing, she thought. He had slipped his serpent's tongue into her ear on mid-summer's day on a strand in Donegal until he could taste the wax that was there, and, even though she had had it syringed when the college closed and the bus brought her home again, home again, she could still feel the strong, wet muscle of its insinuating saliva.

'There was a twelve-month calendar on the wall over the desk, and a poster of Groucho Marx or someone who was the spit of Groucho Marx or someone who was impersonating Groucho Marx, and there were names on the calendar, Declan and Pauline, mostly Declan, Declan. His name in blue felt marker, Pauline in green felt marker. I don't know whether she was getting into him or getting over him, if he was an ex or an extra-special, but I thought: more power to you, Declan. More power to you, pal. And then, somewhere in every single month, there was a P, a big bloody P in dark red ink, all decorated like a letter in the Bible at the start of a sentence at the top of the page each time you turn it to read the first words. *At that time. In the beginning. God said.* Somewhere in every month, there was the letter P. In August, September, October, November. A big, beautiful capital P. And I knew what she was saying because I wasn't born yesterday. So I said 'Sorry' to the room. I said it as an apology, an apology to her. Because I was trespassing. I was a trespasser. Not in the *trespassers-will-be-prosecuted* sense. I wanted her to forgive my trespass against her. In, you know, the Sunday sense. I shouldn't have known so much about a person without even knowing her name.'

There must have been a scuffle at the doorstep, a kerfuffle of canvas shoes, the liquid snort of a girl giggling outside. But she was suddenly tired. She could hardly stand up. Her leg had gone asleep, fast asleep beneath her on the horrible carpet beside the bucket-bag. It was numb now with a phantom pain of pins and needles. She had been drowsing almost at the gas heater, when you would have thought she would be wide awake, more wide awake and watchful than she had ever been before in the whole of her life. The entire side of her under the warm Wolford fabric prickled and winced minutely, a plaster cast cracked open, hair torn from the calf, the scald of a pubic wax in the beautician's.

'I recognize that knock,' the soldier said, but she hadn't heard it at all. She could hear her heart inside her, like a baby kicking nastily, the jab of its heel, but she hadn't heard the rat-tat-tapping on the door. Outside, it had gone as still as Milltown. The two others, the whosoever they were, would be standing in the street on either side of the chirpy knock of the girl's knuckles, not breathing, holding their breath in, not letting their breath escape, with thick woollen winter socks over their desert boots, like it was snowing over the hedgerows and the ground was treacherous.

'That's a famous knock,' said the soldier. 'It's a riff from something. I know that beat.' And he hummed it himself with his puckered, bee-stung lips like Omar Sharif's in *Dr Zhivago*, the whole six stresses that they still called Beethoven's Fifth for some reason. 'Dum, dum; dum, dum, dum; dum dum.'

'Let me in, Goretti,' said a slovenly voice that was too slurred at the letterbox, like the amateur drunk in the pageant play. 'I'm bursting to go, girl.'

Then he looked straight at her in the most natural way, the way that anyone would, boy or girl, man or woman, parent or child, African or American, wild Indian or West Indian, as she stepped over the tray with the lacquered wickerwork handles and the Kimberley Mikados and the polished print of Venice or somewhere that was utterly inundated and would smell of the sea forever like the menstrual estuary of Belfast Lough.

'Goretti?' he said. 'That's weird. I could have sworn you said your name was Grace.'

—

When she left the house, it was already bright, as bright as Iceland, and it shouldn't have been. It should have been dark, it should have drizzling; it should have been Whitechapel weather, Belfast at its worst, the winter solstice. But it wasn't. Instead, it was broad daylight in the middle of the night-time, with the streetlamps still on everywhere and the traffic lights still changing colour at the junction, red, green, yellow, although there was no traffic to change colour for, and no sound of traffic from left or right or from behind her or in front and all around, as far as the smudge of the skyline. You would think there was a curfew, it was so calm. It was a ghost town, actually. It was a filmset or a set for a soap on the television. It was like the set of *Corrie* that you could tour with a tour guide off-season, a ticketed tour of inspection when they weren't shooting, if you answered three questions correctly with the three correct coupons from the right breakfast cereal and were over eighteen at the time of entry.

What would they have done? she thought? *What were they after doing?*

She stood on the hopscotch squares that were chalked on the pavement by the children who had played there before it grew dark and then darker and then bright again, suddenly blithely bright, not a care in creation, with the moon still risen, yellow-white, ludicrous, low over the slateline and the helmeted chimney pots. You would think from the hopscotch squares that the council were going to move the whole street to higher ground because of subsidence or the water table or earthquake damage, and that they had marked each separate paving stone in pink chalk with a number between one and ten to be absolutely sure that they would place the right ones in the right place at the new location, concrete and sand, sand and concrete, so that everything would be the same, neat and natural, ordinary, orderly, alphabetical almost, and nothing would have changed, nothing would be remotely altered, apart from the elevation. They had done it before and they would do it again, the archaeologists had, with an ancient temple somewhere in Africa, brick by brick or pillar by pillar, saving the ivy tendrils and the swallows' nests and the chiselled signatures of tourists who thought they were travellers, because of a dam or a reservoir or a running tide, and they had reassembled it then at the reassembly point, ten thousand feet above sea-level, in thin air, an ark on a mountain top, wiping the whitewash numbers off the marble blocks, one after another as they went, like a list of hymns from A to Z unsung, a Bingo card unblackening, in a kind-hearted countdown to the ready, the steady, the good steadiness instead of the going, the undergoing, the gone.

If they could do it there, they could do it here, no bother, to a terrace of houses in the back streets of Belfast where there was condensation in midsummer and even the water in a soup bowl shivered at the gas heater, although it was bright as Iceland everywhere and there were more suicides in Iceland during the summer than during the winter, and that was a complete and utter contradiction.

She would not have done it until. She would not have done it unless.

She would go home, so she would. She would go straight home to her bed and get into it and curl into the recovery position, like a foetus, and sleep in the usual way on her left-hand side, the side of her vaccination mark. She would be safe as houses there, with the purple draught-excluder snake at the weatherboard of the back door, where it whistled sometimes in the wind like a denture did, and the blackout blind was bolted down beyond the sill so that the light was bearable, a bearable black and blue even at midday. But she would go by the long route and not by the short one, diagonally and not directly, the same as the practice sessions, through terrain that was alien because it was streets and side streets and sides away from where she lived and moved and had her being, another parish, another postal code, a different paper-boy with the same page-boy haircut, a different Anglia with the same dented fender, another foot patrol at the pedestrian crossing, boy soldiers with Sten guns who had masturbated in their bunks out of boredom or terror. She would deviate and she would decoy. She would zig-zag as far as the peaceline and then double back. She would take in the monastery and the mills and the high-rise housing that had been brand new fifteen years before, but was now being used for a spy film set in the Soviet Union. She would go by the bricked-up row and the burnt-out row, past the broken pram that was short for perambulator, like a bus was short for omnibus, past the window-box with its *Fáilte* sign and its plastic snapdragons, because it was facing north and planting petunias failed, year in, year out; and past the hanging basket over the diamanté bay of the corner house with real white fuchsia, pretty as a postcard and radiant from the Miracle-Gro, that the children wore as earrings when they took out their crystal Holy Communion studs.

They had gone and done it now. But he would have done it too. He would.

She would break into a run at the church railings, startling the vixen who starved there under the Huguenot headstone with the broken column in the high nettles where you would find condoms and Kleenex and a knotted handkerchief from the teargas on the way to school one morning, so that the creature stopped dead, stock still, red-handed at the silver callipers of a corporation tree, and stared at the power-walking woman who was out at this hour, her head swivelled, ears rigid, the brush more brown than Titian, paw poised attentively in the bright mid-air of the small hours that should have been pitch-black. She was like a person pouring tea into a teacup, the vixen was, deliberately but not dramatically, like a ballroom ballerina in the spotlight, up there, in the glare of the hall, wordless, waiting in her costume and contestant's number for the first note, the drum roll, the trap sprung, the thud of the silencer on the starting pistol at the sports' day egg-and-spoon race, to prompt her punctual tumble-turn down into the would-be world through the might-have-been universe into the matter-of-fact early morning light that was only a figment and a fib.

It would have been done anyhow. It would have been done anyway.

She would not get sick into the bucket bag. Even if it were steamed and streamlined and sterilized afterwards, even if you syringed it with adulterated Dettol until it smelled like an operating theatre in a hospital, the hot helium glare of disinfected reflectors in every linen cavity, it would still be something she could neither remember nor could she forget. She would retch instead at the corner near the callipers of the plane tree where the fox had paused, and then, if anyone would see her at it from a front window in the red-brick road, he would think to himself, like the lollipop boy had said out loud outside the De La Salle college after the school céilidh when he confiscated her first and only naggin of vodka: 'Ladies and gentlemen of the jury, this is a clear case of the morning after the night before. This is a scene from central casting.

It isn't *Mise Eire* we have here or Mother Ireland. It isn't Mother Church, and it isn't even mammy, let alone mother. What we have here is Miss Ireland, and Miss Ireland is misbehaving beautifully.'

But they were all wrong. They were all wrong tack, wrong track, wrong-footed. If they would only have come out from behind the curtain, from behind the cooker, from beneath the Huguenot tombstone with the scrunched Kleenex tissue, they would have seen for themselves at a glance that she was stone-cold sober, sober as a judge, with maybe a molecule of alcohol in her whole metabolism, a scintilla of anything lethal, those miniature bottles of Babycham. Otherwise, only a bolus of wet pellets of biscuit with a coconut flavour, Kimberley Mikado if you must, and seeds from the seedless grapes they had bought on that basis and found to be counterfeit. There was no other word for the hoax.

In the cold light of day, it was not even vomit, properly speaking. It was hardly regurgitation, which was too enormous a term for slaver or spittle. It would just be the natural acid reflux of her sputum.

IN THE FORM OF FICTION

Afterwards the two of them went for a coffee in a coffee shop in Palo Alto. They sat together in a pinewood carrel under the anachronistic television set, and one or other of them signalled to the waitress to mute the volume, which she did, so that the semi-omniscient narrator could hear them think.

Actually, the coffee shop was only two doors up/down, depending on direction, from the cinema, but you would not necessarily know from a reference to a multiplex called The Emerald that it was located in California and not in County Limerick, say, especially when the film they were watching was a Baltic movie with subtitles and many of the audience, statistically if not socio-culturally, were South-East Asians. Not that I have anything against South-East Asians. I make that disclaimer at the very outset.

Anyhow, she had a sorbet and he had lemon tea. We are back in the coffee shop. They were communicating quite well, he thought. But it had been subject-verb-object since the start. They had been able to set aside the three tedious stages of gnosis, agnosis and negotiation.

For the record I have nothing against Balts, either. In fact, I have never met one and I do not particularly want to.

'Actually,' he said, 'I'm going to have a cappuccino.' That was because saying the sentence gave him conversational access to an anecdote that came into his mind while he was squeezing the lemon into the glass. Otherwise there would be no intelligible transition, and connections matter. If you do not connect consecutively, you end up not shaving. You end up sleeping in your clothes. This is true.

'Would a cappuccino not keep you awake?' said Beth. She has to have a name, but it is/was not necessarily hers. Besides, pronouns panic at a certain point in time. They experience a vertigo not a thousand miles from Asperger's: a remote, immobilized, concussive, far-fetched focus.

'Only caffeine makes my heart beat faster now,' Peter said. There was the risk of a non-sequitur here, but he might forget to say it later on. So he said it at this stage. Then he remarked, or perhaps he made the remark after he had bought and paid for the coffee, and brought it back to the table to avoid tipping the waitress, 'Do you know the Capuchins?'

'Uh uh,' Beth said, which is to be construed as an amiable negative. Not that there was any negativity in the woman I think I am going to call Beth Ann instead of Beth, because Beth Ann is easier to say than Beth, and I have to name her a fair few times before the end of her say in the story, which is sooner than you might think. Not that I have anything against her. I respect her very much as a person, and have done so from the commencement of the narrative.

'Wait,' she said. 'Are they monkeys who look after paralyzed people? They can brush their teeth. I don't know about the toilet so much.'

'No,' he said. 'They're priests with beards. In Ireland, they run parishes because of the shortage of priests.'

'Shortage of priests with or without beards?' she said. But that could just have been her sense of humour, dark and demi-mondaine. She had had two Hawaiian Anchor Steam beers at the cinema, one before the film and one during the intermission, which was why she had had to go to the toilet for most of the trial scene and two flashbacks. In fact, it was a bit disgusting to think of her mopping her bush with three or four folded perforations of Charmin toilet paper, with her thong down around her espadrilles and one or two corkscrew hairs embedded in the crusted cerise gusset. He was not going to think about that for one moment.

'Go on,' she said. 'I'm listening.'

Maybe she was Jewish or Mennonite. If she were, then rabbis and Mennonite elders have beards, so that she would logically draw a straight line, the shortest distance between two points, leading from religious life to facial growth. Not that Peter had anything against Jews or Mennonites. They are great when you get to know them, but the thing is, you never do get to know them. You are always made to feel like an outsider.

'The point is,' he said, 'they call their acolytes cappuccinos.' And to think that the cappuccino which got him to his paragraph had set him back three dollars, fifty cents. It was outrageous, and without waitress service, either. That in itself was a complete non-sequitur.

'What are acolytes?' she asked him. Well, it was a question. *Asked* is appropriate. *Asked* is all right. Also it is vernacular. Creative writing classes go on and on about synonyms. 'You've said *road* already. What about avenue, boulevard, cul-de-sac, *via dolorosa*?'

'Altar servers,' he told her. This, by the way, is elegant variation. You can find it on the Modern Languages Association style-sheet. It is no great mystery. 'Acolytes are altar servers.'

'And altar servers are …?' Beth queried.

The coffee was lukewarm already. He was going to bring it straight back. Peter felt momentarily yet momentously embittered and disheartened. If he were the president, he would press the thermonuclear button before any of the bodyguards could stop him. Besides, they would be looking at everybody except the president. So much for Central American Intelligence. It is a joke.

'Miss,' he said. Well, he said it out loud. You could say he called, but obviously in the vocal sense and not in the vocational. He didn't drop by. It wasn't Yahweh calling Samuel. Of course, the irony is that the waitress was no Miss. She was a Mizz. She had probably been shagged a thousand times. And was she going to service him? No way. That was because he had gone to the counter for the coffee, to circumvent the gratuity.

'You're always talking about priests,' said Beth Ann. 'You talked about priests before the film. You talked about priests during the film. Here we are, the film is over, the coffee shop is closing, night has fallen, and you are still talking about priests.'

'Well,' said Peter, 'the film was set in a seminary. I am just trying to orchestrate the thematics. After all, I am supposed to be a sexually inexperienced male who impersonates a religious vocation precisely in order to attract rogue females for the purposes of fellatio.'

'Are you going to be a priest?' said Beth Ann to Peter. I am building up to something big in an ascending series of disclosures and deferrals. Bear with me.

He needn't have bought the cappuccino at all. That was the last laugh, but his disheartenment lifted like a migraine, which is rather nice when it happens and even nicer when you put it that way. His embitterment, ditto.

'Yes,' he said. 'I am going to be a priest. I am going to be a priest unless, of course, some beautiful woman bewitches me with her toilette.' He had intended to say 'talents' but the cross rhyme between 'bewitch' and 'toilette' is very hard to resist if you have been born and bred in the assonantal tradition, and Peter had. Alternatively, he might have said 'mysticism', because of the cross rhyme between its sibilant fricative and the tarter in-breath of 'bewitch', like the distant lash of a switch on a chatelaine's ass deep in a Transylvanian castle. Besides, what would Beth Ann know about mysticism? She had never even heard of the strict observance of the Capuchins. She needed a few lessons.

Period; new paragraph. Pause in projected public reading of same.

She had been thinking about what he said all through the *explication de texte* that ends with the words 'strict observance of the Capuchins. She needed a few lessons.'

In fact, by way of elucidating recurrent compositional strategies for the interested auditor/lector/reader, the whole business about the assonantal tradition had as its *raison d'être* the provision of a space of silence for Beth Ann in and by means of which to consider and to contemplate Peter's revelation. She was, after all, a fee-paying sophomore and not a postgraduate on scholarship from Dublin.

'From Dublin?' she said. She ran her tongue over her lips hungrily. That was the sorbet. Or was it a non-sequitur?

'Yes,' he admitted, although it would be perfectly apparent to any discerning listener on the audiocassette, because they had taken such trouble over the accents.

'I thought you were from Limerick,' she said.

'That was the first draft,' he said. 'The only people from Limerick in the United States are illegal aliens, not postgraduates from Dublin on full scholarship.'

The prepositional revision is illuminating. Now there is less chance that anyone, even the discerning, will imagine that the scholarship was *from* Dublin rather than *to* an individual ordinarily resident there. A bit of a bursary from Baile Atha Cliath would go no great distance in a story set not a thousand miles from Silicon Valley where at any moment the President may or may not be running the palps of his fingers over the titanium buttons of the control panel while those awful obese American bodyguards are watching the wrong people, especially the Islamic lab attendants from the sub-continent. How our prejudices can disarm us!

'I think you're brilliant,' said Beth Ann. 'Here we are in the heartless heart of the fifth most affluent nation on the planet if we seceded from the Union. Everyone is fucking everyone else, even though the Pax Penicillin has proved to be a poignant phantasm with the advent of Aids. Everyone is getting their hole, which, as you explained in the cinema after I came back from the restroom, is an Irish idiom that indicates full coitus, and you, in the midst of so much radiant ass, are committing yourself to the most enig-matic vigil of all, the quest *par excellence*, the seeker's search for the sought-after.'

Her nipples had hardened like a nursing mother's under her Oxford button-down shirt. In fact, now that Peter looked at the garment again, its fabric seemed finer, flimsy, a chemise from Victoria's Secrets. He thought he had been feeling a draft.

'Unless,' he said, 'the Lord wants me to assume flesh, to incar-nate my project, to enter the historical process in the community of two bodies.'

'I would love to give you a hug,' Beth Ann said to him. 'I would love to give you a handjob. I only give handjobs on a first date. Blowjobs and I spit on a second date; blowjobs and I swallow on the third. I like an ascending series. An ascending series is more ... eschatological than a mere narrative. It graduates what would otherwise be linear.'

'The shortest distance between two points has its own pathos,' he said. 'To start with a handjob is to begin humbly. And humility is endless.'

'I feel really close to you,' she said. 'Now that you've told me you're going to be a priest, I can set aside the tedious stuff. I can set aside the gnosis, the agnosis, the negotiation. We meet, we greet. I come onto you, you come into me, we come in reverse alphabeti-cal order, I browse some of your philosophy books to determine your patronymic while you evacuate the broccoli from the pizza, because how were you to know that I'm allergic, and then I go home because I really wanted to watch *Rebecca* by myself. It's so shallow.'

'Not necessarily,' he said. 'The Lord can use our superficiality to deepen us.'

'You are so Christian,' she said. 'I honour you. I honour your intention to become a priest. I would not disrespect you by making a pass. You could lick my pussy all night long, until you had lockjaw, and we would not be as close as we are, just sitting here in a coffee shop two doors down from The Emerald cinema in Palo Alto, California, where we've just seen a movie called *Seminarians*, a denotative title, as it happens, in that the film is actually about young men studying for the priesthood in the course of an investigation by the DA's office into bullying in the workplace that is spearheaded by the same woman who plays the lead role in that other film we saw last week about the mad president who wants to press the button while his bodyguards are looking at everybody else. I say *film* because *film* is more of an Arthouse word than *movie* which is demotic, although *movie* is contextually accurate as current American usage. On the other hand, *film* is something I would say as a Jewish-American princess with pretensions.'

'Wait a minute,' Peter said. 'This is our first date. We have long since established that. Ergo, mention of another film/movie completely invalidates the premise, destabilizes the confidence of the listener/lector, depending on whether it's a public reading or a private reading and on whether the vocalization is live or on audiocassette in an automobile. I could say car, but I am long enough on the West Coast to have acclimated; and that acclimation is reflected in, and revealed by, localized diction. Additionally, you cannot know about the mad president. That is between me and my pre-frontal cortex. My narrator is not omniscient. Nor are you. Accordingly, you could only know about the mad president if you had heard me talking in my sleep, and we have never slept together. Anyway, I never talk in my sleep. I take a half Mogadon every night.

Finally and fundamentally, you are not a Jewish-American princess. You may be Jewish, you may be American, but you are not East Coast elite. Dream on, baby.'

'Well,' said Beth, a beautiful Hebrew word that means house and carries immediate connotations not only of an abode but of an abiding place, a base as in Bachelard's benign phenomenology.

'Well, what?'

This was Peter, but at a certain point you don't want to impede the forward impetus of the dialogue by interpolating redundant nominations, unless, of course, the repetition expedites a motive of biblical stateliness or of exponential ridicule; or both.

Her eyes had filled up with tears, or perhaps she was wearing contact lenses and he was smoking. Perhaps she had put the contact lenses in during the film when she went to the john.

'You know me as I am,' she said. 'There's no BS between us. We're like me and my girlfriends. I can even fart in front of them and not be embarrassed. We would just move on from there. I think I could pass wind in front of you this moment and not mind at all. That is the greatest compliment I have ever paid to a man.'

His eyes filled up as well. He was wearing contact lenses too, and had completely forgotten. That was not like him. He took off his tortoiseshell glasses, the NHS prescription spectacles he had inherited from his grandmother on the sad occasion of her sudden death at ninety-three, and put them away into the breast pocket of his reefer jacket.

'I love you, Peter' she said to him.

'I love you too,' he said. 'But my name is not Peter. It is too obvious. It is a canard. Even fictional human beings have fictional human rights.'

'Beth is too breathy,' she said. 'And I've never met a Jew called Beth anything. But there you are. Besides, you might have been called Rocky.'

'Uh uh,' he said, which may be construed as an amiable negative.

'Peter is black comedy; Rocky would be farce. There would be doors opening and closing all over the place. There would be ithyphallic undertones to Rocky or subliminal cephalic resonances from the Judeo-Christian texts.'

'We have transcended the sexual,' said the woman, who obviously had no notion what cephalic means. 'If we can transcend things, surely we can transcend the names of things. We are so much at one on this page of the story that I could mop my bush with three or four folded pieces of Charmin toilet-paper, with my thong down around my espadrilles and one or two corkscrew hairs embedded in the crusted cerise gusset.'

'I found that disgusting the first time,' Peter said. 'I am not into body fluids.'

'Me, neither,' she said. 'That's why I said what I said about the fart. If I wouldn't be embarrassed to fart in front of you, that would signify a relationship amounting almost to stereoscopic simultaneity, or, in the expression of the Hebrew Bible that Christians continue to denigrate as the Old Testament when there is nothing old about it, to Oneflesh. No hyphen. Period. New paragraph.'

'Sir?'

It was the waitress, exactly at the midpoint. Nobody had anticipated this. It was the very same as the scenario with the president. You are always looking in the wrong direction of the story. It is a classic Hitchcockian manoeuvre.

'Please don't smoke in the non-smoking section,' the waitress said. 'The non-smoking section is for non-smokers. That repetition is redundant, but redundancy functions rhetorically as a form of ridicule.'

'I'm not smoking,' Peter said. 'Neither is Beth. Enough is enough.'

'I could have sworn you were,' she said. 'I could have sworn I smelled smoke. There's no smoke without fire. Besides, my eyes had begun to fill up and displace my disposable contact lenses.'

Peter looked at her angrily.

'Why are you looking at me so angrily?' said the waitress. 'Have you something against South-East Asians?'

'Your being South-East Asian didn't even register with me,' said Peter. 'I thought you were Norwegian. Not that I have anything against Norwegians.'

'I may be a Norwegian national,' said the waitress, 'but I am racially S.E.A. I was airlifted out of Saigon when that city fell/was liberated, which is appropriate, in terms of my age-profile, for an anthropology teaching assistant who will celebrate/commemorate the twentieth-five anniversary of her neo-natal separation from her birth mother in two weeks' time.'

'You see,' said Peter. 'The little shit didn't even bother googling a Vietnamese patronymic for the birth mother. How long does it take to google these things? It takes seconds on broadband.'

'He called her Ng in an early draft,' the waitress said. 'Imagine that.'

'You'd know he was prejudiced,' said Beth-Ann to the waitress, 'There was a disclaimer at the very outset. And the Torah-Talmud thing is that a character only disclaims the desires he/she/it admits to privately. Surely you've heard?'

'I was listening on audiocassette,' said the waitress. 'The quality is very poor, but they have obviously worked on the accents. The Irish accent is spot on. I would place it within ten miles of Limerick. Norwegians shop there regularly.'

'He didn't even bother to give me eyebrows,' Peter said. 'I don't mind saying it.'

'They'll grow back,' the waitress said. 'He put an ST in my lunchbox. He has a thing about periods. It's so creepy. It's so prurient and patriarchal. Did you know that the Barbelo-Gnostics in the second century AD used to drink menses instead of communion wine at their nocturnal Eucharists? Because I didn't, either.'

'AD is so in your face,' said Beth. 'He knows perfectly well that the polite thing nowadays is to say common era.'

'AD might be a *mea culpa,* Peter said. 'Eyebrows is vindictive. You don't not think about eyebrows. They're staring you in the face.'

'I tell you what's staring you in the face,' said Beth. 'He has given me long axillary hair that is auburn, and all the fraternity jocks love to inhale it.'

'Wise up, woman,' said the waitress, who felt momentarily yet momentously disheartened and embittered. 'He has given me a cold sore. He has given me a period smell. I am supposed to have a whiff like the warm Mediterranean, and he thinks that is a compliment. He thinks that is the greatest compliment a man can pay a woman. Well, I can tell you this for nothing. I do not have a whiff like the warm Mediterranean. I do not have a whiff at all. Once upon a time perhaps, when we all lived happily ever after, I may have had a whiff. My mother, the Lord have mercy on her, as Norwegians say, had a nose like a bloodhound. But I have stopped having periods since the time I developed anorexia because my whole life is a complete non-sequitur.'

'He wants me to undergo a real religious conversion after only three blowjobs,' Peter said. 'In the second draft, he promised me hundreds of them. My grandfather used to call them gobblejobs, which is Hiberno-English argot, but that is beside the point. I get three blowjobs. Then I enter the Jesuits which takes fourteen fucking years before I'm ordained and rogue females find me irresistible again. By that time I'll have forgotten what it feels like to have an erection. The whole thing is completely unbelievable, as far as I'm concerned.'

'Peter. Beth. The South-East Asian waitress. It stinks,' said Beth to Peter and the waitress.

'Do you know what I would do if I was standing beside the presidential button on the control panel at the heart of the military industrial complex?' asked the teaching assistant. 'I would be tempted to press the damn thing. It wouldn't be the end of the world, as far as I'm concerned. It would certainly be better than having anorexia, a cold-sore and a salty whiff of the Mediterranean for the rest of my life.'

'I was supposed to self-harm in solidarity with El Salvador,' said Beth. 'That is completely foreign to my family values. Besides, El Salvador was twenty years ago. Nobody gives a shit about El Salvador anymore. He could have googled the Sudan in a split second.'

'Why don't we go home?' said the waitress. 'Why don't we shut the fuck up and go home? Home is a beautiful Hebrew word that means house and carries immediate connotations not only of an abode but of an abiding place, a base as in Bachelard's benign phenomenology.'

'Where is home and how can we get there?' Beth said. 'There is nothing outside the coffee shop except a multiplex called The Emerald, which is two doors up or down, depending on direction, and in which the current programme includes a Baltic movie with subtitles called *Seminarians,* and where many of this evening's audience, statistically if not socioculturally, are South-East Asians. Not that I have anything against South-East Asians, least of all those bi nationals who have adapted to the rigours of the Norwegian climate.'

'I would not go to that multiplex if I were bursting to go,' said the waitress. 'Bursting to go is a Hiberno-English idiom that refers to bladder control. I have inhaled it by osmosis.'

'Why would you not go there, even if, as you say, your bladder control was precarious?' said Peter, who sensed a complete non-sequitur.

'I went in there earlier,' said the waitress, 'because there are no toilets in this coffee shop. The doors advertising rest rooms are facsimiles stencilled on beauty board. So I went to The Emerald, because it would have taken me several pages of paragraphs to access the departmental john that is used by the anthropology TA's. There would have been no intelligible transition, and connections matter. There is such a thing as the subject-verb-object structure. The species arrived at it by dint of much travail. I object to being subjected verbally to anything else. Then, when I did go in, I found two corkscrew hairs embedded in the crusted cerise gusset of a thong. It was so disgusting.'

'That is not me,' said Beth. 'That is him talking. He has a thing about it. It is really gross. It is harassment in the workplace.'

'The specificity has a certain frisson,' said Peter. 'But he cannot even make a simple transition, such as I am making now, effortlessly, and without drawing attention in an attention-seeking manner, to my having done so. Remember when it took him three pages to get the trophy Oriental babysitter from the microwave to the tumble-dryer?'

'That was before my time,' said the South-East Asian waitress.

'*Moi aussi*,' said Beth. 'It must have happened while I was at French class.' Her accent was really beautiful. She was the business.

'Listen,' said Peter. 'That is the first *explication de texte* for ages. We are not forgotten.'

'You're right,' said Beth. 'It is the first *explication de texte* for quite some time.' But she said it even better than he had, after years at the Alliance Française, not to mention the timeshare in Èze.

'It is far too late in the day to bring in new cultural references,' said the waitress. 'That is page one territory.'

'He is off the lithium,' said Beth. 'That is the long and the short of it.'

'He's been off the lithium since Easter Sunday,' said the waitress. 'He is off the periodic table. He has even been writing verse again.'

'Say no more,' said Peter and Beth simultaneously, as it happened. If that was gospel, it was very bad news. It could kickstart all the old stuff again: the gnosis, the agnosis, the negotiation.

'I am supposed to walk home from here,' the waitress said. 'I am supposed to walk all the way to Menlo Park. How am I going to manage in these shoes?'

Sure enough, she was wearing espadrilles, the very same as Beth's/Beth Ann's.

'He only knows espadrilles,' the waitress said. 'Espadrilles and court shoes and slippers with pompoms. He knows moccasins but he cannot spell the word and therefore avoids it assiduously. I am not asking him to be a foot fetishist. I am only asking him to do some basic research.'

'Me too,' said Beth. 'He has me rooming with an elderly psychoanalyst who eats hash brownies because of irritable bowel syndrome. It is all so unlikely and heavy-handed. When I get home tonight, if I get home tonight, in the comprehensive absence of avenues, boulevards, cul-de-sacs and *viae dolorosae,* I encounter a deer drinking from the deep end of the swimming pool. He/she/it is antlered. The tongue tip radiates ripples on the heavily chlorinated and quite impotable surface of the water. Its slow, successive sips, in contradistinction to the cacophony of the actual swallowing of liquid from a stream/waterhole in such scenic areas as Yosemite wilderness, are dumbfoundingly silent. I am not to intervene to prevent gastric complications in a protected species. I am not to throw my espadrilles at it. I suppose I am to emit another whiff of the warm Mediterranean, forgetful of the fact that the cult black-and-white movie *Rebecca* is about to begin on PBS, and that nothing but caffeine can make my heart beat faster now.'

'But there has been absolutely no prior reference to deer,' Beth said, 'even by way of a natural decollation on the wall of this coffee shop or over the patented warm-air hand-dryer in the restroom of The Emerald. He has not even bothered his arse to invoke either *The Deer Hunter* or *The Yearling* or the classic Walt Disney cartoon *Bambi,* any one of which would have introduced the motif with an economy amounting to elegance.'

'There has been absolutely no prior reference to raccoons, either,' said Peter. 'But I am scheduled to have an epiphany involving racoons at some stage. What happens is, I go home, I am seized by a sudden desire to launder my linen during the small hours, I act upon this impulse, I enter the basement facility and am solicited immediately by two Bahai Iranian/Persians who are proselytizing on behalf of their syncretistic system after dark. In the aftermath of this importunity, as I air the freshened linen on the balcony of a high-rise student apartment, I notice a raccoon among the garbage at ground level. He/she/it has jammed their snout in an empty aluminum can, and the jagged metal serrations have pierced the membrane of the eye-lid and are fretting the retina irreversibly. Now what has that to do with anything?'

'Local municipal ordinances make it very unlikely that careless waste disposal would result in such injury,' said Beth. 'Besides, it is much more likely to have been a skunk.'

'It is just the *ex nihilo* negligence of the whole thing,' Peter said. 'He does not give a damn anymore.'

'On the other hand,' said Beth, 'it suits the priestly scenario. There is something solemn and sacerdotal about it. Whereas I have to go home and feed a fox. I kid you not. Not that I have anything against foxes. I make that disclaimer at the outset. I have never met a fox and I do not particularly want to. This fox comes into the kitchen and drinks pasteurized milk from the cat's saucer. But it must be a vixen, because there are cubs at the door. Now it is a whole menagerie. Yet I can smell zilch. Suddenly polyps have developed in my sinuses. Yet there is no hint of an antihistamine anywhere in the foregoing.'

'It is more than beastly,' Peter said. 'It is bestial. It is anencephalic, whatever that means.'

'We should do nothing,' the waitress said. 'The thing to do is to do nothing. Neither should we say anything. If we say nothing and do nothing, he will no longer have *carte blanche* to carry on as he likes. Our silence will silence him. There can be no *explication de texte* if there is no text to explicate.'

Her French accent was almost as good as Beth's. They had been locked in mimetic conflict for years, of course.

'He can still hear us thinking, is the problem,' Peter said. 'He still has a pass key to the paschal mystery of the prefrontal cortex.'

So one or other of them signalled to the waitress to turn up the volume of the anachronistic television set over the pinewood carrel, and she did. The president's voice was in perfect lip-synch with the movements of his mouth. He was surrounded by awful obese men, not that I have anything against obesity.

Pause. Period. New paragraph.

But this is what I love the most. This is the moment I have been waiting for. They are motionless. They are mute. Now and only now can I begin to hear the *a capella* of the dustmites in their eyebrows. Even in Peter's lack of them can I hear the sound of it, the soprano line and the solitary counter-tenor, where the follicles are multiplying minutely as I intimate them. I can even hear the doxology of the bacteria in his lower intestine, and the great Amen of the sperm awaiting Easter in the scrotal sac. Now and only now can I see the ultra scans of the great-grandchildren of the South-East Asian waitress. Now and only now can I touch her recessive genes with the palps of my fingers. Now and only now (and even then, only now and then) can I taste the molecular disturbance of Beth Ann's sorbet. Now and only now can I inhale by osmosis the warm saltwater whiff of the Mediterranean.

Now and only now. And even then, only now and then.

For I have made intelligible transitions and material connections. I have been involved in a character-building exercise. I have built characters. They are great when you get to know them, but the thing is, you never do get to know them. You are always made to feel like an outsider. But I am not going to think about that for one moment. It is a complete non-sequitur. I do not want to end up sleeping in my clothes. I do not want to shave my clerical beard. I do not want to end up with an encrusted cerise gusset. It is/was not necessarily mine. Besides, pronouns panic at a certain point in time. No, I am not going to think about that for one moment, unless the Lord wants me to assume flesh, to incarnate my project, to enter the historical process in the community of two bodies who communicate quite well.

This is true. I do not object to being subjected to verbs.

They are, after all, recurrent compositional strategies. They are dark and demi-mondaine disclosures and deferrals that lead me by drives and boulevards and cul-de-sacs and *viae dolorosae* to the auditor/lector/reader, to the paused pause button on the audiocassette, to the enigmatic vigil.

INFORMATION FOR THE USER

1. PRELIMINARY WARNING

Read this.

Do not read this.

Read this leaflet carefully.

Better still, read it carelessly.

It has been prepared and prescribed for you and for no one else. Do not offer it to others. It may destroy them, even if their pathology is the same as yours.

If you are a carer or you are assisting someone else in the search for sanity, please think twice about your first impressions before you give that person a dose of your own medicine.

This leaflet is about peace of mind (or trademark PM).

In this leaflet you will discover what peace of mind is and what it is used for. You will learn about the possible side effects of peace of mind and how to store it away safely out of the reach and the sight of children.

This leaflet can be read in silence in approximately fifty minutes. That is the average duration of a private session of psychotherapy; but this leaflet will not dump on parents or engage in the blood sport of blame. You (singular) are the greatest problem in your own life.

You will not have to pay the price of audition at this time. You may pay it beforehand or afterwards. You may pay it sooner or later. You may pay it in instalments or as one lump sum. You may pay it on the way out if you prefer not to pay it on the way in. All the exits are clearly marked: Entrance-Danger-Keep Out.

In other words, you are not being taken to the cleaner's, cherished reader. You are not being taken to the cleanser's, either. You are not being cleaned or cleansed or even laundered in a maudlin manner. You are not being washed or hand-wrung. You are not being hung out to dry. Your shirts will not surrender on the washing line. They will not be white as a sheet in the storm of the slow cycle.

Instead, the purpose of this leaflet is to pray that the Holy Spirit will renew the face of your dirt and restore you to the pure filth of the world. That is our beautiful duty.

Lord, hear your predators as we prey.

The response to the bidding prayer of this leaflet is commonly *Amen*, but the more inclusive *Amended* or *Mended* is preferred. *Minded* is also acceptable, and, in England, a discreetly non-productive clearing of the throat that sounds like *Ahem*.

You may now respond in your own time and place.

—

FIRST THE HOW

DOCTOR: How are you today?

PATIENT: Not too bad, Doctor.

DOCTOR: Not too bad. Not *too* bad.

PATIENT: No.

DOCTOR: Sorry?

PATIENT: I mean yes. Not too bad.

DOCTOR: They say that in French too.

PATIENT: What?

DOCTOR: Not too bad.

PATIENT: Do they?

DOCTOR: They do. Where I go. In Cathar territory.

PATIENT: Right.

DOCTOR: They say *Pas mal*. *'Ca va?'* says the butcher, the baker, the candlestick-maker. *'Pas mal,'* you say back.

PATIENT: Not bad.

DOCTOR: Exactly.

PATIENT: No. I mean your accent.

DOCTOR: *Merci, monsieur.*

PATIENT: Welcome.

DOCTOR: Another odd bod, that one. *Merci. Merci* for thank you.

PATIENT: Why's that?

DOCTOR: *Merci* sounds like Mercy. *Merci Dieu* sounds like Mercy, God. More terror than thanks, I always thought. Of course, I did Pass French in the Leaving Certificate.

PATIENT: How did you get into medicine with Pass French?

DOCTOR: It was different in those days. *Merci Dieu.*

PATIENT: They say the opposite, actually.

DOCTOR: The opposite of what?

PATIENT: They say *Dieu merci*.

DOCTOR: I see. Well, they're not very religious where I go. The church is on all the postcards, but I looked into the confession box and what did I find?

PATIENT: What did you find?

DOCTOR: I found a vacuum cleaner.

PATIENT: A vacuum cleaner?

DOCTOR: I wanted to tell my neighbour, but I couldn't think of the French for vacuum cleaner. Do you know what the French for a vacuum cleaner is?

PATIENT: It'll come back to me.

DOCTOR: I tried *Oover*, without the H. Wasn't *Oover* anyway. Or *Nilfisque*. As well as that, I still have to think a sentence through, word by word, in English before I can say it in French. I can't go straight to French.

PATIENT: I can't go straight to English.

DOCTOR: You can't go straight to English?

PATIENT: Not really. No Irishman can.

DOCTOR: I see. That's very interesting.

PATIENT: You go diagonally.

DOCTOR: Diagonally?

PATIENT: A joke.

DOCTOR: Not bad.

PATIENT: Not too bad. Thank God.

DOCTOR: Not too bad at all at all. Is not too bad a bit better than not too good? Or a lot better? Or a whole lot better?

PATIENT: What do you mean?

DOCTOR: Or is it much, much, much better? Is it the best you can be in this worst of all possible worlds?

PATIENT: Not too bad is not too bad, thank God.

DOCTOR: Thank God.

PATIENT: Yes.

DOCTOR: You're always thanking God.

PATIENT: Am I? Thank God for that.

DOCTOR: You know yourself. You're always at it. The small print at the end of the contract. The contract contracting. Terms and conditions. They used to write *PG* in letters. They used to write *Yours in JC*. It was always *TG* in diaries. *TG* beside the moon waxing; *TG* beside the moon waning. '*Was friends with X. A good day, TG.*'

PATIENT: Yes.

DOCTOR: When you say it, though, it's more than 'like'. It's more than 'you know' or 'you know what I mean'. It's more than when they say 'innit' in London; every second word is 'innit' over there. It's more than when some fellow in Sallynoggin says fuck at the end of every sentence. Thank God.

PATIENT: Yes.

DOCTOR: When is it Tourette's and when is it poetry? That's what I wonder. When is it an intellectual tic and when is it total insight? 'I'm feeling great, thank God.' No problem with that. But six weeks ago, here it is, word for word, in the red accordion file.

'I am in hell, thank God, and I am going to die, thank God.' That was the day you ate all the cheese you'd been stashing away. But you didn't die of the cheese; and you could have, on the tablets. You could have died or been brain-damaged if the cheese had been better quality, not processed. If it had been runny Brie or feta. You vomited it all up in the handicapped toilet and then you went and ate the vomit off the tiles and you still didn't die the second time.

PATIENT: Thank God.

DOCTOR: Now you're talking. Now-you-are-talking.

PATIENT: Always and everywhere.

DOCTOR: Always and everywhere?

PATIENT: Thanking.

DOCTOR: Thanking God?

PATIENT: Yes. Always and everywhere thankful.

DOCTOR: A motto. A mantra.

PATIENT: Yes. A and E.

DOCTOR: A and E?

PATIENT: A for always. E for everywhere. A and E.

DOCTOR: As in Accident and Emergency? As in Casualty?

PATIENT: Just a coincidence. As in *Semper et Ubique*. A slogan.

DOCTOR: My daughter says Omigod. Omigod this; Omigod that. Omigod, Daddy-dear. But that's not Moses on Mount Sinai. That's MTV. That's her iTube and her YouPhone. That's her voice going up at the end of a sentence like an American. But who is this God you're so terrified of you have to be thanking him, thanking him, thanking him, all the time?

2. PEACE OF MIND (or PM)

Peace of mind (or trademark PM) is a placebo. It contains: the smell of fresh toast, serotonin, the alcohol molecule, REM sleep, silly memories, phrases from Mozart, the scent of infancy (especially the nape of the new born neck), nicotine, the burial of the father, the feel of your mother's cashmere cardigan with her own eau-de-toilette, and the manual male orgasm with or without stapled periodicals.

Other ingredients in peace of mind may include the death of enemies as a temporary antidepressant. Urinating and defecating on other people can be very consoling too, but it should be carried out in conjunction with a regime of aromatherapy under the supervision of a medical doctor who is also a reversible tattoo artist. If you must self-harm, please do it in henna.

Peace of mind is used to treat the following conditions:

Moderate to severe insight;

The species' obsessive-compulsive search for meaning;

Minor episodes of a sudden fundamental terror at the thought of it all;

Minor episodes of a sudden fundamental euphoria at the thought of it all;

Major episodes of guilt, grief, and other good things without which we would not be *sapient sapient* or even *sentient sentient*, but simply *homo homo*;

The gut feeling of gastric crisis, unrelated to sugar lows, swine fever, or slimming laxatives;

The knowledge of good and evil;

The second law of thermodynamics, if it is found to be non-falsifiable;

Purging and persecuting.

In conjunction with antihistamines, Australian white wine and gas-fired central heating, peace of mind may also be used to treat:

The counterfactual fantasies of the Sermon on the Mount in the Gospel according to Matthew;

The involuntary ruminative rituals of touching our forehead, belly-button and nipples when we pass the large, listed buildings that are hard to heat where consenting female adults gather on Sunday mornings among many plus signs to hum in unison to their favourite imaginary friend for a period approximating the length of a single session of psychotherapy or the total duration of this outburst.

Peace of mind may be used to anaesthetize the tender bewilderment of each and every stage of human weight gain – breakdown, breakup, and brokenness itself – between adolescence and dementia. It is safe in small doses for embryos and for elders in a vegetative stupor. The biochemical mnemonic may be helpful here: Peace to the goo-goo and the gaga only; the ghastly bodies in between must be agog.

However, PM is not always recommended for pregnant women. Peace of mind can pass through the placenta and give the foetus ideas above its station. Breastfeed gingerly.

Come, Holy Spirit, and renew the face of our dirt. Restore us to the pure filth of the world.

Lord, hear your predators as we prey.

You may now respond in your own time and place with *Amen* or *Ahem*.

NOW THE WHERE

PATIENT: Where do we go from here, Doctor?

DOCTOR: Where do we go from here? You think this is a journey?

PATIENT: Isn't it?

DOCTOR: Beginnings; muddles; ends. Maplines; lifelines. A mystery tour. In the midst of all this terror and euphoria, you're so … empirical. There has to be a story.

PATIENT: There is a story. Once upon a time, there was a man. He was living happily ever after.

DOCTOR: Then one day.

PATIENT: Then one day. 'Then one day' is the most terrible phrase in the English language.

DOCTOR: It's not as terrifying as 'Care in the Community'.

PATIENT: You have me there.

DOCTOR: Still: 'then one day'. The plot thickens; the cemeteries incinerate. I blame the Booker prize. I blame the Puffin Club. I blame novels.

PATIENT: Novels?

DOCTOR: The interaction of character and incident to produce a coherent narrative. That's not life. That's literature. Or a curriculum vitae. All fibs; all fiction. You've spent too long in Waterstone's, dear boy.

PATIENT: Hodges Figgis.

DOCTOR: Tweedledum, Tweedledee. What are you reading?

PATIENT: *The Hunchback of Notre Dame.*

DOCTOR: My point precisely.

PATIENT: What are you reading?

DOCTOR: *Marriage, Monogamy and the Thermonuclear Family,* (Volume 47). Edited by twelve psychogeriatric cellbates in the Society of Jesus.

PATIENT: I want to go back, Doctor.

DOCTOR: To Hodges Figgis? Or to Waterstone's?

PATIENT: To my parents.

DOCTOR: All roads lead to home. That's novels again! If you feel like Solzhenitsyn, there has to be a gulag. There has to be a motive, a message, a meaning. The universe must be a crime scene and not simply an accident waiting to happen.

PATIENT: My father exhaled his cigarette smoke through his nostrils with his head down. My mother through her mouth with her face lifted. Everything made sense in their living room in front of a blazing television.

DOCTOR: If you imitate normality, you will become normal. That's your man. That's your mantra.

PATIENT: We watched colour films in black and white. We were in black and white too. When the picture turned to a ping at close-down, we could see ourselves in brown and taupe for a moment, staring at the screen.

I saw *The Bridge on the River Kwai* again a few weeks ago, but it was better in black and white. So was *The Guns of Navarone*.

DOCTOR: When I say novels, I mean films too. And plays. What I mean is *stories*. We aren't stories. We are histories. We are stranger than fiction, as Our Lord used to say. You follow?

PATIENT: I follow.

DOCTOR: The life you follow is stranger than the life you lead. The life you lead is neither here nor there. The life you lead is anecdotal. The life you follow follows you everywhere.

PATIENT: Tell me about it.

DOCTOR: On the other hand, you can bake beautiful apple tarts. You couldn't do that before. You can make a Blindcraft light shade now or a four-legged stool for a toddler. Opportunity knocks; knocks too can be opportune in occupational therapy. Plus you can write with your left hand because of what you did to your right hand with the secateurs in the potting shed. You're ambidextrous, almost. These are all … anecdotes.

PATIENT: I am more than I mean. That is the worst thing of all.

DOCTOR: That is the worst thing of all. You are more than you mean.

PATIENT: I have a history.

DOCTOR: You have a history. For the time being, at any rate.

PATIENT: If you have a history, do you have a future?

DOCTOR: You can have a future history. I can foretell that.

PATIENT: You can foretell that?

DOCTOR: I can foretell everything except the past. The past is always changing.

PATIENT: And what can you foretell for me?

DOCTOR: There'll be a huge loading on any insurance policy or mortgage endowment. So what? The average life expectancy of an EU citizen retiring at sixty-five is only two years anyway.

PATIENT: Right

DOCTOR: You won't be able to adopt that oriental baby girl. So what? Foreign adoptions will probably be the subject of criminal tribunals in thirty years' time. Hounded grandees flocking into court with their heads covered or their pixels blurred, and a flash photography caveat on the newscasts for the epileptic community.

PATIENT: Right.

DOCTOR: Public-sector promotion is out of the question. So what? You'll be energized by grievance until you retire. A decent dose of self-pity is a spur to sanity.

Now I must call a halt. In fact, I must call my daughter. My daughter in France. Do you know my poor opposable thumb is sore from texting that brat?

3. CONTRAINDICATIONS

Peace of mind may harden your heart. If you feel your heart hardening, talk in confidence to your personal trainer. Avoid the breaststroke, all tumble-turns, and watch a compilation of your favourite television commercials again and again and again. Foremost among them in present polls are the Milk Flake ad in 1971and the Lady Loves Milk Tray, third series.

Peace of mind may cause calcification of the bones of the inner ear so that you may listen intently but just not get it. If you cannot read this leaflet properly, for example, you may be suffering from too much peace of mind. PM can promote the accumulation of wax in the eardrum such that you hear voices and the crow family in mono or not at all, not at all.

You should not drive or be driven or open your Facebook account in this state.

Peace of mind may give you tunnel vision or peripheral vision or religious visions, whether A, B, C, or D (Abrahamic, Buddhist, Confucian, Daoist). If you feel that you cannot see beyond your own septum, talk to your psychiatrist. Do not bother talking to psychologists. They may have doctorates but they are not doctors. They cannot write prescriptions. What use it that? Pharmacy is the answer to most fears. Barley came before wheat, booze before bread. Did you know that? Screw psychologists before they screw you.

Dropped or droopy eyelids can also indicate toxic peace of mind. Use gummy stamps from a reputable philatelist, workplace Post-its cut to size, or small slivers of Scotch tape to prop up your eyelids and see the world for what it is: an enormity. That is how Aristotle Onassis coped with his condition, and he could have paid for any surgical procedure if it had existed.

Peace of mind may prevent inner commotion, existential tremors of a pseudo-Parkinsonian kind, conscience-stricken seizures, passion and compassion, the acoustic of three-in-the-morning deep in the mortgaged dormitory suburbs. PM may also make you speechify when you should be speechless, a chatterbox when you should be shattered. If you are gibbering ten to the dozen as I am now, if you are only tongue-tied when you are French kissing, there is a strong likelihood that you have nothing whatsoever of any worth to say.

Peace of mind may prevent internal bleeding, cardiac arrhythmia, and weeping wounds. These are great losses in the long run, as are anxiety, impulse, dread, exhilaration, shame, and desire. The greatest loss of all is the sense of loss itself: the looking back, the lingering, the belatedness, the saline tears of Lot's wife and Eurydice's husband. We would not be human if we were not the present absentees of our own existence, the illegal aliens of the material realm.

Peace of mind may inhibit that sinking feeling, which is core to our spirituality and to the slow cultural evolution of our religious infrastructure, the ecumenical church of upright primates. If the sinking feeling returns, double your dose of PM and eat salt-and-vinegar instead of cheese-and-onion Tayto crisps. Mouthwash frequently out of consideration for others.

Peace of mind may stimulate self-confidence and other morbid failings. It may have an eventual contraceptive effect. If you are serenely sleeping spoons with a woman you would have shagged in the dog in a Renault 4 twenty-five years ago in Ballyferriter at the full moon, you are unlikely to have a runt in your litter at this late stage of your docile, your indolent fertility.

Peace of mind may increase or decrease sexual function, as if it weren't functioning perfectly well already. It may cause long-standing erections which you are impotent to do anything about or it may potentiate erectile dysfunction, whichever. I say tomatoes, you say tomatoes.

It may also retard genius and other related disabilities like self-effacement, modesty, and mindfulness.

Come, Holy Spirit, and renew the face of our dirt. Restore us to the pure filth of the world.

Lord, hear your predators as we prey.

You may now respond in your own time and place with *Amen* or *Ahem*.

THEN THE WHO

PATIENT: Who are all the priests?

DOCTOR: The priests?

PATIENT: In here. All the priests in this hospital. All the patients pretending to be chaplains and not inmates. It's like the segregation unit for the paedophiles down on the Curragh. A priest smoking at every sand bin in the corridor.

DOCTOR: They're safer in here. You're safer in here. In here is mental illness, but out there, out there is madness. You can treat mental illness, but you can't treat madness.

PATIENT: What madness?

DOCTOR: The current craze. Ireland as Auschwitz under the swastika sign of Saint Brigid. That madness. We're running out of things to hate. That's why I love the mentally ill, dear boy. They only hate themselves, and they're allowed to smoke. Normal people hate everyone else bar none, and they grind their teeth on their Nicorette chewing gum. It's a collective psychosis. You can't treat a collective psychosis. All you can do is hide. All you can do is find a safe place, a safe house. That's what asylum means in Greek: a safe house.

PATIENT: What am I hiding from?

DOCTOR: Your perishables. We've sorted every dry recyclable, every plastic container, every Sunday supplement. It has to be your perishables. Sloppy, slippery stuff, somewhere between compost and diarrhoea. Excrement marks the spot. It always does. We stink, therefore we are.

PATIENT: What are they hiding from?

DOCTOR: Who?

PATIENT: The priests. The childless fathers. The fatherless children.

DOCTOR: They're hiding from the posse. The impossible posse. The only way to be ahead of the posse is to be part of the posse, but they don't know that. They're pillars of salt and not pillars of state. The columns inch towards them. The columnists surround them. It's the Little Big Top. It's Babi Yar. It's bogeyman time. It's the Celtic Terror. Or maybe …

PATIENT: Maybe?

DOCTOR: They're waiting for their mammies to die before they quit the ministry. The trouble is, those witches with their bitch-craft are good for a century. They're not just Marian; they're mari-nated. I curse their corporate uterus.

PATIENT: Can I ask you?

DOCTOR: Ask away.

PATIENT: Are you a practising Catholic?

DOCTOR: Am I a practising Catholic? I'm certainly a practiced one. Perhaps I'm a practical one. If I look at the writing on the wall behind your head, I discover to my amazement that I'm a licensed catholic practitioner. Is that the same thing?

PATIENT: Nobody practises anymore. Nobody pretends.

DOCTOR: That's because rehearsals are over. Even the dress rehearsal. This is your big day. It's your first night as a committed Christian. You've been committed by your wife, your brother, your children, and your chiropodist. That's a lot of commitment, and you're feeling stage fright. Besides, people with your particular predilection tend to be smells-and-bells sorts. I kid you not.

PATIENT: But you can help me?

DOCTOR: Of course I can help you. You're ill enough to be helped. Isn't that wonderful? Pity those who aren't. Pity the poor folk on the commuter trains, hanging from the handcuffs of the straps on a Monday morning. Pity the poor folk on the gridlocked motorways on a Monday evening. Pity those who come twentieth and twenty-first in a class of thirty students. Not for them the scholarship programme. Not for them the special needs assistant. They are alone with their ordinary torments. You are the lucky one. You should be grateful.

PATIENT: How can you help me?

DOCTOR: How can I not?

PATIENT: My life is pear-shaped. My tears are pear-shaped. My shit is pear-shaped. The only thing in my life that isn't pear-shaped is the fruit on the pear-tree where the partridge sits.

DOCTOR: Your life isn't pear-shaped. It's not oblong. It's round.

PATIENT: I didn't say it was oblong.

DOCTOR: I always thought oblong was pear-shaped. Is it obloid?

PATIENT: No.

DOCTOR: What is it so?

PATIENT: Pear-shaped is a tapered sphere in solid geometry.

DOCTOR: Of course, I failed General Level Maths in the Leaving Certificate.

PATIENT: How many subjects did you pass in the Leaving Certificate?

DOCTOR: Tapered sphere is pretty, but let's say a circle instead. Your life is a circle. Because it's a circle and not a straight line, you're afraid it's a zero. You play with the sign of nothing at all like a child with a hula hoop. Actually, it's rather beautiful to watch. The Kleenex, you know, are not there just for the client.

PATIENT: It may be beautiful to watch, but it is not beautiful to be.

DOCTOR: Try to be kinder to your cortex. Weigh yourself in the morning and not in the evening. Be still and know that none of us is God, thank God. If you have to pray, pray that you'll be spared any other significant human experience for the duration. There are three-hundred-and-sixty degrees in a circle; but there are three-hundred-and-sixty-five days in the year. Stitches drop. Fittings alter. Things get messy. They are meant to.

PATIENT: I thought you failed Maths in the Leaving Cert.

DOCTOR: Some things get beaten into you. In a manner of speaking. Now I must text my daughter in France. The sat nav tells her that she's reached her destination, but she's just pulled into a war-graves cemetery somewhere in the middle of nowhere.

4. HOW TO REGULATE YOUR PEACE OF MIND

Peace of mind is a mood stabilizer. It should always be taken with a pinch of salt, preferably lithium. Pinches of such salt may induce an initial sense of buoyancy and flotation, familiar to those who have bathed in the Dead Sea and bobbed about in its swampy, stinking surfaces, two thousand feet below sea level, for year after year after year, till their great-grandchildren grow beards as long as rope ladders; but this sensation will eventually mature into the strong sense that you are lying eternally on a memory-foam mattress beside an infinity pool, which ends in a frozen waterfall, a cliff-hanger on ice under skies that are parting at the speed of continents, a micromillimetre per millennium. Your renal func tion will be grievously insulted at this point. That is to say, your kidneys will be wizened giblets. If and when this happens, switch from liquid anaesthesia to pot. Lebanese Red in biscuit form is recommended over inhalation of weed for respiratory reasons.

Peace of mind in the form of pinches of salt like lithium should be taken with lots of water, either still or sparkling (Please buy Irish). Yes, yes, yes, this will bloat a woman's biomass to the point of obesity, but a third of something is better than a half of nothing, the perfect is the enemy of the good, that's life, *mar a deirtear*, and let it be said that anything worth doing is worth doing poorly, et cetera, et cetera, as the American Psychiatric Association voted by acclamation at their EGM car-boot sale on the Great Blasket in 2020.

Peace of mind should never be taken lying down. We are a species who think on our feet. Take your tablets in the living room, standing tall, back straight, wearing a necktie and button-down collar, looking at the black-and-white mantelpiece memories of the dead and the dying and the undead on the marble slab of the fireplace over the smoke and embers of your barbecue in a bag.

Swallow your peace of mind whole. Do not chew on it. You may be a ruminant, but you do not have the stomach.

Do not use your peace of mind to live in the minute. That is what our zoological colleagues in other classes and categories do. It is what aardvarks and geckoes, hooded cobras and store-cattle do – in fact, all animate entities bar us. We are something else altogether, God forgive us.

Do not use your peace of mind to predict the past. The past is always ahead of us, out of sight, out of mind, out of minding; mutating, mutating. The past has an inexhaustible future going forward.

Do not use your peace of mind unless you have to. Otherwise you will degenerate into an after-dinner speaker, a beloved public figure, a national treasure, a hardy laureate, a person who feels that he, she, or it is entitled to inherit his, her or its *curriculum vitae*. A *curriculum vitae* is the opposite of eternal life. Only the virtues that ruin us are real.

Flagellate yourself. This is how sperm start out, by self-flagellation, and look where they end up. In the best possible place:

the portals of debutantes, the dowager vaginas of our sweet sego-
tias, Lord have mercy.

On which note: Come, Holy Spirit, renew the face of our dirt.
Restore us to the pure filth of the world.

Lord, hear your predators as we prey.

You may now respond in your own time and place with *Amen*
or *Ahem*.

THE WHEN

DOCTOR: When was the red telephone?

PATIENT: The red telephone was when I got lost in the North of
Ireland.

DOCTOR: You left the path and you went into the greenwood.

PATIENT: I left the path and I went into a dark forest. I couldn't see
the wood for the trees. Every signpost pointed to atrocities in the
same language. Every place name ran like colitis down the callipered
legs of the metal posts. Wherever I turned, I came upon myself.

DOCTOR: What were you doing there in the first place?

PATIENT: I was buying Cadbury's chocolate Buttons.

DOCTOR: That was when you were little. What were you doing in
the North of Ireland?

PATIENT: I was buying copies of *Mayfair* and *Men Only*. Those
women would be grannies now with bright blonde hair and lasered
eyes.

DOCTOR: That was when you were an adolescent. What were you
doing in the North of Ireland?

PATIENT. I was buying contraceptives. I was buying Trojans; but
the Trojans lost.

DOCTOR: That was when you were married. What were you doing in the North of Ireland?

PATIENT: I was having dental implants on the cheap. My mouth was like stalagmites. I couldn't shriek.

DOCTOR: And you saw the red telephone?

PATIENT: I saw the red telephone. Deep in their dark territory. With a manse to left and right of me. Where even the Methodists are meant to be Antichrist.

DOCTOR: Never mind the Methodists. Tell me about the telephone. What was it like?

PATIENT: It was like the lantern in *Narnia*. It was lucent; it was light. My cardiac muscle opened like an orchid. In I went.

DOCTOR: You went in?

PATIENT: I went into the tabernacle. The reasonable, the right-thinking Ark.

DOCTOR: You were home again. Home again.

PATIENT: It did not smell of urine or cheroots or the anthracite of corpses. It smelled of the *Golden Pages*, of the Esperanto of suitors, and the deep decency of England. I inhaled it like hash, so I did. I weed myself a little, like a dachshund, with regret and gratitude. The North roared at me through its mullions with abominable breath, like dolmens round my childhood the Northern poets loomed; but the red telephone rang true. Its pitch was perfect: mild, mindful, moon-bathing. I said: '*Buíochas le Dia.*'

DOCTOR: Thank God. Irish was obviously compulsory in the Leaving Certificate, but it could be compensated.

PATIENT: Not Thank God. More like Thanks be to God. It's a pious ejaculation. It's the burst of breath in the *Buí*.

DOCTOR: But you went and you weed there, damn it. You went and you weed. Which dovetails, doesn't it, with the dream of everybody sitting down to dinner, everybody bending over and turning away from each other like they were saying the rosary in the old days, bottom to bottom, and then shitting on the place-settings together. You see how they dovetail, dream number one and dream number two?

PATIENT: I did not dream the red telephone. It imagined me.

DOCTOR: But you dream the impossible dream repeatedly.

PATIENT: I dream that everybody brings something to the table. In a rational state, we'd shit together and eat apart. We'd fast as one and we'd breakfast by ourselves.

DOCTOR: But why in the invalid's toilet? Why not in the men's? Why not in the women's?

PATIENT: The invalid's toilet is twinned with a torture chamber in Argentina. I write my Amnesty International notelets there between the chains and the hoist.

DOCTOR: Do you see yourself as an invalid? Do you see yourself as a victim? Are you part of the *veni-vidi*-victim chic?

PATIENT: Did you do Latin in the Leaving Cert?

DOCTOR: It was obligatory long ago. In the good old days when things were obligatory and you obliged.

PATIENT: I take my meals into the toilet. The fish smells of chicken. The chicken smells of fish. Bread is asbestos. The plastic cutlery snaps like ice-cream sticks. It makes a sound like the fraction of the host before the bread-line forms at Mass. My wrist leers up at me.

DOCTOR: You're afraid they're listening.

PATIENT: I turn on the taps so no one will hear me do what I have to do in the toilet. I turn on the cold tap and the hot tap and the faucet tap to drink from. The faucet tap to drink from is the loudest, but it stops after fifteen seconds.

DOCTOR: You're afraid they'll hear the terrible sounds of the loo.

PATIENT: I activate the warm-air hand dryer. I step into the cubicle, lock the stall door, lift the lid of the seat in one silent, succinct motion, depress the chrome lever, flush the bowl loudly, whistle something Country and Western …

DOCTOR: 'Tie a Yellow Ribbon'?

PATIENT: Or 'Sylvia's Mother.' Sometimes 'I Wish All My Children Were Babies Again.'

DOCTOR: I love that one. And the B-side: 'You Never Can Do Wrong In A Mother's Eyes.'

PATIENT: I whistle something country and western so they'll think I'm at the urinal, not in the you-know-where about to you-know-what. The ghastly, God-awful sounds.

DOCTOR: And then?

PATIENT: Then I do it.

DOCTOR: Good.

PATIENT: I open my lips. My mouth proclaims my teeth.

DOCTOR: Good man.

PATIENT: I eat. I ingest. I wolf down.

DOCTOR: Good man yourself.

PATIENT: The broccoli. The burger. Pigs' trotters. Sheep's brains. Mutton dressed as ram. The Lamb of God.

DOCTOR: Down the gullet into the gut and on to the winking sphincter. More power to you.

PATIENT: The chewing is drowned out in the lavatorial orchestra. The mastication goes unnoticed as the waters rise around me. The cruelty of incisors is not heard. The swallow itself is inaudible, lubricant drool and saliva. The drip-feed; the drop zone. The sound of a man consuming; the sound of a man consumed. The sound of a mammal cannibalizing creation.

5. MONITORING YOUR PEACE OF MIND
Stop your present course of peace of mind and consult your doctor immediately if:

You're a forty-five-year-old alpha-female who wants to marry and have a baby;

You're a forty-five-year-old alpha-male whose children are bonding blithely with their new father, fuck him, give him pancreatic cancer, God, four weeks and whoosh, he's soot in the columbarium. You pass the party balloons on the wrought-iron wicket gate of your late-Victorian semi, a twenty-year tracker; you do not go past. You do not pass Go. You listen to the pizzicato of the drizzle in your pre-frontal cortex. You hear the chromatic harmonica of the wind.

Stop your present course of peace of mind and consult your doctor immediately if:

You're a parent of any gender whose child is power-walking through the darkness past the photographs of missing kittens and disappeared teenagers;

You're a parent.

You're a child.

You're a married child, yet your bus ticket says: 'Single Adult. One Use, One Way.'

You're alive and ill and living in the world. Your brain has a mind of its own. Your mind is electrical offal. Your mind is offal with voltage.

You realize that the weight of the world on your shoulders is the chipped crash helmet of your own consciousness and not just the force of gravity, although the pressure of the latter does indeed amount, more or less, to three tusked Indian elephants on top of your tonsure at any one time.

Your guardian angel has died and risen again in a *papier maché* impersonation as the angelical *Guardian* newspaper. You take it into bed with you where your wife used to lie through her teeth, two Belfast crowns that cost a K. You lay it down, a scroll of the law, beside the poker and the flash lamp.

You walk home instead of withdrawing money for the Dart fare to Balbriggan because there's a schizophrenic with strawberry-blonde hair sitting under the ATM in D'Olier Street with a sign that says *I thirst* pinned like a bib to her blouse. Is that copy from a Guinness Lite commercial or something Jesus said at the wedding feast in Cana?

You count the CCTVs on the way to work, on the way from work, at work, out of work, between jobs, the grey and grainy multiplication of your three-piece suit subtracting among the hoodies and the pyjama bottoms and the high heels, among the starved secretaries in their pinstripe skirts-to-the-knee and Nike sneakers.

For the purposes of this outburst, male baldness can be every bit as bad as bereavement. Worse, in fact.

For the purposes of this outburst, you may pray to the Father and the Son or to the Mother and the Daughter. We are all in this together, for fuck's sake.

For the purposes of this outburst, peeing in a wetsuit to warm it up before you go into the great unwashed of the deep is not a perversion. It is just a bit kinky. Live and let live.

For the purposes of this outburst, heterosexuality is regarded as a statistically overrepresented, non-pathological variant on the gay, lesbian, bisexual, transgender, and queer community norms, to be accorded equal solemnity and self-importance.

Finally, for the purposes of this outburst, fundamental human rights to outpatient care are accorded to our synanthropic brothers and sisters in the bonobo, chimpanzee, and dolphin traditions. As a result of the State *versus* the Equality Commission and Max the three-legged dachshund (2011), pet cemeteries may now be incorporated sensitively into human crematoria, but the sepulchres should be proportionate to the dimensions of the deceased (see the Office of Public Works *versus* Harry the Hamster and the monumental treadmill in Glasnevin, 2010).

Come, Holy Spirit, and renew the face of our dirt. Restore us to the pure filth of the world.

Lord, hear your predators as we prey.

You may now respond in your own time and place with *Amen* or *Ahem*.

FINALLY THE WHY

DOCTOR: She forgot to take her contacts out and to put her tablet in. That's how smashed she was after the pre-debs. Woke up in the afternoon with a migraine and a missing M.A.P.

PATIENT: What's M.A.P.?

DOCTOR: Morning-after pill. Mutual assured peace of mind. Truly, truly I say to you: He who hath children hath given hostages to fortune. I'd already spent a few grand on having her jaw reconstructed by a plastic surgeon to make it less masculine. Take out the wisdoms. Deepen the dimples.

But why am I telling you these things? I'm the patriarch; you're the prodigal.

PATIENT: We're swapping crosses. It's an Irish pastime. Go on.

DOCTOR: Where was I?

PATIENT: Stansted. Ryan Air. Thursday the nineteenth.

DOCTOR: If you don't book ages in advance, they crucify you. It cost as much as Aer Lingus to Heathrow, and then, to add insult to injury, they took my aftershave away. Christian Dior Eau Sauvage in the duty-free. The large atomizer. You can only get it in Brown Thomas otherwise, and when am I in town?

PATIENT: Rarely.

DOCTOR: Never. Never.

PATIENT: How was she afterwards?

DOCTOR: She was all right. She was fine. We did the business. Then I took her to *The Lion King*. Paid through the nose for the dress circle, of course. But she loved it. The mango and raspberry ice-cream from the cone was running down her hand onto her lucky-charm bracelet. She was mesmerized.

PATIENT: And now?

DOCTOR: A1.

PATIENT: Thank God.

DOCTOR: Absolutely. At least I know where she is. Wouldn't want her in Hersonissos or pole-dancing in Puerto Banus. The stories you hear.

PATIENT: They're all ... anecdotal.

DOCTOR: True for you.

PATIENT: Abort is a hard word. It's the B and the T together, with the O in between.

DOCTOR: We didn't abort. We removed a microscopic blood clot. We aspirated a gestational sac. Life is a hard word too.

PATIENT: It is. Sort of wistful. I suppose it's the L and the *fuh* sound at the end.

DOCTOR: Aspirate is nice.

PATIENT: Aspire. Aspiration. *Aspirateur.*

DOCTOR: *Aspirateur?*

PATIENT: The French for vacuum cleaner. You found one in the confession box. That was an *aspirateur.*

DOCTOR: Gas. Where were you when I needed you?

PATIENT: On Thursday the 19th?

DOCTOR: No. In Cathar territory with the butcher, the baker and the candle stick maker. Thursday the 19th is ancient history. Of course, it's modern history too, in another way.

PATIENT: How so?

DOCTOR: Something pretty important happened on Thursday the 19th of May.

PATIENT: What was that?

DOCTOR: After *The Lion King*, in the hotel, we watched it together, herself and me. She fell asleep with her glasses on, but I stayed awake. I had a sense of the history being made. I took off her glasses, opened the minibar, and got stuck into Sky.

PATIENT: Sky?

DOCTOR: There I was on the corner of Covent Garden and the Donmar Warehouse in a top-tier suite in London, the bed turned down and a chocolate crème de menthe on the two batik pillows, while the Queen of England was making a speech in Irish at a dinner in downtown Dublin. The wife was there in her Marc Jacobs fun fur. It's not Kennedy or the Pope being shot, but still.

PATIENT: But still.

DOCTOR: Admissions rose dramatically that week. Did I tell you? All over the country. Brother Albert was on his knees at reception kissing the palms of their hands as the families signed them in.

PATIENT: Admissions always rise at the start of summer. Then they fall again when the evenings shorten and the darkness goes without saying.

DOCTOR: This was no plateau. This was a peak. The manics and the paranoids peaked. There's a paper in it.

PATIENT: But I was well. I was never weller.

DOCTOR: If you imitate normality ...

PATIENT: We will become normal.

DOCTOR: Well, *you* will, anyway. I'm already a veteran.

PATIENT: I was at work. I was working away.

DOCTOR: Down in Docklands.

PATIENT: Down in Docklands.

DOCTOR: Across from the conference centre.

PATIENT: Across from the conference centre. Near Misery Hill at Blood-from-a-Stone Street.

DOCTOR: You were breadwinning.

PATIENT: I was breadwinning. I was charging sterling on the clock. The client was in Strabane. By God, I was beavering.

DOCTOR: And will again. And will again. But remember: fewer Magnums, more opus.

PATIENT: I came up in the bubble lift with a SWAT team. With six clean-shaven snipers. The snipers were smaller than they should have been, but they said the height requirement had been axed by the ombudswoman. Most of them had shaved their heads to hide their baldness. People are so sensitive about hair loss. Even snipers.

DOCTOR: How do you know they were snipers?

PATIENT: There were telescopic sights on their rifles. The rifles were much lighter than they looked.

DOCTOR: They took out my father's femur and put in the captain's prize. But it weighed nothing. That's platinum for you. Or is it plutonium?

PATIENT: The bullets were soft, they said. They were specially made. They'd detonate in the target like a dum-dum, bulge and burst there, and not exit or ricochet and run riot. Otherwise they could hurt somebody, they could kill somebody, a prefix, a suffix, a first secretary with his only grandchild sprung for the day from a private Montessori. Then they'd be handing out saline solutions in sub-Saharan Africa until they needed a drip stand themselves.

DOCTOR: The same consideration for others produced the red telephone box.

PATIENT: I brought them decaff coffee up on the roof and six small Twixes from the Latvian's hospitality trolley. Regular coffee can produce a tremor. You don't want that, obviously. But they all took sugar, except the one who was spreadeagled on the Astroturf among the satellite shields. He said that, no, he used sugar substitutes, Hemesetas and/or Canderel, and he swore by them. He had lost pounds, he told me, since the start of Lent.

DOCTOR: Time will tell. Time will tell all.

PATIENT: I came down to the atrium by the back stairs where the anorexics practice. Up down, up down, up down, both of them, whenever it's too wet to walk, but the sky was back above me, a blue helmet, a peacemaker. A black-backed gull coasted through my floaters, flicking them deftly downriver. The shutter speed of the lightning flash in the lobby photocopier copied the replica flash of the flash photography in the street outside as the pod of the motorcade passed.

DOCTOR: It was a perfect match, a match made in heaven.

PATIENT: I imagined myself. It was all mirrors and no smoke in the restroom. It was all Eureka and no karaoke.

DOCTOR: You had imitated normality and become normal.

PATIENT: The man on the flat-screen set in the unisex toilet was reading the numbers of the Lotto jackpot. His voice went low and slow and solemn when he read the numbers out, like a priest reciting the words of consecration one after another, first-the-bread-and-then-the wine, twelve, twenty-eight, thirty-two, forty, forty-five, all the good years, all the in-between times, all the dry land and the solid ground of my life so far and no farther, rainbows over the white fuchsia, meltdown of February, ground-swell of March, the new script; and I watered the spider plant that was there with sparkling water from a source deep in the limestone Burren, and the spider plant trembled as it drank and thanked me in Greek for what I had done and for what I had failed to do.

DOCTOR: I wish I could give you a bear hug. I wish I could clap you on the shoulder. I wish I could punch you in the stomach. I wish I could play with your hair. This new no-contact policy is a bugger for the shrink and for the shrunken. But I can still blow you a kiss. I can still give you the thumbs up, and I don't care a damn what it looks like on the CCTV camera.

6. FINAL CLAIMS AND A DISCLAIMER OF ANY FINALITY WHATSOEVER (insofar as finitude is not the problem. Finitude, in fact, is a dividend and not a deficit. The difficulty is not that we are

finite, but that we are finite *and* unfinished. There, in a nutshell, in the serum of our sperm, is the shit storm.)

Peace of mind is marketed as a hard capsule in other countries under the following brand names:

In England, peace of mind is called Optimize. It can be purchased in twenty milligram amounts available generically as Home Fires Burning.

In France, peace of mind is called Irony. Irony can be administered at will in situations of schlock, schmaltz, and devious sentimentality. It has many mineral preservative properties, but can result in loss of feeling in the digits and diverse arterial complications. Symptoms of irony closely mimic mercury poisoning.

In Germany, peace of mind is traded as Guilt. Everything in Germany is guilt-edged, and no wonder, by Christ. But there comes a time when guilt is itself a form of denial.

In Ireland, peace of mind is available as Faith and/or Fatalism, hence the trade-mark *Faithalite* in blistered foils and in peppermint-flavoured rosary beads.

In Russia, peace of mind is black-market contraband bartered as *Hope* with a very small H. Sometimes the H is not even aspirated. Hope is an herbal remedy and is therefore uninsurable. Its shelf life is continental.

In the United States, on the other hand, Hope is a dead comedian who was never as funny as our grandparents always insisted, but it's still *de rigueur* to snigger at his double-entendres to Bing Crosby when they regurgitate the road movies in the stupor after Christmas and before the New Year.

In Texas, where human sacrifice is commonplace in the death chambers, hope is a prohibited drug, but major tranquilizers like Melloril and Largactil are offered to clients up to seventy-two hours before execution as a part of the chaplaincy protocols. Capital prisoners on major tranquilizers should avoid direct sunlight and trips to the beach.

In Italy, peace of mind is added to the water supply like fluoride in a form that dissolves into non-partisan laughter and a ludicrous attachment to the good old human body, the *bella figura,* particularly the female pelvis and the male posterior, in spite of everything that's been said about Brother Donkey and Sister Ass down through the ages.

Californians call peace of mind something else altogether; and it is. They habitually confuse it with peace and quiet.

Peace of mind is free, gratis and for nothing in Monte Carlo, Liechtenstein, and the uninhabited interior of Antarctica, but it is largely unavailable throughout Africa, Asia, South America, and all chainstore turf accountants in the North world. Bookies cannot guarantee it. Neither can books, not even the Good One.

In Israel and in the Vatican, peace of mind is known as *Shalom, Pax Prophylaxis,* and colloquially as Godspeed, which is, incidentally, the best speed of all. Available in suppository form to rabbis and bishops whose lips are sealed.

Come, Holy Spirit, renew the face of our dirt. Restore us to the pure filth of the world.

Lord, hear your predators as we prey. Hear too our prey as we predate.

You may now respond in your own time and place with *Amen* or *Ahem*.

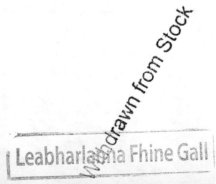